LOKI'S LUCK

A BAD BOY BIKER ROMANCE

STEAMY BIKER ROMANCE SERIES

MONIQUE MOREAU

Cover Design by Cover Couture
www.bookcovercouture.com

MEET MONIQUE!

Join Monique's Newsletter (and receive goodies and release information)
https://bit.ly/SteamyReadNewsletter
Follow her on TikTok
@moniquemoreauthor
Like her Facebook Page
https://bit.ly/MoniqueMoreaufb
Follow her on Instagram
https://bit.ly/MoniqueMoreauIG
Follow her on Book Bub
http://bit.ly/MoniqueBookBub
Learn all about Monique's books
MoniqueMoreau.com

1

LOKI

Loki's eyes snapped open.

Soft light from the parking lot outside bled through the partially opened venetian blinds and slashed over his prone body. He rubbed his closely shaved head and propped himself up with his elbow. The futon he was laying on didn't offer much padding between him and the hard floor of his office in the Box.

It was a little past six a.m. He knew because his body woke up at the same time every day, without fail. No alarm clock. Nothing, except his own mental regimen. The hours he'd put into the boxing gym the Squad had recently purchased, and that he'd assisted in converting to accommodate MMA practitioners as well, were grueling, but he welcomed the nonstop work. So what if he dragged out his futon and slept on the floor of the office he shared with Cutter? Massaging his left shoulder, he rolled his rotator cuff until the stiffness eased.

Taking two ends of his sheet, he folded it into a perfect square and then rolled up the futon and tucked his bedding away into a near-empty closet. He scratched his abs. His palm slid down, paused on his erection, and gave it a hard squeeze.

Gritting his teeth, he could almost feel the snug tightness of a woman's pussy.

One stroke, and he released his cock.

Abstinence might not come naturally to him, but it was a choice. One that he renewed every damn morning. Why? Because every morning, he woke up knowing he was alive and Chopper was dead. Abstaining from pleasure, from comfort, was both a penance and a reminder that Chopper was dead and that Loki didn't deserve to live. Chopper had been the better brother. If life were fair, he would've been saved, but Loki learned early on that there was little justice in the world.

Padding out into the hallway, he stepped into the gym's tiny kitchen and grabbed a bag of Arabica beans from the freezer, his only indulgence. Using a hand grinder, he ground the two ounces he'd measured on a small kitchen scale. Eyeing the coffee machine, he sighed, scooped in the ground-up coffee beans, and poured water into the side receptacle.

Kingdom was stopping by to go over the renovation plans for the unfinished rooms. It'd been a year since they'd opened the gym, and finally, there was enough money to fix up the rooms that languished in the back of the renovated warehouse. Thank fuck. Hopefully, one of them could be converted into another office because he was getting sick of sharing with Cutter. The brother was a fucking slob. He didn't know how Greta put up with it.

Espresso cup in hand, Loki roamed around the cavernous main floor of the gym, pulling up the blinds of huge floor-to-ceiling windows. Loki had meditated, showered, and dressed in his self-imposed dress code—black Henley, black jeans, and his cut—by the time Kingdom waltzed through the entrance, a takeout bag tucked in the crook of his elbow.

He strode into the kitchen with a "Whattup?" Loki took a

seat on a stool at a high table near the lockers and waited for Kingdom to get his coffee.

Minutes later, he dropped a wrapped egg-and-cheese sandwich beside Loki's empty espresso and slid onto a seat across from him.

"Sandwich smells good, but I'm fasting today," Loki gently denied the offering.

"You don't eat. You don't fuck. All to punish yourself for Chopper's death. Don't see how that's helping you, but hey, it's your life. Hope your dick doesn't shrivel up and fall off from lack of use," Kingdom said.

"Ha! You did this shit on purpose," Loki retorted.

"You're one suspicious asshole, but not this time."

"I'm suspicious 'cause you're the asshole," he scoffed.

Kingdom didn't negate his claim. Slurping on his hot coffee, Kingdom peered at him over the rim. "You're lookin' chipper this morning."

Loki sent him a doleful look. "You wanted to talk, so get talking."

"Yeah." Kingdom paused. Not a good sign. "It's about the self-defense class you're teaching tomorrow. The women's social worker will attend."

Hold up, what the fuck? Kingdom *knew* Loki didn't like being micromanaged. After over a decade in the military, he joined the Squad because the loose confederation of brothers gave him a sense of community without the oppressive set of rules. He was done with rules and regulations. Put up with it in the military because he loved what he did, but he wasn't gonna take any shit in the civilian world. The whole point of leaving was to be free.

Loki slitted his eyes, stretching the skin around the scar that crossed through his eyebrow, passed close to the outer corner of his eye, and ended on his cheekbone. "Don't trust me?"

"'Course, I trust you," Kingdom scoffed, "You're the most qualified brother there is to teach this class. But they're survivors and the woman in charge wants to be present in case the lessons bring up shit for them. Ya know, be there to give them support, that kind of thing."

"I'll be there for support. Christ, you know me. I know exactly the kind of pussies who beat on women, and I despise them for it."

"Brother, we have a contract with a government agency. You know as well as I do, government means bureaucracy. If we do it right, more work will flow in, and we need that flood of cash, get me? If this is how they want to play it, then that's how *we're* gonna play it. End of story."

Loki's jaws clenched. "The contract didn't stipulate a supervisor overseeing and controlling me during my fuckin' class."

"Loki," he sighed, "They don't know who you or the details of your qualifications. All they know is they want one of their own present to make sure everything runs smoothly. I understand that it's a hard concept for you, but we gotta be flexible."

Flexible. He didn't do flexible. He did control. Craved it, in fact. Kingdom knew that. The idea that he wouldn't be able to control what happened in the classroom, to protect the women from any issues that came up, was preposterous. Through sheer force of will, he'd become the opposite of his father. But, he hadn't been named Loki for nothing.

Loki was a trickster, and beneath the veneer of impenetrable control lay an ocean of seething rage. It rarely came out nowadays, but after Chopper's death, his loss of temper was so prolonged and memorable that the brothers christened him Loki.

The Viking god didn't play well with others, and neither did he.

Peering down at his cell phone, Kingdom said, "Fuck, Kite's blowing up my phone."

Loki straightened. Kite was the president of the Jersey chapter of the Demon Squad. He was involved in negotiations with another MC, the Dark Horsemen. There was bad history between the clubs because they'd fucked with Cutter's old lady, Greta.

"What's the problem?"

"Seems like Shadow is fucking with Kite in little, passive-aggressive ways. Apparently, Shadow wasn't happy with our intervention."

"Kite must be irate if he's texting you this early in the morning."

Kingdom grunted his assent.

"Too fucking bad for Shadow, though," said Loki. "He shouldn't have messed with Greta. That's on him."

"Yeah," Kingdom responded absently as he shot off a text. "Gonna set up a time to talk with Kite and get a lowdown on the situation. Shadow's a damn pussy. He can't do anything. Not at this point anyway. Taking over as president isn't easy in the best of times. He doesn't have the clout to start in on another MC."

Pocketing his cell, he looked up at Loki. "Now where were we? Oh, yeah. The supervisor doesn't know you. It's not personal, you know," Kingdom clarified. "She's real particular about her clients."

"She's not the only one *real particular* about things," Loki grumbled. "I'm the one certified to teach self-defense to vulnerable females. Christ, I don't gotta give you my résumé. You know who I am and what I've done. What I don't need is the distraction of some random bitch intruding on *my* class, especially when I've got to establish trust between me and the women I'm working with."

"Okay, she's not a random bitch. She's been working closely with Greta and Sage. It ain't personal," Kingdom repeated in an exasperated tone. "It's for her clients."

"Fuck her. I can handle anything that goes down during *my* class."

"Try telling her that," he muttered.

"What'd you say?"

"Look, Abby's normally chill and down-to-earth, but there's no denying she can get uptight when it comes to taking care of people. You know, like a mother hen."

"You knew my mother," he relied dryly. "Does mother hen sound like something I would know jack shit about?"

"It's not a big deal, Loki. You know, it wouldn't hurt to have a female with you the first couple classes."

"The deal is, Kingdom, that I know what I'm fucking doing. I don't need someone to babysit me to make sure I don't —what? Scare them? They're not gonna be scared of shit when I get through with them."

Kingdom snapped his fingers as if reminded of something. "That's right. She also wants to observe because she's planning to go through the same certification process."

"Whatever," Loki ground out. Kingdom had already made up his mind. He could see he wasn't gonna win this round. "Sounds like it's easier to deal with it than argue over it."

"You don't know the half of it, brother. She's become tight with Sage and Greta through the domestic violence cases they've been taking on."

Christ, that explained it. Both Kingdom and Cutter were pussy-whipped. He'd figure out a way to get rid of the pesky social worker on his own. He wasn't about to have some know-it-all chick meddle in his class. The class had to be successful, and the only way to guarantee that was if he did it his way. Not only for the influx of cash, but because he knew a thing or two about self-empowerment. No one would stand between him and the women he was helping.

2

ABBY

Abby whipped into the newly paved parking lot in her little cherry-red Nissan.

She'd been determined that the first car she bought would be red. Of course, the only way it was affordable was to buy the smallest one on the market. But she'd succeeded and she was damn proud of her little Nissan. Riding with the windows down, she rolled to a stop in a parking spot near the door.

She'd been comfortable in her pantsuit back at her frigidly air-conditioned office, but now she was overdressed for the summer weather. Regardless, after hours cooped up in a windowless office, nothing could ruin the lovely breeze of fresh air coming through the windows.

The oldies radio station began playing "Like a Virgin" by Madonna, so she turned up the volume. Her mother, a diehard Grateful Dead and Phish follower, was a closet Madonna fan so she'd grown up on songs like this one. Anyway, trashy 80's music was a thing, and it was meant to be blasted out of a car on a sunny day.

She peered up at the boxing gym, where she was meeting

Sage and the instructor of the self-defense class. It was a little rough around the edges, but the new blacktop showed that they had their priorities straight. Put money into the basics instead of dolling up the storefront and leaving the rest crappy.

Sage had assured her that the clients would have their own entrance so they wouldn't have to walk through a floor of people punching bags and kicking each other in the face. As her clients grew in confidence, they'd be moseying through the front door, just as she was doing right now. But in case they were still nervous, they'd have the option to continue using the side door. Options were important for survivors.

Abby was excited for this class. It was her first foray into taking charge of activities outside of the Agency. Which meant there was no room for failure. Her boss lady was no joke, and Abby took every opportunity for what it was. An honor and a test. If she crumbled, if anything went wrong, it was her butt on the line and she'd be waiting a good long while for another chance to come her way.

Stopping at the front desk, Abby checked out the surroundings. The wall of floor-to-ceiling glass was impressive. So was the expanse of space. Sounds of grunting and whacking of flesh on flesh, or flesh on leather, echoed off the high ceilings.

Suddenly, Sage slipped in front of her. "Hey! Hope I didn't keep you long. I was in the middle of an emergency call. It's hard to get off work in the middle of the day, if I'm not at court."

"You didn't have to come," Abby lied.

Sage was a badass defense attorney, professional to the nines. If she felt it was imperative to step out of the office to facilitate this meeting, then that wasn't a good sign. *Again, not my problem. I've got to make this work. Period.* Abby couldn't imagine what the problem could be, but then again, this club had been their best choice. The price was right, and with the budget cuts the county had imposed, that was imperative. Plus, apparently the instructor was top-notch. Truth was, they'd lucked out that Sage knew him personally and that the club was new.

After a quick hug, Sage gave Abby a cursory tour of the main floor. Guiding her down a hallway, she pointed to the alternate entrance for the class participants and then swung open a door. She was attentively listening to Sage as she entered an office, but when she turned her head to face forward... whoa, what the—*gorgeous.*

That one word rolled through her mind. *Gorgeous, gorgeous, gorgeous.*

He was one big, bold, and beautiful specimen of a man. Abby's breath hitched as her eyes wandered over his wide chest, broad shoulders, and stubbled, angular jaw before resting on a pair of gorgeous blue eyes. All that olive skin and broody masculinity made her forget why she was there. Her nipples pebbled underneath her blouse and she quickly folded her arms over her chest.

The biker—Loki was his name—stretched like one of those massive lethal felines one would see on a nature documentary. He settled back into a relaxed pose on the couch. Apparently this was his office.

His eyes settled on hers. They didn't exactly radiate friendliness, but they demanded her attention. The pull she felt was like racing down a fast-running river going in one unforgiving direction toward a run of rapids. No matter what she did, no matter how much she fought it, she was rushing downstream over those torrents.

As she stood before him, her sex clenched, and she pressed her thighs firmly together. Good Lord, the way she was reacting, one would think she'd been raised in a nunnery. A slight smirk on his face told her that he'd noted her discomfort. There was that pull again. This time, tugging low in her belly. *Crap.*

Sage began introducing them, "Abby, this is Loki. A member of the Demon Squad, supervisor of the Box, and the instructor for the self-defense class."

He partially rose from the couch and extended a hand. She stared down at his outstretched hand, as large as a bear's paw, and a frisson skittered down her spine. The energy coming off him was intimidating. He wasn't scary, per se, but the authority vibrating off him unnerved her.

Peeking up at him for reassurance, she was faced with perfectly sculpted features devoid of expression. He didn't crack a smile. No crinkles fanned around the corners of his eyes. No laugh lines at the edges of his lips. Nothing. *This dude kills it at poker, for sure.*

And, then there was his scar. Whew, that was one wicked-looking injury. It started at his hairline and barely missed his eye.

A survivor.

She recognized him instantly. Above all else, she respected survivors. Unlike her mother, who'd fought the good fight, but didn't survive.

"He looks menacing, but he's very capable. More feral than domesticated, but loyal," Sage prattled on.

Capable and loyal. Sage hadn't mentioned gentleness, which would've been more comforting considering her group of clients. The feral qualities were evident. If pressed, she'd describe them as grizzly; not one cuddly, teddy-bear characteristic hung about him.

Abby's hand was engulfed by his much broader palm. Static crackled when their skin came into contact. She hurried to withdraw her hand and rubbed her sweaty palm on her pantsuit. He didn't frown, exactly. His expressionless visage didn't change perceptively, but she was almost certain a ghost of a scowl crossed his face. As if he didn't like her reaction. But that couldn't be right. A man dressed solely in black, with a hard jaw and sharp, cerulean eyes under heavy brows didn't care what a girl like her felt or thought. It brought up a bubble of irritation from the years of putting up with her older brothers' bossiness.

She blew out a breath, waving away the fringe of chin-length hair framing her cheeks. "Glad to meet you, Loki. I'm sure we'll get along fabulously well."

Sage's gaze flittered between them; a notch of concern lodged between her delicate brows. She could understand why. He had the bearing of a soldier. A hardened soldier. Broad shoulders bulged beneath his biker's vest. His black T-shirt broadcast prominent biceps with delicious veins popping out from his olive skin. Given half a chance, she'd tongue the edge of that fat vein down his arm, and between his knuckles. Flutter her tongue between his blunt fingers before sucking the tip of one into her mouth.

Okay, what the fuck? Is this what happened when a person was severely sex deprived? *I guess it's to be expected from a woman who'd had sex all of one, single time.* There was no other explanation for her fantasies about a bad-boy biker like him, who didn't go more than twenty-four hours without pounding into a woman. Unfortunately, that thought led to a lascivious image of Loki lounging on the couch, a woman between his legs, going down on him. Annnd...she was wet. She stifled a groan. *Just great.*

Of course, looks could be deceiving. Both Greta's and Sage's boyfriends doted on them, and bikerness bled out of every pore in their bodies. It was his overwhelming charisma.

It was addling her mind like scrambled egg. *Snap out of it, girl!*

"Are you okay?" Sage peered at her. Abby blinked a few times and flashed a practiced, reassuring smile. "Yes! Of course."

She cringed at her overly enthusiastic response. A little over-the-top, for sure.

"I thought we lost you there for a moment," Sage said, studying her carefully.

Suddenly, a hand wrapped around her elbow, and Abby was being guided to a seat behind a monstrous desk. Another electric jolt ran up her arm, and she reacted to the zing by struggling against his clasp. Loki tightened his hold and commanded, "Sit."

Her butt plopped down instantaneously. His voice was like bourbon, dark and heady. Her pulse roared as she gazed up at him, hoping to see a reflection of the same desire strumming through her body. A knot lodged in her throat. No such luck. His expression was as cool and smooth as ever.

His gaze sidelined to Sage, and he gave another order. "Water."

Sage scurried off to the water cooler. A gurgle of bubbles in the tank broke the silence. Loki knelt; worried eyes lit on her. His broad hand wrapped around her knee. It was like a punch to the gut and her shoulders gave a slight shudder. He squeezed. Heat lit up a bonfire between her thighs, which she clasped together in desperation.

Whatever Loki saw on her face must have finally registered because Bunsen burner–blue flames flared in his irises. In a tone bleeding molten sensuality, he cautioned her, "Stand down, little girl. I ain't the one for you."

Oh, yes, you are. You so, so are.

Her body was screaming out that he was exactly the one

for her. His eyes turned icy, or rather icier. Firming her lips, she swiped at his hand, but it was a useless gesture. He only tightened his hold.

A paper water cup was thrust in her face, breaking their staring contest.

"Here, Abby, drink this."

Then, Sage's hand was shoving at Loki's shoulder, and his grip slipped away, leaving a cold spot where his flesh had wrapped around hers.

"Do you mind, Loki?" Sage's face swam in her line of vision. "Drink up. Are you okay? Maybe it's the heat. Lower the thermostat, Loki. She looks like she's about to have heatstroke."

Abby guzzled down the water and cleared her throat. "Yes, it is hot in here."

Sage turned a narrowed-eyed stare of blame onto Loki. "Why do you keep it so hot in here?"

"No, it's not his fault," she hurried to say. "It's so cold at the Agency that I'm always over-dressed in the summer months." She gave a little shrug. "You know how I'm a jean shorts and T-shirt kind of girl." Embarrassment seeped out of every inch of her skin. She was a professional, dammit. This was so unbecoming. Straightening her shoulders, she took in a deep breath and firmly reminded herself to focus.

3

LOKI

ean shorts and T-shirt kinda girl, huh?

The image made him swallow hard.

Yeah, he'd love to see her in cut-off jean shorts showcasing her thighs and a tight shirt stretched over her full rack. Standing with his fists on his hips, Loki frowned down at the slip of a girl, sitting on the edge of her seat, thighs pressed together. Because...she was young.

Her wide, innocent eyes alone broadcast her inexperience. Innocence wasn't the only thing swimming in those remarkable, copper-colored eyes of hers. Blatant desire, as well. That was a powerful combination for a man like him. He practically reeled back on his heels.

She looked close to passing out. An intense craving to sweep her onto his lap and cradle her in his arms seized him. Sage had to shove him out of the way because he didn't want to break the charge of energy volleying between them. Those large puppy-dog eyes of hers flashed up at him as if he were a god or a gentle giant. Nothing could be further from the truth. There was zero softness left in him.

His gaze glided over her sweet little body. Pixie girl. Nice curves. A pouty bottom lip that teased the fuck out of him. Sexiness, he could handle. But fuck-me eyes like hers, shimmering with guilelessness, and his heart stuttered in his chest. If he closed his eyes, he could taste her brand of innocence. He'd guess it tasted like sunshine, wrapped in honey, dipped in fucking sugar crystals.

Fuck his life. His cock was coming to life. In public, no less. He couldn't remember the last time that happened. He was a former solider and now a biker. If he dared to touch a bright-eyed fairy like her, he'd break her to pieces.

Not. Happening.

The back rooms were always hotter, and with his tendency to save money, he didn't lower them until a couple of hours before classes started in the training rooms. He left the room to decrease the temperature on the thermostat. Marching back in, he was pleased to see that the whoosh of cool air flowing out of the vents was blowing wisps of blonde pixie hair from the crown of Abby's head. They looked so soft, floating there. Begging for his hand to smooth them down. Or tug them. He felt an unfamiliar twitch on the edges of the severe, straight line of his lips. Almost like a smile.

Over her shoulder, Sage winced and said, "You're scaring her with that look on your face." Shooing at him with her hands, she snapped, "Go do something."

"No," pixie girl peeped up. "It's not him." Her voice was like honey, smooth and sweet. A slow ache settled behind his sternum as if she'd reached out and rubbed her small hand over it.

"Are you sure? He has such a bully vibe," Sage returned, still glaring at him from her seat beside Abby. Ever since her pregnancy, Sage had been snappier. Lines creased his forehead. He couldn't remember what he'd seen in her, at one time. The contrast between her and the sweet, tasty treat beside her couldn't be greater.

Dragging a chair over, he sat down close to Abby and wrapped his arm around the back of her chair. He was crowding her, but he couldn't keep his distance if he tried. She jumped, as if startled, but then leaned in ever so slightly. His cock pulsed again. Being close to that juicy little morsel did that to him. He canted his head to the side. Her flushed face and dilated pupils told him that she was literally juicy. He wanted to run his palms up her thighs and search between her legs. Check out for himself just how wet she was.

"So," he began, "I heard that the supervisor has issues. You work with her, right? Let's address those first and you can take the info back to her before tonight. Then I'll go through the lesson, step-by-step."

Across the back of Abby's chair, he let his hand drop, the tips of his fingers brushing against her shoulder, and he felt a jolt of electricity. Christ, she was so aware of him. He didn't touch, much less toy with females, but something about her messed with his internal control.

His hand was slapped off, and he leaned forward to glare at Sage, sitting on the other side of Abby. His gaze was caught in the gap in Abby's shirt, and the top swells of her tits.

Sage harrumphed. "Loki! You're flustering her."

"No, he's not!" Abby denied vehemently, her blush deepening. Fanning herself, she plucked at her dressy, ribbed cotton sweater.

It's not just the heat, sweetheart. Normally, he ignored chicks. Yet he couldn't seem to stop himself with this one. She was like a ray of sunshine, a drop of raw honey on the tongue. He wanted to curl up and soak up her warmth and dip his tongue in for a taste.

Sage slapped at his hand. Instinctually, he growled, "You're not a fuckin' guard dog."

She inhaled sharply and her eyes began to water. *Fuuuck*, he'd hurt her feelings. She was sensitive as hell lately, and Kingdom would go ballistic if he found out that his woman, his *pregnant* woman, was upset by something he'd said. Closing his eyes, he sucked in a breath and did what he had to do.

"I didn't mean that, Sage. Sorry," he muttered.

Sage's lower lip trembled slightly, but she got herself under control. Rising to her feet, she said, "I've got calls to make. Abby will be in all the classes with you." Turning to Abby, she said, "I'll wait for you outside to talk after you hammer out all the details with Loki."

After giving Abby a quick hug and him a final glare, she left. The door clicked softly behind her, leaving them alone in his office. *Alone.*

"Christ," he mumbled low.

A pair of big doll eyes turned on him and a hand gently, cautiously, inched to his thigh. The muscle jumped upon contact. "It's not your fault. It's the hormones talking."

Was this little pixie girl trying to comfort him? That was bold of her. There was a spine under all that softness. He almost barked out a laugh. Something niggled at him. What did Sage say before she left? Abby would be at *each* of his classes. *She* was the supervisor. Sage hadn't specified that the supervisor was coming and when he laid eyes on the girl, with that fairy air about her, he assumed she was an assistant of some kind. Oh. Hell. Fucking. No. *Just no.*

※※※

"Listen, I don't appreciate anyone supervising me like I don't know what the hell I'm doing," he bit out.

Abby drew in a sharp breath and retracted her hand from his rock-hard thigh. That was a quick turnaround. She craned her head back to get a better look at him. Where was this defensiveness coming from? "I'm not supervising you."

"Aren't you a supervisor at the Agency?"

"I am a supervisor, but my intention is not to supervise you."

He looked at her askance. "Yeah, if that's the truth, then don't come tonight."

"It *is* the truth, actually, and I plan to attend for my clients. They're my priority and several of them are in vulnerable states, at the moment. One has recently started a twelve-step recovery program for drug abuse. A few others suffer from psychological and emotional issues, including panic attacks. Practically all of them have some form of PTSD." Loki's large frame stiffened beside her. "It's my duty to be present in case they need me."

"I'll be there. That's enough. I've been a trainer for years. I can handle anything that comes up."

Abby's blood pressure shot up and waves of heat spread over her face. She stared at him in disbelief. How dare he? "Do you have specific experience working with this kind of population?"

"See, there you go questioning me. Someone at your agency reviewed our proposal and my résumé. There were competitors, but we won the contract. Wanna know why?"

She opened her mouth to answer, but it was a rhetorical question, of course. He didn't give her a chance to answer, but went on, "Because we know what we're doing."

"I'm not questioning whether you know what you're doing, having seen your résumé, but..." she paused as her eyes surveyed him from head to toe, "you're a large man. It could potentially be intimidating."

One of her favorite and most sensitive clients, Alex, didn't take to large men, and Abby was most worried about Alex. She might have conceded to Loki's wishes if Alex wasn't participating, but she was, adamant about "getting strong." And when Alex got on a kick, there was no stopping her.

Loki snorted through his nostrils.

Glowering at him, she asked, "What was that for?"

"You're overexaggerating. Don't know why you've got to coddle these women. Whatever they've been through, they need to dig in deep to their inner core and build on it."

He thrust his face in hers until there was a hair's breadth of space between them, the intensity of his forceful stare scorching her to the bottom of her soul.

"That's what you're doing, you know that, right? Coddling," he spat out like it was a curse.

Insulted, she gritted her teeth. She did *not* coddle. He didn't even know her or her working methods. Abby's hand twitched with the urge to smack the arrogance off his face because she doubted a man like him knew much about damaged women.

Straightening her spine in preparation for a battle, she retorted, "If there's any issue, any backlash, that comes from taking your class, then who do you think will be picking up the pieces? Hmm? Answer me that." She paused meaningfully before forging on, "Me. That's who. Therefore, I decide how to handle it, and I've decided that I want to be there to take care of any situation that might come up. It's my prerogative and I'm taking it, so stop whining like a baby."

Staring into the composite of ice shards that were his

pupils, she decided to double down on her stance. "If you have a problem, feel free to take it up with my supervisor. But be forewarned, as far as the well-being of my clients goes, my word is law, and I won't take shit from you or anyone else. However," she swept her hand out grandiosely, "feel free to try."

Loki's jaws clenched hard, a muscle ticked away at the bottom of the left side, but she was not daunted by his irritation. She wasn't budging on her decision. When it came to Celine, Alex, and Jenny, she'd fight tooth and nail.

Eyes flashing with cold fury, Loki leaned back in his chair, crossed his thick arms over his broad chest, and gave a shrug.

"Fucking fine. Have it your way." He lifted his forefinger. "Once."

4

LOKI

Those trusting amber eyes of hers looked even better sparking with annoyance, flashing with grit.

How had he imagined that she was soft and pliable? Oh, right, because she was having a heatstroke. Turned out, once recovered, she could slug it out like an MMA fighter in a cage.

Which only increased his attraction to her. She was more than curves that begged for his hands or full tits he could feast on for days. No, she was much *much* more. There was fire in that tasty little package, and it stirred his heart and his cock. But none of that matter, he reminded himself sternly. Either way, she was not for him.

Reaching over his desk, he slammed his laptop shut and dropped it over his crotch to cover the erection that was about to bust out of his jeans from their little tit for tat.

The flags of pink on her cheeks told him that she was feeling him as well. He bet the honey from her pussy would be tooth-hurtin' syrupy. Sticky. Like biting into a caramel apple. Caramel apples were for little boys, and he'd left boyhood long ago. By fifteen, he was swinging at his shit-for-brains father like a champ, and by eighteen he was signed up for the military. Got him out of that run-down shit town he'd come from and into basic training. He fucking loved it. The rules, the cleanliness, the control. Life was simple. Men acted like men. There were a few assholes, but they paled in comparison to the fucker he'd grown up with. For the most part, they were honorable.

Deep down, he'd recognized that he could never be as good as they were, but at least they gave him a model to strive toward.

Rules worked for him, until they didn't. They couldn't save him from the guilt. He'd lived under the illusion that he was a better man until the day Chopper up and killed himself. The guilt consumed him and the rules were no longer boundaries, but barbed wire wrapped around his throat and he had to get out.

Jolted by the memory, his chair screeched away from Abby. There was no way he was touching a feisty busybody like her, with more sass than was healthy. She was trouble with a capital *T*, and he'd known trouble his entire life. At his age, the whole point was to avoid accruing any more. She was the epitome of everything he didn't want in his life. Didn't deserve.

Deserve. Want. Same difference.

The little witch tapped her foot impatiently, arms crossed over her plump chest with tight nipples that made him salivate.

Waiting for his response after she dared him to go to her supervisor, aware that he'd do no such thing. She had the upper hand, and she knew it. The fingers of his left hand twitched at his side with the maddening urge to rip off those fitted pants and swat the bubble of her ass until it matched the color of her cheeks.

He swiped the sweat building along his temples. Hot. Damn.

Slamming the laptop down on the desk, he leaned over and gripped her chin. Tilting it up, he snarled in her face, "You get one class to supervise. One class and that's it."

Ripping her chin away, she snapped, "More like observe. Again, you're taking this the wrong way. I won't judge you. I'll be there for my clients. Seriously, what is your problem?"

Loki's gaze pierced hers, and she scooted her chair back.

Between clenched teeth, he said, "It's my class and I decide how to run it. You wanna observe? You get one class. Nothing's gonna go wrong. I'll prove that to you, and then you're gone. Hear me, woman?"

She hadn't debated that, but he had to put his foot down about *something*, dammit.

"Oh, I hear you, *man*."

He groaned internally.

There she went again. Her smart mouth begging for a swat on that plump ass of hers. Fuckin' *pleading* for a rectification on his part. He ground down on his molars.

"I'll be here at six," she gritted out between clenched teeth.

She stood up and shimmied past him, her free hair swinging, leaving behind an intoxicating scent of oranges and sunshine. Did he just think the word sunshine? His life was a tundra. No sunshine. No warmth. He balled his fists in his lap, mesmerized by her twitching ass as she marched out the door.

Slam. The heavy door reverberated in its frame.

He dragged a hand down to his hard cock and palmed it.

"Christ*fuck*. I'm screwed."

✳✳✳

MARCHING down the corridor leading to the main floor, she balled her fists and punched the air a few times. To think she thought he was hot. Ugh, more like an overbearing oaf.

Her pussy fluttered when he barked orders in that growly voice of his, trying to bully her. Those cerulean eyes, whirling with a critical mass of emotions. And an inflexible pride that took her presence in his class personally. He was trouble and she worked with troubled people all day, so she sure as hell didn't need to date one. She snorted, highly doubting that a "date" was in his repertoire.

Plus, she couldn't trust a man like him. A biker who dripped sex appeal from his pores. He was a manwhore, for sure. Not a bone of monogamy resided in that tall, delicious body. To her dismay, her first reaction to him was absolute: he was *the one*. She knew all about *the one*. She grew up listening to stories of how her parents had met and fallen in love at first sight, blah, blah, blah. But that was her body talking.

Abby was certain that he was basically worthless for anything beyond dirty, sweaty fucking. She paused midstride. Come to think of it, sex with Loki would solve one of her lingering issues.

Resuming her determined pace, she shook her head. She'd have to keep her heart out of it. Abby snorted as she walked into the main area, the thumps of punching bags and grunts of fighters permeating the air. Considering how rude he was, it wouldn't be a difficult thing to do.

Skirting around the large boxing ring, Abby surveyed the floor for Sage. Her primary impediment to lusty sex was lack of expertise and a wandering mind. Her first time had been abysmal. She learned a two-fold lesson: never lose your virginity to a virgin and experience matters.

Once the mortifying hymen was gone, she figured she could afford to wait. Of course, she hadn't expected almost three years to pass with no more than oral sex as a follow-up. On her journey of self-discovery, she found that she had to be in full-on lust mode to escape her persistent thoughts.

During her last hookup, not only had she dried up like the Sahara on the Equinox, because, hello, that's what lube was for, but she'd been so bored that the guy actually noticed. And commented on it. She shuddered at the memory. There was no need to remind herself of how that episode ended. He accused *her* of being a wet blanket.

As if.

Pfft, not with the way she masturbated.

Not with the purple rabbit vibrator she used. Heck, no.

Abby spotted Sage sitting at a high table with her laptop open, typing furiously as she spoke into her cell phone. Rows of boxing gloves hung on the wall above her, along with vintage framed posters of boxing and MMA fights.

She slid onto the stool beside Sage, who lifted her index finger and mouthed "sorry" before returning to her conversation with whichever judge's clerk she was speaking with.

While waiting, Abby mused about how Loki checked off certain boxes. The moment her eyes landed on those thick biceps and the scar running down his left cheek, her pussy went *ding ding ding! Ladies and gentlemen, we have a winner!* Her body shivered like a Carnival dancer's feathered headdress in a Mardi Gras parade.

Sure, she was treating him like man flesh. She should probably feel bad for objectifying him. Really, she should.

She gave a little shrug. Heh, what he didn't know wouldn't hurt him.

Sage dramatically tapped several times on the "end call" button on her cell.

"What a miserable bastard," she exclaimed about her caller. "Did you finish hammering out the details with Loki?"

"That's one way of putting it," Abby huffed.

"He's prickly, for sure. I apologize on his behalf if he was being difficult. He tends to be...controlling."

"You can say that again," she rejoined.

Grabbing Abby's shoulders, Sage gave her a quick squeeze. "Despite his gruff exterior, he's actually the best at what he does. I wouldn't have pushed for him if I didn't trust him implicitly. He's like a temperamental artist, and like with anyone who's temperamental, it's best to simply ignore the grumpiness."

"Oh, grumpy is an understatement," Abby grumbled as Sage led her out of the gym. Clearly, that had little impact on her reaction to him. If anything, it might be part of the attraction.

God, she was so screwed.

5

LOKI

"We have a situation, and it could get ugly," Kingdom intoned, deep creases lining his forehead.

Loki folded his arms across his chest and settled down on the arm of the couch in Kingdom's office at the Squad clubhouse. His eyes scanned over the other brothers present. Cutter, Puck, and Prez were either sitting or standing around the room. Besides Kingdom, Cutter looked particularly agitated. There wasn't a whisper of a smirk on his lips, which was a rare sight for him.

"Kingdom, give them the specifics," ordered Cutter.

"It's Shadow," he admitted.

Puck groaned from his place, leaning against the wall.

No wonder Cutter looked like he was about to rip shit apart. Greta and Shadow grew up together in the same fucked-up, destructive MC, the Dark Horsemen in Jersey. After ignoring her ass for a decade, he decided to steal her from Cutter when he took over the club from Greta's father, who was on his death bed.

"He's not getting her," Cutter growled. "No way, no fucking how."

Loki clapped Cutter's shoulder. "We know that, bro. No one's suggesting otherwise. We took care of this before and we'll take care of it again. Greta is Demon Squad pride. No one's touching her."

Cutter's eyes slanted over to Loki, and he nodded in gratitude for his support. It was proof of how far the two of them had come.

"Greta is one of ours. Don't care that she was once a Horseman. Don't care what that motherfucker wants with her," Prez chimed in. "She's your old lady. She wears your property patch. I don't know what the fuck he's thinking. Unless he has a death wish, he won't touch her."

"Not sure what his game is, to be honest," added Kingdom. "Kite from the Jersey Squad chapter has been texting me updates. From his intel, it seems that Shadow doesn't have the backing of his entire club. Maybe he's starting shit with Kite to divert attention from his own problems or to drum up support by creating trouble with another club, making it out like they're an outside threat."

"Or he could be pissed off because he looked like a fool after Greta dissed his ass in front of her father and his officers," suggested Loki. "That old son of a bitch might be dead, but I was there during the negotiations, and he reamed Shadow's ass in front of a dozen Horsemen about how he was too much of a pussy to keep hold of Greta."

Greta's father, Scorpion, had been a bastard, through and through. Cutter had urged Greta to attempt to reconcile with him on his deathbed, and for his effort, Scorpion did everything he could to undermine their love. Almost broke them up.

Kingdom sent Loki down to Camden separately to deal with Scorpion because Shadow had lurked in Squad territory like the little bitch he was. There were strict rules about spying on another MC's property. As if sniffing around an MC's biker bitch wasn't bad enough, he approached Greta while she was under Squad protection. Direct violations had to be dealt with.

By the time Loki showed up for the sit-down, the place was fucking mayhem. He snorted softly to himself. Such a Greta thing to do. That woman was a fucking whirling dervish. Only a brother like Cutter, with his special set of bedroom skills, could bring her to heel.

"Either way, I got a call from the Dragoons MC up in Newburg," revealed Kingdom.

"That's only half an hour away," said Cutter.

"Yeah, and apparently, they had a biker hit them up for business. And guess who the motherfucker was?"

"Shadow," Cutter replied, seemingly already in the know by the growl in his tone.

"Yup. I don't know what the fucker thinks he's doing, but we need to be on the alert. Greta's an obvious mark, but everyone must be on watch. I don't think it's time to bring in the entire club, but we need to monitor the situation."

"You sure we shouldn't call Church? A meeting of all the patched brothers might be the best thing we can do, in case shit turns ugly fast," suggested Prez.

"I get your point, Prez, but I don't know if we should call a special session just yet or wait till the next scheduled Church meeting."

"Fair enough," replied Prez.

"All right, that's it for now." Kingdom wrapped it up with, "I'll keep you posted."

Puck swung the door open and waved them out. "Let's go get us something to drink."

"Nah, I've got to head back to the Box. My first self-defense class starts in less than an hour. I've got some supervisor lady coming to boss me around. Got to make sure everything's copacetic so I can get rid of her ass pronto."

"You talkin' about Abby?" Cutter asked, eyes gleaming with humor. "You're not gonna get rid of her, bro."

"So you say, but I say otherwise," replied Loki as he followed Cutter out of the office.

The fucker simply chuckled and said, "Good luck."

Loki scowled because he looked too mighty pleased with himself for Loki's taste.

6

ABBY

"Don't be a victim. Be aware of your surroundings. Awareness and safety are interconnected concepts."

Loki paused in his lecture to give Abby a cool nod as she entered the room. Spine plastered to the wall, she crept to the back, where she willed herself to disappear. Despite her best efforts not to interrupt the class, a few of her clients shifted their heads in her direction.

"I'm going to repeat this frequently," he resumed his lesson.

Running late, as usual, she'd missed the introductions.

"We don't see ourselves as a potential victim. We don't see, ahead of time, a situation that can turn ugly. The truth is that much violence can be prevented without resorting to physical self-defense, and nonphysical means carry a far lower risk with a higher chance of success. The first two tools in our arsenal are awareness and prevention."

He paused for emphasis before continuing, "Most people do not *need* to learn boxing or martial arts skills to protect themselves from violence. We will certainly get into those, but the takeaway tonight is that we shouldn't have to use any of those skills. The first and most important objective is to avoid dangerous places and people."

Christine raised her hand.

Loki paused and, pointing to her, said, "Yes, Christine."

Huh, he's already memorized their names.

"I would love to never see my husband as long as I live but I can't avoid him during custody pickups and drop-offs."

"There are ways to minimize danger, such as meeting him in public places or with another person present who can supervise the transfer of custody. It is important to bring up the subject with your counselor or social worker to determine and outline safer measures. But if that's not possible, then yes, we'll learn how to deal with unavoidable dangers."

Loki's gaze flickered to Abby and then scanned the rest of the women sitting cross-legged in a semicircle around him. "Any other questions?"

No one raised their hands.

"Lesson one is avoidance. For a predator to attack you, he needs three things: intent, the means, and the opportunity. If you deny him one of those three things, it will be impossible for him to attack. Let's talk about what other ideas would keep you safe."

Alex raised her hand and answered, "Being aware of your surroundings."

Thatta girl. She spoke up even though Abby could see the tremor in her raised hand.

"Absolutely," Loki answered. "That's a fundamental lesson. How many of us have walked toward our car in a parking lot while checking our text messages?" Loki raised his hand. "I caught myself doing that last week. I'm usually the last one at the Box, so I end up locking up for the night. It was past midnight and I was on my way to my car, checking my texts. Here I am, a self-defense and martial arts instructor, and I violated one of the cardinal rules. Anyone could have taken me from behind in a bear hug and tackled me to the ground."

It was immediately obvious that Loki was exceptionally good at what he did. The women were riveted by him, a few of them nodding their heads as he described his mistake and the potential consequences. She was enjoying watching this hot-as-sin biker, with his mixture of solidity and sensitivity, instructing the group of vulnerable women.

"By being aware of your surroundings and paying attention to warning signs, also called pre-attack indicators, you can mark a predator and deny him access to getting close to you. Let's take a step back and discuss avoiding dangerous places. You're probably thinking to yourself, I don't live in a dangerous neighborhood, I don't work in a dangerous neighborhood, so I'm good. Unfortunately, every neighborhood, no matter how safe it's supposed to be, has something called 'in-between places.' These in-between places are hot spots. They're places where people commonly pass through, but not too frequently. Think parking lots, jogging or hiking trails, isolated side streets or back alleys. Even going to the mail room or the laundry room in a perfectly safe apartment complex can be dangerous. Attackers lie in wait in these places, knowing that few people will pass through, and that they will have time alone with their victim."

Suddenly, Alex shot to her feet. Rooted to the spot, she began to shake uncontrollably. Her entire body trembled as tears streaked down her face uncontrollably. Her chest convulsed in great heaves, and clutching her throat, she rasped shuddering breaths. Loki was already by Alex's side before Abby got the chance to shove herself off the wall and go to Alex.

In a shaky voice, another participant exclaimed, "W-what's happening to her?"

Loki raised his forefinger to his closed lips to silence her.

Standing close, but maintaining a far enough distance, he faced Alex and spoke in a smooth, calm tone, "Alex, what's going on? I see something's upset you. Whatever it is, we can take care of it together. You're safe here. I won't let anything happen to you."

Alex turned her head slightly toward him, but otherwise remained in the same comatose, frozen state. He didn't attempt to touch her in any way.

"Alex, listen to me. I'm going to take your hand. Okay? Nod yes if it's okay."

He waited until she gave a slight shake of her head, then approached closer and touched her hand. She flinched but didn't move away. "I'm guiding you to the mat so you can take a moment and regroup."

Loki glided a finger over the top of Alex's hand. Her hand twitched and she clasped his hand forcefully, crushing it in her grip.

"Good girl. I'm right here. You're going to follow my hand guiding you down to the mat. Okay? Nod if you hear me."

Unseeing, Alex nodded again.

Slowly, he knelt and guided her hand down, her torso following until she was kneeling beside him.

"That's right, sweetheart, you got this. We're going down a little more." He tugged at her hand, and she shuffled on her knees until they were on the mat. Little by little, he tugged until she stretched out on her side.

Cross-legged, Loki placed her head gently on his lap and slowly stroked her hair as if she were a child.

Over his shoulder, Loki's sharp gaze fell on Abby, and he ordered, "Grab a cold towel and a glass of water."

Abby hurried out the door. Returning with the wet towel and glass of water, she slipped back into the room and found Alex and Loki in the same position. A circle of women formed around them. Over their heads, she saw Alex breathing calmly, staring up at Loki with trusting, unblinking eyes.

Loki's eyes were on Alex, nodding approvingly, while softly stroking her hairline with the back of his knuckles. Abby's heart pounded in her throat. His complete focus was on her client. The only thing that mattered for him was her safety and comfort. He'd guided her every step of the way, and she'd come out on the other side of her panic attack.

The back of Abby's neck felt hot and her stomach unclenched. She hadn't trusted him, and he'd proved her wrong. So very wrong.

She was having trouble reconciling this man with the one who'd stuck his angry face in hers earlier that afternoon, looming over her in a threatening manner that had simultaneously disturbed and excited her. His burly body, the one without an ounce of fat or softness, lounged in a comfortable yoga-like pose, cradling Alex's head in his large hand, fingers caressing her forehead. There was no denying that he had the situation firmly in hand.

Hopefully, he'd allow her to return because she fully intended to continue with his course. But, instead of checking on him, next time her goal was to learn from him.

7

ABBY

Greta had offered to pick Abby up with the excuse that club parties could be intimidating, but she was having quite the opposite reaction.

Sure, she partied in college like any young adult, but since then, her life had been uneventful, and since starting at the Agency, her social circle revolved around work friends. The idea of going to a club party with new acquaintances promised excitement. There was also the off chance that she might see that sexy, broody man candy, Loki.

Greta told her to dress casually, which was her jam, so she wore a pair of jean shorts and a form-fitting top that, with her chest size, was sexy. Checking out the people around her, she was relieved to find that she blended in, although she was definitely leaned on the clothed end of the spectrum compared to some of the women.

Most people seemed to know one another, and everyone was enjoying themselves, laughing and joking. The atmosphere was easygoing, like a bar of regulars, and even though she'd already gotten separated from Greta and Cutter in the rowdy crowd, she felt at ease.

Abby wriggled between two huge guys and grabbed onto the edge of the bar before she got whisked away by the crush of bodies. The downside of being so petite is that it was easy for her to shoved aside, but Abby didn't mind because she was so happy to be at the party. By some miracle, the bartender heard her yell out for a beer before she was moved half-way down the bar. He grabbed a slick wet bottle, popped the cap off and slammed it in front of her. She shouted out a thanks, although she wasn't too sure he heard it over the din.

Turning toward the crowd, she went on her tiptoes to scan the crowd in search of Greta, Sage, or their partners. She was also hoping for a glimpse of a certain enticing male. Since the first class, he'd routinely popped into her thoughts. She'd felt an intense physical attraction from the get-go, but to watch him handle her clients with such care made her see him in a new light. He was his résumé, and more. You couldn't fake the kind of experience and sensitivity he'd shown Alex.

The excitement of the crowd and loud music pumping through the speakers hanging on the walls reverberated in her body. She began shaking her hips a little to the music when she noticed the curious, yet hungry, smirk of a large biker peering down at her. Her heart pattered irregularly like a drunken tap dancer. He gave her a slow, appreciative look-over. Abby took a swallow of her beer to cover her nerves.

"Hey, girl, you're new. First time here to party, huh?"

"Yup, first time," she croaked out. Normally, she wasn't so nervous, but this guy was big and rough around the edges. He was sexy as well, but for some reason, he didn't automatically make her feel comfortable like she did with Loki.

"Gotta get on this before the other brothers snap you up," he shouted over the music, grabbing her small hand into his huge paw. "I got a room in the back."

Greta had warned her that bikers could be forward. She needed to be firm and vocal. Niceties were not a priority, Sage had said. Abby was looking for an adventure, but this was more than she'd bargained for.

Her head snapped right and left, searching for a familiar face in the throng of people. No such luck. Heels digging into the floor, she yanked her hand out of his and was about to open her mouth to speak when a sudden jab in her ribs had her sucking in a breath.

A woman, whose breasts practically spilled out of her skin-tight, cut-off top, inserted herself between her and the big guy.

Plastering herself to his side, she crooned, "Hey, Tank, how are ya?" Edging Abby farther away, her tone changed as she gave Abby a nasty look from over her shoulder, "What the hell do you want with a bitch like her?"

Raking her from head to toe with hard eyes and a curl to her upper lip, she spat out, "She looks like a fucking prude."

"Hey!" said Abby. That was a tad bit of a sore spot. She also didn't like when women attacked one another. What happened to solidarity, sister?

Another, younger woman slipped in on the other side of Abby, and waved her arm, trying to flag down the bartender.

"Please, bitch, you don't belong here," the mean one spat out.

The biker guffawed, and Abby felt her face flush red. Okay, Greta had warned her that biker women called each other bitches, but that sounded hostile to her ears.

The young woman beside her whipped around, reached over Abby and smacked the mean girl on the arm. "Please, bitch. Retract the claws. It's not this bitch's fault that your man of the month can't keep his dick in his pants. I recognize her.

She's Greta and Sage's friend. Do you really wanna go there, Kerri? 'Cause you ain't that far up the totem pole to get on the bad side of those two."

Abby watched, riveted by the young woman's self-confidence. She was about Abby's age, but she stood up to a woman at least ten years older than her like she had the right to. She was a bold one. Abby took to her instantly.

"Mind your damn business, Sammi."

"Bitch, treating a guest badly *is* my business. Been in this club *waaay* longer than you," she retorted.

Grabbing the front of Tank's shirt, mean girl—aka Kerri—hissed, "Come on, Tank, you're taking me to your room."

Tank leaned against the bar, grinning from ear to ear, and said, "I love me a catfight."

Sammi's hand whipped out and smacked Tank in the chest. "Seriously, are you that stupid, Tank? You know how messing with other bitches riles her up."

"Sammi," Tank replied nonchalantly. "Please, I saw her hitting up another brother the other day."

Her savior, Sammi, rolled her eyes. "Whatever, that doesn't make you less of a dog." Then she gave him a shooing motion. "You know she's high-strung, so go on and settle her down. I guarantee you do not want Greta on your bad side."

"Tell me about it," he grumbled. "That bitch is crazy. Submissive, my ass. She's the biggest hard-ass there is when Cutter's not around."

"You can't touch her badassery, brother, so don't try," Sammi said with an unladylike snort.

Tank dropped a kiss on Sammi's head. "Second only to you, sweetheart."

Clutching her chest, she batted her eyes at the big guy and said, "Aww."

He grunted, gave Abby a wink and permitted himself be led away by the scary, mean girl, biker bitch.

"Thanks," Abby said loudly, her ribs slamming against the side of the bar as a slew of people roiled past them. "Greta warned me."

"About the bitches?"

"Yeah, but that one was scarier than I'd thought possible." She gave a self-conscious shudder.

Biker chick or not, Sammi didn't look like she'd cower to anyone. She embodied confident sexiness.

"Don't mind them. Kerri's actually sweet when she's not being insecure about her man."

Abby shot her a look of disbelief. Sammi chuckled and held out her hand. "I'm Sammi, by the way."

Shaking it, Abby replied, "So I've heard."

Sammi gave her a confused look.

"Tank said your name. Mine is Abby, obviously."

"Cool. Let's get some drinks and find our way back to Greta."

❋❋❋

Abby was like a lively butterfly, fluttering from nectar to nectar. A fucking gorgeous, little pixie butterfly creature, with her thick, short waves of blond hair with eyes to match.

"You can't keep your eyes off her," Cutter noted.

"The fuck you talking about," Loki growled.

They were sharing a bench during a normal mid-July party in the backyard of the clubhouse. In the middle of the yard, near the bonfire, Abby was chatting with Greta. The light from the fire silhouetted her from behind, her hair bouncing along with her tits as she made enthusiastic gestures.

Whenever he saw or thought of her, the word sunshine popped into his head on repeat. Recalling the sunny landscape that he conjured up as a kid when his mother described her natal home in southern Italy, he bet they'd be one and the same with that girl.

She was like a ball of sunshine and honey. Sunny and sweet. And vanilla. If he was to name the elusive scent that wafted up to his nostrils when he'd crowded up next to her in the office, it'd be honey-sugared vanilla. Besides being so damn pretty and sexy, she exuded a sweetness he'd only seen on sitcom shows growing up.

"Don't snap my head off. Telling you what I see. It wouldn't kill you to admit that you like her."

"Like her?" he scoffed. "I admit no damn thing. She's a pain in my ass, is what she is."

"Not mutually exclusive, brother. I should know. Story of my life with Greta."

After class, the night before last, Abby had rushed up to him, complimenting him on his handling of Alex's panic attack. Pride and pleasure bubbled in his chest at her attentiveness. She'd interrupted the class with her late entry, and he was biding his time to chew her ass out afterward, but the smile lingering on her lips as she praised him had waylaid his best intentions.

From under her eyelashes, she asked in a hesitant but throaty voice, "Do you...um...want to go for a drink or something?"

All the blood in his body headed south to his cock. Glancing down her tank top at the swells of her full, heavy tits added to the temptation to take her. As did her pink, flushed cheeks and warm golden eyes.

Instead of doing any of that, he squashed the balmy heat taking residence in his chest and glared down at her.

Crossing his arms over his chest, he replied with a question of his own. "Why would I want to do that?"

Shrugging a bare shoulder, the strap of her tank lifting and falling over her shoulder as she toed the new padded flooring, she offered, "We could, you know, talk about Alex. How to handle it if another situation occurs in the future."

His brows slammed together, and he glowered. "I handled it. I'll handle anything that comes up. I don't need your help. Hell, I don't need you."

He got that she was trying to make friends with him, but he didn't appreciate a reminder of her lack of complete confidence in his abilities. Shit went down with Alex, and he'd helped her through it. It's what he did. He took care of things. Initially, he'd felt put-upon and had only done it for the money, but helping Alex come out of her panic attack made him feel useful.

As he laid her head on his lap, he was reminded why it was so crucial to commit 100 percent to the class. He'd deal with whatever it brought up for him, because Alex's transformation was worth any kind of shit he ended going through himself.

Undaunted by his cruel words, she went on, "You're obviously a professional, and I realized that I was being overly protective. Maybe a little territorial. Not only do my clients mean a lot to me but a lot of my professional advancement hinges on whether my boss sees the clients doing well in the class. I'm also taking a course to become certified as a trainer, so I need to participate in one myself in order to complete the requirements. More than that, I'd love for us to be able to talk through the class. It's obvious you don't need my help, but I was wondering if I could continue attending for my own education."

His brows shot up. That was unexpected. He pondered on her proposition. On one hand, she admitted that she wouldn't be taking the class to spy on him. She trusted his ability to take care of the women. So much so that she wanted to audit the class for herself. That, he could work with.

"Fine, but on one condition. Anything between us is strictly professional. We will not be *hanging out* or *fucking* or *anything* else. We'll meet after class to review any questions you have, and that's it."

Abby's face fell, her expression stark with embarrassment and hurt. His chest felt tight and uncomfortable. He rubbed his chest, but he refused to back down. Yeah, he shouldn't have been so crass, but he'd needed to shock her a little. Let her know that he was no Prince Charming. He was a demanding mofo. There was no future for him and this cutesy, sassy fairy creature. She sure as hell could never handle him and she sure as hell deserved a lot better than him. They'd never work. Never.

Flattening her lips, her little body stiffened, and she crossed her arms over her chest. She had a tendency to do that when she was upset, he noticed. His fucking heart *ached* to watch the hurt pouring off her, but he was doing this for her own good, dammit. This was him manning up. For fuck's sake, chances were, she'd never survive a man like him.

Although unaware, the protective gesture of folding her arms pushed her plush tits high up in her tank top. A strap fell off her shoulder, doing a damn good job of torturing him. He rolled his eyes as he bit back a groan.

Tough little thing that she was, she rallied. Throwing her shoulders back, she said, "So I can take the class, then? To observe."

"Yeah," he grunted out.

It was the least he could do, considering his blunt rejection.

"Nothing else though?" she asked hopefully.

Damn, she was persistent, showing more mettle than he'd expected. He almost, *almost* caved, but stiffened his spine and imitated her posture, tightening his fingers over his biceps. Although his reasons for doing so were entirely different. For him, it was to keep from yanking her by the shoulders, hoisting her up to her tiptoes, and kissing the hell out of her. The taunting strap continued to torment and mock him, but he'd stay strong, goddammit.

"Nothing," he confirmed.

That was how they'd left it last. Little did he think she'd show up at the clubhouse two days later dressed in a ripped jean shorts and a scrappy tank top stretched wide over her luscious tits. His life was fucked. Seriously fucking fucked.

"Never seen her at the clubhouse before. How did she end up here?" he asked, playing it off as if it didn't matter either way to him.

"Greta and Abby have become friends over the past months. I guess she told her to stop by. Chick bonding and all that. You complainin'?"

"No," he lied through his tight lips.

At that moment, Abby threw her head back and laughed at something Sammi had said to her. The cords stretched over her smooth throat and her mouth opened, letting loose a husky, sultry laugh.

If only she was kneeling in front of him, he'd order her to keep her doe eyes on him while he filled her mouth and thrust his thick cock down her throat. *Fuuuck.* His cock was harder than hard. He refused to masturbate, much less fuck a bitch, so there was no relief for him other than a cold shower at the end of the night.

Whistle approached Abby and handed her a beer. Loki's eyes narrowed into slits.

Oh, hell fucking no. *No.* The pretty boy would have his hand under her skirt in a hot second.

"'Scuse me," Loki grumbled, dropping his beer bottle and standing up.

Chuckling under his breath, Cutter queried, "Where you goin'?"

Cutter followed his line of sight and then belly laughed at his expense, but Loki was too busy getting to Abby to stop and beat his ass. He was going to rip the young pup apart.

A second later, he wrapped a hand around Abby's elbow and yanked her against his side, glaring down at Whistle. "Don't you got somewhere else to be, boy?"

Whistle's eyes widened. His gaze drifted down to Loki's hand, and he mumbled something about a beer and melted into the crowd.

Shaking off his hand, Abby turned on him and accused, "Why did you do that? He was cute."

"He's a *kid.*"

"He's not a kid. I'd bet we're around the same age. He was very attentive, and, God knows, I can't say the same of you. Unless another man flirts with me, that is. You're such an asshole. You can't have a drink with me, but you think you can butt in when I'm talking to someone at a party?"

She poked a finger at his chest. "I don't think so, buddy."

"You don't know what the fuck you're talking about," he fibbed. "Whistle can barely talk. He's an idiot. All he knows how to do is fuck."

Her chin tilted up in the air. "What's the problem with

that? Perhaps that's what I'm looking for. I could do with a good fuck."

Loki felt his face pale. *She did not just say that to my face.*

Stepping into her space, he pushed until his chest grazed hers, forcing her to take a step back to maintain eye contact. Gripping her arms tightly, he seethed through clenched jaws, "You are not going to fuck him."

"Why ever not?" She batted her eyelashes at him.

She thinks she can act cute with me? Yeah, not happening.

Loki pounded his chest. "Because you want me."

"That may have been true *before*," she scoffed. "Since that's not on the table, I'm free to be with whoever I want, in whatever capacity I choose."

Nostrils flaring, he yanked at her arm and stalked off, dragging her behind him. He wrestled through the crowd into the clubhouse, hauled her past the bar, around dance area, and prodded her down an empty hallway.

Swinging the first door he found open, he shoved her inside an office and slammed it behind him. This sexy little pixie being with anyone else was not on the fucking table. If she needed something, he would be the only man providing it for her.

Walking her backward, he watched the various expressions flashing over her face. All good. Her eyes were dilated. Her mouth parted. Then she nervously bit down on her plump lip, her nails scratching down his T-shirt.

He pushed her backward with his chest until her hip knocked against the corner of a desk. Her hand flew back and clutched the table to maintain her balance, brushing papers off the desk onto the floor. Loki kept going, pressing her until her spine hit a wall. Once there was nowhere else to go, he smacked his palms on either side of her head.

Towering over her so she could feel just how much bigger

he in comparison to her, Loki leaned in and got caught up in her vanilla and sunshine fragrance. He might as well have been at the Disney resort in sunny Orlando, Florida. Her scent evoked hot sun, salty waves, cotton candy, and roller coasters.

"What was on the agenda for tonight?" he asked snappishly.

A furrow crinkled between the perfect arcs of her brows. "What are you talking about?"

"If you hooked up with Whistle, how far were you gonna let him go?"

"For the record, I spoke to him for literally five minutes. I had no agenda."

"Fuckin' fine," he bit out. "Let's say you hung out for a while and he suggested you go upstairs with him. What would you have ended up doing?"

Her head canted to the side. "Why are you asking? Do *you* want to do something with me?" She clutched her chest. "Heaven forbid."

Fuck, he deserved her taunts. "Answer the question, woman."

Her gaze sliced over his shoulders for a moment as she contemplated his question. Then her eyes coasted down his cut, hovered at the bulge behind his zipper, and fluttered rapidly. Yeah, he was a big guy everywhere, but he had nothing to hide.

Rage and jealousy pummeled through his arteries, poisoning his heart against one of his own brothers, and he was hanging on to the last thread of his fraying self-restraint. With one hand wrapped around her slender neck, his thumb holding her chin in place. The pulse at the base of her throat was going a mile a minute.

She swallowed and then bashfully dropped her gaze. Fuck, he liked that bit of submission. Nervous, she licked her plump lips with languid slicing motions. First the top. Then the bottom. After she was done with them, they were glossy and succulent, like she'd applied a layer of gloss. Goddamn, his balls were pulling up tight.

"I'd kiss him."

"What else?" he bit out.

To give her courage, his lips brushed over hers. Once. Twice. A third time. Holy fuck, it was official. The chick tasted like fucking sunshine and honey.

His knees almost buckled but he locked them in. He couldn't remember the last time he kissed a woman, but he knew in his bones that he'd remember his first kiss with Abby for-fucking-ever. Like he needed his next breath, he needed her to turn away from her plan with Whistle and turn toward him for whatever she wanted. He'd make damn sure to satisfy every one of her desires.

Pressing against her lips, he murmured, "How far, Abby?"

His tongue swiped over her fleshy bottom lip.

"How far would you have let his lips touch you?" he pleaded.

The palm of his hand drifted down and cupped her breast.

"I'd let him eat me out," she blurted.

As a reward for answering, he slanted his mouth over hers and plunged his tongue inside.

Fuck, that's where the vanilla came from. He'd found the source and, dammitt, nothing was gonna stop him from drinking from it.

A small moan vibrated from her mouth straight to his cock. Fuck, if he could bottle that sound and sleep beside it at night, it would surely banish all his nightmares.

He feasted on her soft, wet mouth as her tongue darted out to play with his. Tentative in the beginning, her kissing built in confidence until she was meeting him thrust for thrust. The image of Whistle's face rose from the recesses of his mind. *That little punk.*

But he was here with her, not the punk. Never the punk. Now, he had to make sure that he imprinted himself on her body so that she never thought of Whistle again.

8

LOKI

Loki broke off the kiss, a growl rumbling from his chest. The thought of Whistle's mouth anywhere on Abby was bad enough. But her *pussy*? He heaved out a breath, the air from his lungs caressing the blond wisps along her temple.

Drilling into her with his eyes, he slowly took a knee in front of her.

Pressing his nose to the apex of her thighs, he took a deep whiff and said, "I'm going to fuckin' devour you."

Her thighs trembled at his threat, but she was so wet he could fucking smell it. The thought that another man might have had the privilege of being in his position almost threw him into a frenzy.

He had to make this good for her. Not just good, but un-fucking-forgettable.

"Holy shit, holy shit, holy shit," she repeated as he undid her jean shorts and yanked them down, uncovering plain white cotton boy-cut panties. *Holy fuck.* Even her panties screamed unspoiled and girly.

Pre-come oozed from his twitching cock. Unable to stop

himself from taking a nibble, he nipped her mons. Nails curled over and hooked into his shoulders. Pulling back to take a good, long look, he stripped her slowly, exposing her velvety skin, inch by fucking inch.

His fingers released the elastic band, and they fell to the ground. "Step out of them."

For once, she did as he ordered. Rushing, she tried to step out of her panties too quickly and her feet got caught up. His hands flew out and caught her by the hips.

"Slow down, Pixie, we have all the time we need," he soothed.

Abby regained her balance and roughly kick her panties away, leaving him eye level with the prettiest little cunt he'd ever seen.

Caressing her thigh, he ordered, "Spread those creamy thighs for me and show me your pussy."

"Yeah," she breathed out, nodding vigorously as she did what she was told.

It was a heady sensation watching her instantly follow his commands.

With his pointer finger, he traced a circle around her clit and parted the lips of her heat. Her pussy was a beautiful flower. Glistening wet petals parted to show her hidden treasure of glittering, sparkling dew.

He ran his nose along the slit, inhaling her honeyed vanilla scent and couldn't help but give it a quick flick of his tongue. Hot *damn*. Tasting her for the first time, he heard angels. He lapped at her honey and twirled around her clit a few times.

Above him, Abby was panting hard.

He hooked one of her legs in the crook of his elbow and spread her wide for his viewing pleasure. "You've got a sweet-tasting little kitty for me, Pixie."

A guttural moan slipped out of her and he almost spent in his damn pants. At the end of his tether, he palmed her ass and dragged her closer so as to better consume his meal. And consume he did. He slurped and licked and nipped to his heart's content. Head lodged between her thighs, he latched onto her clit and sucked down hard as he slowly sank a finger inside her. She let out a yelp followed by a series of hoarse moans.

His finger parted her tight pussy, plunging past one knuckle and then bumping against another as her flesh clamped down on his digit. Damn, she was tight. Abby was young but, chances were, not still a virgin at her age. Although, it was obvious that it'd been a long time since she'd taken a cock into that tight channel of hers.

A grim smile stretched his lips against her pussy. He liked that she didn't have much experience.

He could mold her to his specifications.

The specifications being the width of his cock.

For now, he didn't attempt to add another finger. Even with her juices easing his movements, she was almost too tight. Once his thick finger was completely enveloped, he got her sex dripping into his mouth.

Hands attacked his hair, clutching and tugging roughly, as she rocked her sweet cunt into his face. Grunts and other sounds he didn't recognize sprang from his throat as he alternated between pulsing his finger in and out and suckling on her tight pearl.

Her thighs began to quake. Her pussy clenched and unclenched rythmically. She was getting close. Drips of liquid rolled down and seeped over his knuckles.

His balls, trapped in his jeans, jerked tight. Loki yanked down on his zipper until he felt the air-conditioned air rush over his balls, but it did nothing to cool him off. He slapped his hand around his shaft and stroked it roughly.

Twisting his face to the side, he sank his teeth into her plush inner thigh. Her scream ripped through the air. He continued to finger fuck her while latched back onto her clit. Thrashing above him, her head whipped from side to side and banged against the wall as she came. Her pussy soaked his face as she ground down on him and he drank as much of her essence as he could.

Once she'd peaked, he replaced his finger with his tongue, lapping at her folds until her breathing settled. After one final shudder, she stilled above him.

Unlatching her fingers from his hair, she murmured in an awed voice, "That was incredible."

He lowered her leg beg to the floor with a dull thud. Rocking on his heels, he licked her slickness from his lips before wiping the leftovers with the back of his shaking hand.

That had to be the most satisfying thing he'd done in a long time. His cock had punched out of his jeans, but he'd done enough damage. He forced it back inside its prison of denim and tipped his head back to gaze at her exquisite face.

Cheeks flushed, eyes tearing, and hair in disarray, Loki barely suppressed a fist pump in the air. He swallowed down the raucous whoop hovering in his throat and stuffed down the urge to run victory laps around her. But, most of all, he stifled the drive to flip her on her back and pound into her clenching pussy.

She stared down at him with shock in her wide copper eyes, a trembling hand covering her gaping mouth. "What did we do?"

Heartbeat drumming in his chest, he chuckled. "Well...I'd say I ate your sweet pussy and you creamed all over my face. Came harder than I've seen a woman do in a long time."

Stomping her feet, she tangled with her shorts, pulling them up until it covered her glorious pussy.

Fixated on the wall above his head, she said, "We shouldn't have done that."

He ground down on his back teeth. What the fuck? She'd wanted him before.

"Hold up, you did ask me out," he pointed out.

Her eyes flashed. "That was before you rejected me and told me that our relationship would be strictly professional. What were your exact words?" She tapped her chin. "There will be no hanging out, no fucking, no anything else."

Fuck, if he could get a redo, he'd punch himself in the face before he opened his dumbass mouth. As much as he hated it, facts didn't change just 'cause he'd gotten a taste of her sweet puss. He still didn't deserve a woman like her. But there was no denying, tongue-fucking her cunt had been glorious

"Something like that, yeah," he agreed. "What can I say, I've been a bad boy."

Her brows notched together, and her bow-shaped lips pursed in an adorable pout of frustration. "What does that even mean?"

He shrugged. "Doesn't have to mean anything."

She visibly winced and he clamped his lips together. Fuck, he'd opened his big mouth and spewed out more bullshit nonsense. He sounded like an asshole, but it was for the best. Best for her, he reminded himself.

Her spine snapped straight and rigid as she stuttered out, "I-I see."

Rising, he adjusted his cock to give it a modicum of relief. It hurt to watch the pain crossing her face, but he couldn't exactly admit that he was pushing her away for her own sake. That it was easier for her if he was an asshole because he didn't deserve to have her or any woman. Not when Chopper was six feet under.

He reached for her jaw, but she flinched away from his touch.

"I wasn't using you," he said softly. He had to make sure she understood that much, at least.

Her eyes shattered like firecrackers in a night sky. "Oh, I think that's exactly what you were doing. Your ego got the best of you when you saw one of your friends flirting with me. You couldn't let him have me, even though you don't really want me."

His buzz popped like a balloon. That was the farthest thing from the truth. If he was a good man, an honorable man, if he hadn't let his brother die, proving that he was a piece of shit and nothing more, then he'd snap her up and never let her go.

Gripping her chin, he said, "Not true."

Abby jerked away from him.

Avoiding his direct gaze, she crossed her arms over her chest and demanded, "Then, explain."

He let out a weary sigh. He couldn't explain to her the entire truth. Searching for words, he finally settled with, "Babe, I don't fuck women."

Her eyes snapped to his, confusion clouding her golden eyes. "Men? Why would you go down on me if you're into men?"

"Not into men, either. Not that there's anything wrong with that. I haven't touched a woman in three years. Not a one. I haven't touched myself in that amount of time either. That should tell you the power you have over me with that sexy, tight body of yours and that tasty pussy."

Unable to help himself, he smacked his lips while gazing down at her delectable curves. His fingers twitched to grab her. "You're one hell of a temptation, I'll give you that much."

"Three years," she repeated. Her hand drifted down and settled on the outline of his cock. "Want me to—"

Clasping her hand, he dragged it off. "No."

Her brows drew close together, her lashes batting quickly in distress. "But, why?"

He couldn't tell her. After the year of trying to kill Kingdom and hurt himself, he didn't talk about Chopper anymore. Shaking his head, he snapped, "Not your business. It happened, but it can't happen again."

"Why not?" she huffed, reaching out, molding her small hand around the outline of his shaft and squeezing hard one more time before her hand slipped off him.

"Because it can't," he bit out. There were no words that could explain his predicament. The humiliation. The remorse. The abstinence. How could he explain the pact he'd made with himself to be abstinent, self-flagellation in retribution of Chopper's death?

Her chin lifted haughtily. "Fine, then I'll find someone else to take care of my needs."

She was goading him, but his stomach roiled at the thought of Whistle, or any man, on his knees with his nose in the pussy that he'd just made come.

His hand captured her jaw, not painful but enough to make a point. His eyes turned into angry slits. "Not a brother or any man I know. I'm warning you, Abby. I can't be with you, but I will hurt any man who touches you. Don't play me. I'm a jealous, vindictive son of a bitch when I want to be. I'm a Pandora's box you don't want pried open. It won't end well for anyone."

Grasping his hand, her nails scratched him, reminding him of the love marks she'd left on his neck and scalp.

He pulled away and took a few steps back. Sweat rolled down the length of his spine. Letting her walk away took every ounce of self-control he had, but there was no other sane choice. Bad enough that he'd slipped in a big, motherfucking way. One that would take years of his life to rectify because, standing there with her luscious curves in hand's reach and his cock about to explode, he would've sold off his left nut to have her.

Turning his back, he gritted out, "Go, Abby. Get the fuck out of here and go home."

He heard her shoes scuffing against the concrete floor, her hands struggling with the doorknob, the bounce of the door against the wall.

Her ingenuous vanilla scent was whisked away from him by a rush of cool air from the open door.

Head bent, a splash of white on the floor caught his eye.

He picked it up and nuzzled the sweet scent lingering in the gusset of her panties.

Fisting his hands, he punched the air. A left hook, a right hook. Left, right, left, right. Swinging his leg into an arc, he kicked the office chair. A series of arm and leg combinations burst out of him, and he attacked phantom fighters until he had to bend over from the stitch in his side.

Curled over himself, he fell to his knees, clutching the scrap of cloth in his fists, and howled in the empty space.

9

ABBY

*id every man lick a woman's pussy like it was his one
and only mission in life?*

Loki and his talented tongue were...just wow.
Abby twitched from the memory of him between her thighs. A
Cheshire-cat smile spread on her face. She was kinda proud of
herself. Despite his whatever was holding him back, she'd
managed to not only get him to touch her, but she had him
between her legs. While she'd been angry and sexually frustrated, it had been a relief to find out that it wasn't about her.

Loki was twisted up inside, roaming the earth like a
wounded animal. Her heart squeezed at the thought of him
suffering, and not only because it was her life's mission to help
people in pain. It had been difficult to watch the anguish
sweep over his stern face, witness the self-hatred etched on his
features. As much as he enjoyed what they had done, he
looked crushed, as if he'd failed someone. She wanted to
reach for him, comfort him, but she knew better than to
attempt it. His pride and the self-recriminations would've
prevented him from accepting her help.

Flicking the end of her pen on the notebook in front of

her, Abby fixed a look of interest on her face during the staff meeting. Seriously, though, back to her question. Did men routinely go down on women like that? Was this a routine part of a woman's sex life? She hadn't ever had a man's mouth on her before, so she didn't personally know the answer to that question, but it was burning her up. Not only had she gone mindless with lust, but now knowing what she'd been missing for years, she was hot under the collar. And that had only been his *tongue*. Who knew what it would feel like to have his cock inside her, moving in and out, in and out.

Sweet Jesus.

She screwed her eyes shut.

"Abby?"

Abby cracked one eye open, heat rushing up her throat and cheeks. She was caught out fantasizing about a man in front of her boss, Caroline, and eight of her closest colleagues. Yikes.

Sitting up in her chair, she replied, "Yes?"

"How is it going with the class at the boxing place?"

"It's boxing and MMA," she clarified.

"Excuse me?"

She cleared her throat and shifted in her seat. "The facility engages in boxing and MMA, that is, mixed martial arts. Loki teaches and trains MMA fighters."

"Loki? The trainer? I thought his name was Brandon."

"Yes, it is, but he goes by Loki. I guess it's like a stage name," she clarified.

"Oh, like a wrestler going with a stage name."

Yeaaah, let's go with that and bypass the whole biker thing, shall we?

"This works with the women?" Caroline asked with curiosity in her eyes.

"Oh, yes, they adore him. He's a military guy. Army something or other and he's built. Huge, really, but he has a way that inspires confidence in them. I also think that he models appropriate male behavior. He's clearly protective of them, but he maintains rigorous boundaries. No flirting or anything even vaguely inappropriate. I was a little concerned in the beginning, but a client had a panic attack during class and he handled it impeccably. I didn't even have to intervene."

Caroline gave her a thoughtful look. "You're certainly singing his praises."

Abby's entire face flushed. She was certain she'd gushed like a girl crushing on a boy. "My biggest concerns have been relieved, yes, and I will continue to attend the class since I'm going for my certification as well."

An amused smile spread on Caroline's face. "How old is he?"

Aww, shit. She loved Caroline, but that woman was like an octopus. Plus, she was around Loki's age. Abby gulped. "I'm not sure. Hard to tell with these types."

"Are we going to get a chance to meet this Loki?"

God, I hope not. Caroline was a black widow when it came to men. Mated them, burned them to a crisp, and then ate them for breakfast the following morning. A subtle shiver ran through her.

Tongue-tied, she said, "Of course."

Luckily, Abby's response was satisfactory. Caroline checked the meeting agenda and moved on to the next item.

Turning her attention to Deborah, who headed their largest annual fundraiser, she asked, "How are things going with the location? Did you secure the same location as last year?"

With the focus off her, Abby melted back into her seat with a relieved sigh, grateful that she managed to avoid any more Caroline's incisive questioning. She was the director of one of the largest and most effective programs in the county, but her sharpness also intimidated Abby, even after working under her for several years. Speaking of their annual gala had images of Loki, deliciously filling out a tuxedo, dancing in her head. With his shaggy dark hair, his scar, and his overall protector vibe, he'd look like a dirty dream in a tux. Yum.

※※※

HE WAS ADDICTED to her taste.

What man in his right mind wouldn't be?

Thank fuck he'd gotten that punk Whistle out of the picture before he got a taste of her sweet pussy. He had no intention of getting attached to her in any way, shape, or form, but one taste and *fucking hell*, the floodgates had been kicked open.

All day long, he walked around with the hard-on to end all hard-ons. If his life wasn't miserable enough before, touching her had made it exponentially worst. The more he tried to suppress thoughts of what he wanted to do to her, the more his dreams haunted him and worsened his disturbed sleep.

Every morning, he woke up with spilled come on his sheets. It was downright demeaning. He was stronger than this. Three years and he hadn't touched a woman, but one taste, *one* taste, and he was screwed.

Apparently, his usual dose of grumpiness had become unbearable. At least that was Cutter's complaint when the bastard cornered him after shuttering the doors of the gym.

"Bro, you're losing your fucking shit, and I've about had it. We need to talk," Cutter began.

"The hell are you chattering about?" Loki countered.

"*Brah*," Cutter said in an exasperated tone.

"What?"

"You're fucking shitting me, right? You must realize how you're acting?"

Loki stared at him blankly. Maybe if he was silent the fucker would get on with what he had to say.

"You're barking at everyone. Jackie came to me in tears because you reamed into her about some shit."

Loki's head snapped back. "She forgot to clean the last stall of the bathroom. I had to go behind her and clean up her mess. Didn't finish up before eleven fucking p.m. because of her."

Raising his hand as if trying to soothe Loki, Cutter said, "Dude, I get it, but you can't scream at people. You could have left it for her the following morning."

He gave Cutter a droll look.

"Or, barring that, because you're an anal neat freak, you could've cleaned it and, y'know, talked to her about it the next morning. Like a human being. Jackie's not a one-time incident. Only time you come up for air is when you gotta prep yourself for your class with the females. Other than that, you walk around acting like a righteous asshole. And that's on top of your usual, everyday assholery. You gotta get a grip before you run off our employees."

Cutter was right. Even he had to admit that he was amped up. Every reaction was extra. And he knew the culprit.

Cutter canted his head to one side. "What the fuck is going on, Loki?"

Loki collapsed on the couch between his and Cutter's desks. Tilting his head, he banged it against the wall a few times and then settled to stare up at the ceiling. There were spider webs in one corner, the spider busy working away on another strand of its web. Fucking Jackie. Truth be told, they needed to suck it up and employ one more janitorial staff, but Loki couldn't justify the expense. Unfortunately, the downward sprial in his attitude came from another source. Was he willing to breach the issue with Cutter?

"I can't help you if you won't talk to me, and if you don't spit it out, I'll be forced to bring Kingdom into the conversation," Cutter reasoned.

Loki groaned. "Not that fucker."

"Just sayin'. You deal with me or with him. Your choice."

"Christ. All right," he grumbled.

Cutter pulled out a vape. His so-called "transition" into a new, smokeless lifestyle. Lighting it, he leaned back, tipping his chair on its back legs. "Come on, out with it. I know what it is anyways."

Loki lifted his head and zeroed in on Cutter's arrogant smirk. "Yeah? What the hell do you think it is, smartass?"

"Two words. Abby. Sex."

Loki scrubbed his eyes. *Fuck me, I'm that obvious.*

"Don't worry, no one else knows you hooked up with her."

Shooting up onto his feet, he stalked toward Cutter. "How the fuck do you know?"

"I ain't blind. I saw you follow her at the club party. A little while later, she walked out, her hair sticking up like she'd been fucked seven ways to Sunday. By the way you're actin', I'm thinkin' you didn't actually fuck her. You wouldn't be wound up like you are."

Baring his teeth, Loki stalked away and flung himself back onto the couch.

"I'm right," Cutter said.

Loki glowered at him.

"Yup, I'm right," he repeated. "You'd have told me to fuck off if it wasn't true. Look, you gotta do something about this.

It's bad enough that you haven't been with a woman for ages, but now it's damage-control time, yo. For the sake of our workplace, if nothing else."

Loki scraped a hand over his jaw and muttered, "I should've never tasted her."

"You're not going to like this but I don't give a fuck so listen up because I have the solution."

"What could you possibly advise me on? You like to tie them up, for chrissake. We're not playing in the same league," Loki griped.

"We never have before, but your situation has changed over the years. The way you wanna fuck ain't the way it was before Chopper's death."

Gritting his teeth, Loki questioned, "How in the fuck would you know this?"

"Because you crave control. You won't fuck, but my educated guess is, that if you did, you wouldn't be satisfied with the normal, vanilla shit. Not anymore. Dominance rolls off you, bro. The only way you can control the feeling is by controlling a woman while you fuck her."

Loki's jaw dropped marginally. Crazy as he sounded, Cutter's words resonated, like when he was in the zone while cleaning his katana, his Japanese sword.

He pinched the bridge of his nose. "If what you say is true, then I'm in a bad fucking way. Have you seen Abby? She's like a fairy, waving her wand and throwing pixie dust everywhere. They don't get sweeter and more innocent than her. She'll never want an ugly, old motherfucker like me."

"True dat. She is all those things, but don't make the mistake of assuming she's weak. She is most definitely *not* weak. Annnd I'm gonna tell you something that will make all your problems go away."

Cutter gave him a meaningful look that he couldn't decipher.

Loki demanded, "Well? What is it?"

"Don't shoot down what I'm about to tell you. Think about it first," he cautioned.

Loki nodded and made a gesture for Cutter to continue.

"She's a submissive."

Loki barked out a laugh. The short laugh rolled into another and another until he was laughing so hard he doubled over. Abby a submissive? Most ridiculous thing he'd ever heard.

"You are so wrong. She looks like she'd cry over a paper cut," he panted out when his laughing finally tapered off.

"I didn't say she was into pain. I said she was into being dominated. I'll bet my left nut that she's got the taste for some good old-fashioned bondage, too. You'll have to build her pain tolerance slowly because you're the one who likes to inflict a pinch of discomfort. No worries though, 'cause she's a good little subbie, and she'll do what you want."

Surveying Cutter from top to bottom with an incredulous expression, Loki asked, "Have you lost your ever-fucking mind? What are you? The subbie whisperer?"

Shrugging, Cutter grinned widely. "I know what I know. Anyway, I'm good. You're the one losing your damn mind. I've got a woman to fuck and dominate. Every. Single. Day. You're the one in trouble, not me."

Abby a subbie? Abby a *subbie*. The words echoed in his mind, strengthening with each subsequent loop in his brain. Could it be true? "Let's say, hypothetically, that you're right. I don't do women. You know my stance on this issue."

"I get you," Cutter nodded, sagely. "But you're losing control. That shit is gonna spiral and take you down with it. I ain't in the mood to get you committed any sooner than necessary."

"Ha. Fucking funny."

Cutter pocketed his vape. "Point is that you need this. It ain't about turning your back on the oath you made to yourself since Chopper. No one gives a shit about that oath, by the way, but you. Don't know where you came up with it, but I can guarantee you that Chopper wouldn't appreciate anyone taking on a 'no bitches' rule on his behalf. He was all about the bitches."

Loki's belly clenched. Only Cutter, the fuckin' jokester, could get away with throwing shit out like that and then move on as if he hadn't mocked a man's vows.

"This is about regaining control," he continued. "Let's face facts, you need control. It's the bedrock of your life. I know because I have the same urges. I've just learned how to handle it. You fuck her, get control, and then cut her loose. Easy."

A hunger tugged low in his gut. One that insisted *more, more, more.* Although he couldn't have everything he wanted, a normal life—girl friend, old lady, wife, children, *family*—he'd make an exception and get what he could to regain control of this never-ending thirst. Fuck her and then cut her loose. For once in his life, Cutter was talking sense.

10

LOKI

"You're not following the other women home. Why me?" Abby challenged him, sitting on one of the mats lined up against a wall of mirrors, changing from sneakers into flip-flops. Loki's eyes twitched in reaction to her tone of voice. She stared up at him expectantly, waiting for him to answer.

Class had ended, and even Kerri, who had joined the class as a survivor, had given up on flirting with him and left. Abby had waited because she had a few questions about a technique he'd used during class.

Things had changed since the night he went down on her. She didn't trail after him the way she had after the first class, when she'd propositioned him, but there was an undeniable tension between them. Every word they'd spoken to each other was fraught with innuendo. She also started testing him every chance he got. She'd been getting bold, and he was damn near close to cracking and putting her in her place.

After they'd finished talking about the class, he'd spontaneously informed her that he'd follow her home to make sure she'd be okay. That was when she landed a question he had zero intention of touching. He'd never admit it out loud, but that the idea of anything happening to her on her way home made him want to rip the universe to shreds.

He'd already let her go home twice alone, and it near drove him crazy. He was gonna make sure she got home safe.

End of fucking story.

When he refused to answer her question, she rolled her eyes at him. Her blond hair made her look like a cute pixie angel and that snarky eye-roll made him want to turn her over on his lap. Grabbing her bag, she stood, heaving out an exasperated breath. At the sight of her chest rising and falling, his mind veered off course into porn fantasy territory. Despite the powerful netting of her sports bra, each upward movement showed off the swells of her tits, his cock growing harder with every subsequent breath she took.

"If I allow you to follow me—"

Stalking toward her, he pinned her against the wall mirror, and cut her off mid-sentence. She let out an audible gasp, which he felt gust over his neck. Her huge tits pressed against his chest and, swear to God, he'd never experienced sexual frustration like he had in the past two weeks.

"Allow me? Babe, you don't allow or disallow anything with me, you hear?" he growled in the shell of her ear.

"Whatever," she muttered, batting his arm with her hand. "You don't want me driving you all around the city before I shake you off, which I will inevitably succeed in doing, because I know how to lose a tail."

That sass. Fuck him, she knew how to get under his skin. His cock thickened further, and he dug it into her belly.

Unable to help himself, he groaned and nuzzled into her fragrant hair. "How the fuck would you know how to do that?"

"I learned from a law enforcement officer to teach my

clients if any of them were being followed by their deadbeat loser boyfriends or husbands."

Bracing a hand on the mirror, he lifted a shoulder in acceptance of her explanation. "Random, but okay."

"If I *allow* you"—Loki groaned and pushed his erection deeper into her— "to follow me home, then you'll have to come in for a chat."

"You're negotiating with me? Most women would be flattered with the stalking alone. A bit demanding, aren't you?"

"I'm not most women," she replied pertly, raising her chin and boldly locked eyes with him. "Either you come in afterward or you'll never know if I end up home. I may decide to stop at a bar or hit up a friend." She looked down at her nails nonchalantly. "It's a Friday night, after all."

Christ, he wanted to smack that bratty ass of hers because she had him. He'd lose sleep if he didn't know where she was. A bar? On TGIF? Where this little pixie girl would get hit on by a dozen drunk assholes? *I don't think so.* So long as they were in each other's lives, at least for the duration of the class, he didn't want her gallivanting around town without him. Yeah, he got that he was a caveman, and he gave zero fucks about it either.

"Fucking hell. You win. Go to your car."

✳✳✳

STOMPING UP HER STAIRS, Loki paused behind her as she fumbled with the keys in the dim light. He squinted at the wall lamp beside her door. How many watts was the bulb? It was a low-as-shit voltage, is what it was. He was already strategizing how he could come back when she was at work and change it for her.

Standing behind her, he looked down at the doormat and saw the thing had butterflies and ladybugs, with the words "Home Sweet Home" written in looping cursive. A wreath of silk sunflowers hung on the door, covering the peephole. Hers was the only door with decorations in the open-air hallway of the quiet apartment complex.

Abby jiggled the lock a few times before managing to get the door open, stepped into a small foyer, and hung her keys on the tail of a small cat-shaped key holder.

Speaking of cats, a little red tabby greeted them by the door, instantly twirling around Loki's leg.

Abby peered down and noted, "Ginger seems to like you. Huh. She's usually shy with strangers."

"What can I say, pussy cats love me," he replied with a twinkle in his eye.

On her tiptoes, hooking her purse on the back of the foyer closet door, she threw him a grin over her shaking shoulders. "Couldn't help yourself, could you?"

"Nope," he replied, unrepentant. "Am I wrong?"

"Oh, no, definitely not wrong," she answered with a light laugh that sounded chimes to him. Buoyant and joyful, just like her.

Slipping off her flip-flops, she pointed to a cozy couch in her compact living room. "Make yourself comfortable. Do you want a beer?"

"Got anything else?"

Padding across the parquet floor to her kitchen, which was separated by a bar with three stools, she opened her fridge. He caught a flash of her heart-shaped ass as she bent over to inspect the contents. Fuck, he wanted to glide his hand all over her sweet ass. He shifted until he found a position that gave his dick a little more breathing room. He was going to broach the subject of benefits with her. Since they wouldn't be friends, because he didn't want or need a friend, the topic would be strictly about benefits.

"Lemonade. Orange juice. Water."

"Water."

"Ice?" she called out.

Loki eased his aching muscles into the comfy pillows and let out a sigh. "No."

Being in her space was so different from his hard futon at work, and his even harder mattress at the club. The place fit her perfectly, cozy and relaxed. Lots of stuff on the walls— posters of flowery shit—and little knickknacks on her book- shelves and fireplace mantle. There was a cat bed and a scratching post. Cat toys were scattered on the floor. Her honied vanilla fragrance was everywhere, weaving around him, and making him a little drowsy.

He'd been working out harder than usual in a desperate attempt to get a handle on his runaway libido, but it was catching up to him. Tomorrow he had to take a day off to rest his body.

Abby stood before him, holding the glass of water and a beer. Frowning down at him, she asked, "What's wrong?"

"Nothing."

"You're wincing. I know you're an old man, but still," she teased.

He snorted. "I'm thirty-eight. Not *that* old, yet." His gaze raked over her, "How old are you?"

"Twenty-two."

"Who's the old one now? I didn't think you were a day over twenty-one," he shot back.

She lounged beside him. He took her beer bottle from her hand and twisted the cap off before handing it back to her. A quick smile and she tipped the bottle to her lips. He had to stifle a moan when he watched the glide of her slender throat muscles working the liquid down her throat. He had more than one beer that he wanted to shoot down her throat. Fuck, thoughts like that were not helpful.

"I've been told I look young for my age. It's so annoying. I'm the only one who gets carded when I go out with my coworkers on Thursday nights."

"Did you start working at the Agency right after college?"

She nodded. "I interned for them when I was doing my master's in social work, and I interviewed with them a few weeks before graduation. After I graduated, I took a few weeks off to visit one of my brothers, who lives in the Virgin Islands, and then started right when I got back. Been there ever since. Barring anything unexpected, I expect to work there until I retire. It's everything I've always wanted to do."

"You always wanted to work with battered women? That's a tough job," he observed. She might be young, but she was focused on her career. He liked that about her. She took her work seriously, and he'd helped out Sage and Greta at their law office, so he knew it wasn't an easy job.

"I do mostly work with women, but I have several male clients. Yes, since my first psychology class in undergrad, I knew what I wanted to do. Help people. Work with them to break away from harmful relationships and grow into healthy, independent human beings."

Loki took Abby's legs onto his lap, pulled off her shoes, and began massaging her feet. She was a hard-working woman. It'd been a long week for him. He doubted it was any easier for her.

A small moan slipped out of her mouth and she wiggled into the cushions to get into a more comfortable position.

Her eyelids drooped slightly. "What about you?"

His hands stopped working the arches of her foot. "What about me?"

"When did you become an MMA expert?"

"I was always into weapons and self-defense. Didn't realize how much I liked it until boot camp when I was eighteen. A buddy of mine was a black belt and he taught me when we had time. On tour, there were long boring stretches of downtime in Afghanistan. Once I came back from my tours, I started going to fight clubs. Underground fighting. That kind of stuff."

Abby spread her fingers over her breastbone, eyes wide. "Why?"

"Life is simple in the cage. It's you and the other guy. The rules of engagement are straightforward. You defeat your opponent using any skill you've got. Nothing's off the table." He shrugged. "What's not to love?"

"But the risk of injury..."

"Is real," he finished. "It's brutal and dangerous, but it's when I felt alive, honestly. But I had to stop."

"Why did you stop if you love it so much?"

Because he didn't deserve to feel alive. And because he'd promised Chopper. At the time, he figured he'd finagle his way out of his pledge, but Chopper knew what he was doing. Asked him, knowing he was gonna kill himself and that Loki wouldn't go back on the oath he'd made to his dead little brother.

Loki pushed Abby's legs off him, stood up, and began pacing. "It's not something I talk about it."

Abby dropped her feet to the rug and gingerly placed her palms on her knees, her eyes following his path to and fro. "You're shutting me out."

Loki's gaze slashed to hers. "I don't recall ever letting you in and I don't recall asking you to care."

"It's not the kind of thing one needs permission for, it just happens. There's nothing you can do about it and there's nothing you can do to stop it," she replied calmly.

Beneath her sweet pixie exterior, the girl had grit, he'd give her that. "Yes, I can."

Abby grasped his hand as he stalked past her and held on. "Loki, please, don't act like this. Most people are happy to have someone care about them."

Shaking her hand off, he drilled into her, "I'm not one of your damaged victims. Someone to pity. Someone to save. I don't need your fucking help and I sure as hell never asked you for it."

"I've never pitied you," she called after him as he stormed out and slammed the door behind him.

Yeah, and he wouldn't give her the chance to either. Time to deal with his frustration on his terms. He was gonna take care of his cock with his own hand.

11

ABBY

Abby hadn't seen him since the disastrous confrontation in her apartment.

He'd looked so good, all gruff and prickly, sitting on a couch too small for his frame, in her living room. Massaging her foot, talking about herself, asking questions about himself. He stormed out, but she hadn't taken it personally. She knew a tortured man when she saw one. He'd picked the wrong girl if he thought to scare her off with his outburst. If anything, it had only strengthened her resolve. She had a proposal for him, one that would mutually benefit the both of them, and she wasn't going to be cowed by his brusque mask.

"I didn't take you for a coward," Abby stated, deciding it was best to face this head-on.

Facing away from her, Loki was wiping down the mats after the last student left the room. He was bent over a mat, giving her a perfect view of his ripped muscles beneath a black T-shirt and his delicious ass encased in athletic shorts. His quads bulged as he crouched over, and she had to bite back a moan.

"Don't start with me, Abby. I don't have anything good to give you, believe me," he said in a low rumble.

"On the contrary, you *do* have something I want. Badly," she argued.

Jumping to the door, she firmly locked it, and placed her shoulders against it, arms crossed over her chest.

His head whipped in her direction. Rising to his feet, he stalked over to her. "What the fuck, Abby?"

Heart beating against her chest, she held out her hand and spoke rapidly, "I know what kind of man is attracted to me, and the kind of man I will end up with. You're not for me long-term, but you're perfect for my current needs. See, I'm inexperienced. I want to learn and I want you to the man to teach me." She swallowed hard and clarified, just in case she hadn't been clear enough. "To have intercourse with me."

He halted abruptly midstride, then resumed his prowl toward her. Although much more carefully, as if *she* were the wild animal here.

Good, she'd caught him off guard.

Eyeing her up and down, he clarified, "You want me to fuck you? Did I not already tell you I'm celibate?"

Abby averted her eyes. "Yes, but I thought you might make an exception for a-a... friend. I know it's a bit of a hardship, what with the women you had sex in the past, but I'm asking as a favor."

"With me?" he stressed.

She rolled her eyes and huffed out, "Of course, with you. I'm attracted to you, and after seeing how you handled Alex, I know you'll be gentle and caring. What with your control issues, you won't ram into me like a bull and tear me apart. Honestly, my first time was awful, and I haven't found anyone I wanted to try with again. I want to erase the memory of losing my virginity and add new ones on top of it. I want to learn about sex, how to enjoy it, how to offer it to someone else. I know you can help me with this, Loki, and I trust you."

Scrutinizing his stoic expression, she fidgeted, and caught a lock of hair around her finger. She'd laid it out there, alright. Having never been this bold with a man before and choosing Loki was nerve-wracking, at best. Maybe he wasn't interested, and she'd misconstrued the night he went down on her as more than a one-off. Just because she was attracted to him didn't mean it was mutual, but she'd come this far so the only thing to do was keep going.

He hadn't moved an inch, which only added to her roiling tummy. Nervously, she prattled on, "You could get drunk. That could definitely help."

He scowled deeply, the skin pulling on his scar, making the thin line flash white. "I don't get drunk."

"Hmm. How about weed? Drugs?" she suggested.

"Nothing," he gritted out. "I don't do any of that shit."

She pursed her lips, thinking hard as she scanned her body with a critical eye. She wasn't like Greta, tall and slim with perky breasts. She was too short, curvy with breasts the size of melons that didn't match the rest of her. Her chest was almost obscene—in her eyes. Yet, they were her only advantage because, while a man might pass over her plain face, he commonly paused on her chest. It didn't hurt that she showcased them tonight, instead of covering them up like she usually did.

"Maybe I'm bigger than the women you're used to, but I'll think of something. I could buy skimpy lingerie. Make it more enticing for you," she mused.

A low rumble reverberated in the empty space. "I don't need you to dress like a stripper to fuck you, and don't you dare lose your curves. Christ, what is it with women and their weight?"

Shaking his head, he concluded drily, "I may not have fucked in a while, but I enlisted when you were a little girl. I've been with many women in my time."

She glared up at him. The way he'd causally thrown out how *many women* he'd been with dug into her chest with an unpleasant sensation she'd never experienced before.

Jealousy?

She frowned. That was a first, but, seriously, the urge to mow down the throngs of women he'd been with like Freddy Krueger pumped through her veins.

Oh, Lord, not good.

Lifting her chin at a haughty angle, she said, "You're not a liar, so don't start for my sake. We both know the type of women you're used to. You don't have to get defensive again; I'm just trying to make this easier on you."

Eyes blazing fury, his hand slipped over the curve of her hip, then farther down, and squeezed her butt a little harder than she'd expected. It felt surprisingly good. Almost like a claiming act.

He leaned down and scented her below her earlobe. "Babe, you're cute. I don't do cute, but you got the kinda tits and ass men pay to jack off to, feel me?"

A giggle bubbled in her chest because his words sounded so ridiculous, but she wasn't going to disabuse him of the notion, no matter how unhinged he sounded. His compliment soothed her, especially considering she was feeling vulnerable after her proposition. Glancing up, she caught him watching her intently. As in, his entire attention was on her. It made her want to melt in place and run away at the same time.

He swiped his hand over his chin and tugged, as if he was still considering her proposal, still not won over by her arguments.

"It's the celibacy, isn't?" she asked.

"Yeah, but hell, I'd already jacked off to keep myself sane. What's one time," he replied, suddenly sounding resigned, exhausted.

"Is it a chore? Because I have much less experience than the women you've been with in the past?"

"Not a fucking chore, Abby. That's not the issue." His face hardened. "But there is an issue and if I do this, break my celibacy to help you out, then there will be rules. Clear fucking rules. It's a one-time thing, hear me? One night. One all-night fucking marathon where I'm going to make you so many times I'll ruin you for any other man, but if you're willing to risk it, then I'll do it.

Her entire body flushed.

"But that's it. It's the only way I can manage this in my head," he insisted.

The flush receded just as quickly. What did she expect? She didn't deny he would likely ruin her, but she'd never get an opportunity like this again so if she only got one night, then she was going to make the best of it.

On a bit of a high from the surprise of having won her point, she impulsively reached up to his jaw, caressed it for a moment, took hold of his nape and pressed her lips against his. Again, she heard the low rumble from the back of his throat she'd heard during their first kiss. Standing on her tiptoes, she licked the seam of his mouth. Once his lips parted, she plunged her tongue inside. His rich taste, like slow flaming bourbon, titillated her taste buds. She burned for him. *Burned.*

Loki took her by the hips and turned her toward a desk standing near the entrance. His hand swept piles of clean towels off and effortlessly lifted her on top, spreading her thighs wide. Stepping between them, he thrust a big hand beneath her shirt, pushed her sports bra up and splayed his hand over her breast.

Swiping over her nipple, he groaned.

He gripped the back of her skull and he took over their kiss. With a grunt, he bit into her bottom lip and held it. The *tug, tug, tug* of his teeth around her swelling flesh reeled her in, and she arched to push more of her breast against his wide palm. His fingers latched onto her nipple. Twisting and releasing it, Loki built a pressure strong enough to cause discomfort, but she leaned into it. He was going for what he wanted, and she would let him because she'd chosen him, would be guided by him.

His other hand went for her mound, pressing the heel of his hand against her clit in a lazy rhythm, like they had all the time in the world. He grasped the sides of her yoga pants and tugged, about to rip them off. She pushed against his chest and he allowed a couple of inches between them.

Her voice unsteady, she said, "No, not here."

"Yes, here." He captured her chin and gave her a mocking look. "You aren't the one in charge, baby girl. You asked me to fuck you and I will. That's where your power ends and mine begins. Get used to it because this is how I fuck, and it's how I'm gonna fuck you."

He crushed her nipple between his thick thumb and forefinger to prove his point, then freed her breast, gave it a quick slap that had her gasping, and stepped back. "If I wasn't afraid of hurting you, because I'm assuming it's been a while, I'd have my cock up your pussy so deep, you'd be screaming and creamin' on it right fucking now."

He blatantly adjusted his erection in his jeans in front of her. Dang, she loved that he was so hard and uncomfortable because of *her*. It gave her a bit of a head rush, to be perfectly honest.

"Doesn't mean we can't play," Loki said, tugging on his zipper. Freed, his cock slapped against his abs and Abby gave a start. Sure, she'd seen a bunch of penises before and touched him in the clubhouse, but—hot *damn, this* was something else. Fisting his thick shaft, he thrust into his hand a few times.

She tilted her head to the side and frowned. *Is that going to fit?* Huh, she wasn't so sure. He pulled on his dick again and liquid heat gushed out, soaking her panties. Who would have thought that she'd have this big badass, scarred biker jerking off in front of her, right outside of the hallway. Granted, not many people used the space they were in, but her gaze flicked to her door.

"The lock engaged," he confirmed, sparks glinting in his eyes. "Now, on your knees." His tone softened a touch, although a needy edge tinged his next question. "You wouldn't get me riled up and leave me hurtin', would you, Pixie? That wouldn't be very nice, and you're a nice girl."

"The gym is crawling with people, Loki," she tried to reason, but quickly realized she'd undermined her argument when Loki caught her licking her lips. In any case, the expression on his face told her that it wasn't up for discussion. Her gaze landed on his flared crown and wandered down the thick vein snaking lazily on the underside of his shaft.

"I may only have had sex once but I've given quite a number of blow jobs," she boasted.

"Glad to hear of it," he snorted, wiping the pre-come off his penis and slipping the wet thumb between her lips. "On your knees. And start sucking."

Freeing his thumb where she'd caught it between her teeth, she sank to the padded floor. Impatient, she yanked her tank top and bra off. Her breasts slipped out and quivered in the fresh air, her nipples as hard as diamond points. Eyes hooded, Loki's breathing came out harshly.

Cradling the root of his shaft in her hand, she slid it up to the tip and then back down before taking him deep to the back of her throat. A gurgling sound burst out of him. Excited by it, she purred around his cock.

"You look so hot sucking my cock in that pretty little mouth of yours. You're pussy might be inexperienced, but that mouth is..." He shook his head from side to side. "Straight-up nasty."

She moaned hungrily before swallowing around him again. His taste was to die for. Seriously, she was ready to die. A heavy fog of desire wrapped around her head. He enfolded his hand around hers, and urged her to move faster, harder, not letting go until he was certain she got the rhythm right. Abby dug deep into the experience she had and went at him with ferocious determination. She licked the tip, swirling around until he was cursing at her. Then she sank down on his shaft, sucking out her cheeks, hitting her tonsils again and again. Huffing through her nostrils, she cut off her own breathing to prove herself to him.

He yanked her off him by the hair and gave her a quelling look. "Too much."

"I want to please you," she panted.

"You please me, more than you can imagine. Stop trying so hard. When I want you in pain, I'll take care of it myself. When I pull your hair back, it means you're going too fast. Y'know what? Hold still. I'm taking over."

Her hair was long enough for him to loop it around his fist once. Once in total control of her head, he thrust into her. "See, that's more like it. Good thing I like to take control because," he thrust, "an inexperienced girl requires guidance."

She glared up at him. If she could, she'd remind him she'd given blow jobs before. His cock went down her throat deeper than she'd imagined and she concentrated on relaxing to give him the space he sought. Loki made a delicious sound of approval and pulled out.

"I like guiding," he grated out. "You might not have much experience, but you're my good girl, letting me do what I want to you. Such a good little slut, letting me fuck your sweet mouth hard, the way I like it." She shivered, his filthy praise getting to revved up.

"Take a breather but keep stroking," he ordered.

She wrapped her hand around him and brought it up and down.

"That's a good girl."

His hand was on her breast, again, plucking her nipples until she was squirming in place. No guy had touched her before when she opened her mouth for them.

"Back in," he demanded. "I want to see those pouty lips hit my groin."

She rammed down until the curls at the base of his cock tickled her nose.

A brutal, harsh sound came out of his mouth.

He placed his toe between her legs and ordered, "Rub your clit on my foot while I fuck you."

Widening her eyes, she shook her head. A grimace stretched his scar to a thin white line. "Do what I say."

He lifted his foot and pressed into her pussy, putting pressure on her clit with the tip of his sneaker. She began rocking from side to side, and he stopped moving to let her control the pressure and speed. Giving a blow job to a guy who looked like a dark, sinful god, while he groped her breast and she rubbed on him like a cat in heat, built delicious heat in her.

"You're going to swallow."

Of course she was. Her mouth already got a taste of his salty flavor. She wanted the honor of getting him off. She'd *earned* it. Her own pleasure was forgotten, she was so intent on pushing him over the edge.

Going at him like a beast, she then slowed down to let him feel the outline of her teeth. He hauled in a sharp breath. Suddenly, he stiffened above her, his cock jerked, and his breathing stuttered. His movement became irregular, scraping against her teeth, prodding her inner cheek, and thrusting down her throat until she felt the intense shock of his come spurting out. He pulled on her head in short pulses as he braced his hand on the desk and came until his cock emptied itself.

She'd swallowed as much as she could, but the flood of come was too much and spilled out the sides of her mouth, trickled down her chin and streamed down to her heavy breasts. He took the end of her hair and used it to clean off the tip of her chin.

A grin flashed for a brief, brilliant moment before his expression returned to his normal tight-lipped frown. Oh, he liked it. Abby drew in a breath of sheer, unadulterated pride. She lapped his cock clean until he pulled it away. Loki took his time, no shame or concern whatsoever about people passing in the hallway on the other side of the door. He tucked his cock into his shorts and helped her up.

Looking down at her chest, he said, "Hmm, you look good painted with my come."

She blushed. Grabbing a towel from the floor, he wiped her dry and arranged her bra and shirt until there was a semblance of order.

He swept her come-covered hair over her shoulder and commanded, "Don't clean that up. I want you smelling like me when I come over later."

He slipped a hand inside her yoga pants, molded her pussy in his palm and pressed his fingers against her opening.

"Damn, you're wet. You ignored my instructions. Normally, I won't tolerate that kind of insubordination, but since you're not mine to keep, I won't be breaking you in. Worked out for the best 'cause I want you to stay hot and sticky for when I take you tonight."

"Tonight?" she squeaked.

He frowned again, his downturned lips puckering the skin surrounding his scar. "Yeah, tonight. You've got a hot, wet pussy that's gonna be as tight as a vise. No way, I'm taking a pass." Adjusting himself again, he said, "Hell, I'm getting hard again just thinkin' about it."

"You are?" she squeaked. Wow, that was a quick recovery if she ever saw one. *Gah!* She sounded like an idiot.

"Yeah," he looked at her with the faintest trace of sheepishness. "I can already see my cock won't wanna stop once it gets in that snug pussy. Alright, I've got shit to wrap up here. Give me an hour and a half and I'll meet you at your home."

"Like...umm...okay."

"And, Abby." He waited until her eyes were focused on him. "I want you naked and ready for me when I walk through the door."

12

LOKI

Abby's artlessness had undone him.

The blow job was fuckin' hot. She didn't have the skills she thought she did, but she made up for it with a vigor and enthusiasm he hadn't experienced in a long time. With her nimble fingers, she'd unspooled him like a ball of tangled yarn. Hands down the best blow job Loki had ever had, and this was just the beginning.

It took a lot to shock him, but the girl had succeeded. Twenty-two years old and practically a virgin. If he didn't know Abby didn't go in for pain, it'd be hard to believe she allowed him to push her boundaries the way she did. Guess Cutter was right about her submissive nature. He hadn't taken it easy on her, but she wanted to please him so badly any discomfort she might have felt came in at a distant second.

Already thoughts of taking the knives he lavished so much time and attention on and turn them on her danced in his head. Not to break skin. Just to play. He gripped his forehead. *No, no, no*. There was no way he was going there. He said one time. Teach her how to fuck and then move on. That was the deal.

At her front door, he knocked softly and announced himself since she couldn't see shit through the peephole. Lifting the wreath off the door, he thrust it into her hands when she opened to him.

Head cocked to the side, she asked, "What's this?"

Strolling in, his gaze ran over her. She was wrapped in a fluffy, pink bathrobe reaching midthigh.

"Your wreath. It's blocking your peephole. Security breach. Move it or get another one."

"Umm...thanks, I guess."

Giving her a sharp nod, he turned around to inspect her. She was splendid. She hadn't washed her hair. He noted clumps of *his* come on a few tresses. Her eyes glistened with excitement as she bobbed up and down on the balls of her feet. Pressing his lips together, he smiled inwardly at her enthusiasm.

"W-would you like anything to drink?"

"I'm good," he answered brusquely.

Her hands were in constant motion. One moment, fingers curled a strand of hair behind the shell of her ear, the next moment they twiddled with the belt of her rope. A gratifying thrill flushed through him.

Grasping the tips of her slim fingers, he rumbled, "Relax. Get me a drink."

"Water?" There was a breathy quality to her tone, but at least the halting stutter was gone.

"Something stronger."

A small smile graced her lips. "See, I knew alcohol would help."

His own lips curved in response. "Not for me. Now, go get it."

Turning his back, he took off his cut and laid it carefully over the arm of the couch. She returned with a glass of amber liquor and set it down on an end table. Tucking her shapely legs beneath her, she linked her fingers around her knees, posing like a mermaid basking in the sun on an outcrop of rock. Eager. Dainty. Sensual. A gap in her robe exposed a swath of creamy skin that had his cock pulsing in anticipation.

Glass in hand, he sat down and directed, "Come here."

She edged closer to him. He gave her a chin lift, and, understanding his silent command, she tipped her head back slightly and opened her mouth. Against her lower lip, he laid the lip of the glass and tilted until the alcohol spilled in.

She swallowed once. Twice.

His fingers traced the edge of her robe and tugged it wide. He tipped the glass again, but this time, a thin stream of golden liquid trailed over her collarbone, down her breast and beaded on her nipple. Chest rising and falling like bellows, Abby parted her lips and panted.

Yanking her robe apart completely, he leaned over and sucked her dripping nipple into his mouth. Bourbon combined with the orange and vanilla notes of her tasty flesh. Her hands flew out and outlined his skull, scoring his scalp as he drew on her peaked flesh. He lapped at the blushed tip until only her taste remained. His gaze flicked up to hers.

Handing her the glass, he ordered, "Do the other."

Once the bourbon hit her breast, he latched onto her other puckered tip. Pulling hard, then biting softly around her areola. A moan slipped from between her lips, the gravelly sound so erotic that his balls drew up tight.

Mouth full of her cushiony flesh, he intoned, "The other one."

Bourbon skated down her plump tit. Drops gathered around her nipple and his mouth was instantly wrapped around it.

Alcohol and woman never tasted so good. Loud sucking

noises he barely recognized erupted from his mouth. True, he'd been deprived for years, but there was no denying it, Abby tasted fucking delicious.

The empty glass clattered on the wooden surface of the table, but he paid it no mind. One more hard suck and then his mouth pulled free with a loud popping sound. Heavy-lidded eyes appraised her tits; two equally-matched, brightly bruised buds stared back at him. She melted into the couch, and he was halfway on top of her before her back hit the arm covered by his cut. His tongue playfully darted out for one final taste. The urge to consume her like a wild, starved dog was on him.

Abruptly, he jumped off her and landed on the opposite side of the couch. Too fast. He had to slow it down or he'd hurt her. Traces of longing filled her expression.

She reached for him, gripped the bottom of his shirt, and begged, "Please...take it off? I want to see your chest."

His fingers tore at the neck of his T-shirt. "Tit for tat, baby. Robe off. I want to see your pussy."

He hauled his shirt off and threw it over the back of the couch.

"Oh, God," Abby crooned, gaze riveted on his chest. He knew he was built, with a pair of broad shoulders and a powerful chest, typical of MMA practitioners.

Soft fingertips brushed over his chest hair and scratched the surface of his flat nipples, hardening them. Fiery sparks caught on his skin like nettles. "Death Before Dishonor" was inked in Germanic script across the top of his chest, followed by snipers holding rifles against the background of two halves of the American flag down each of his flanks. The fluttering sides of the battle-worn flag arrowed down his ribs to his hips. Crossing over his heart was the Demon Squad emblem.

Fingertips ran over the ripples of his abs. They flexed under her touch.

"Your body is incredible."

Heat singed the top edges of his ears. "Eh, it's the workouts. No big deal."

Her entire palm and fingers returned to the top of his chest, caressed down to his flat belly, and back up, bumping against the firm points of his nipples. Her tongue found each tat, and gave them some much-needed attention, chasing down lines of ink and laving away at them.

Her fingers fumbled with his buckle, but he dipped his head and stamped down on her mouth, intent on marking it. On bruising it. On fucking it. Beginning slowly, he cupped her nape and licked her lips until she parted them. Slipping between them, his tongue leisurely caressed hers, advancing and retreating in a teasing ebb and flow. Little by little, he increased his thrusts, challenging her to meet his, stroke for stroke.

Soon, she was restless.

On her knees, Abby twisted her mouth over his and sucked his tongue into the roof of her mouth. The suction almost toppled his self-restraint. He clenched the bottom cushion of the couch in his massive fists, beating down the urge to flip her on her hands and knees and ride her for broke.

When he ripped his mouth off hers, she let out an anguished mew. Craning her neck, she attempted to capture his mouth again.

A solid hand landed on her shoulder, keeping her at bay. "Easy, baby. We've got all night."

A strained expression dominated her face, but, after taking a large swallow, she backed up. Christ, she already looked halfway fucked. Strands of hair were in messy knots where his hands had gotten rough. Lips puffy and red where he'd sucked hard on them. Her eyes were bright with lust, mutating her normally copper-tinted irises to amber. The warmth he found in them mesmerized him.

A shadow of worry crossed over the brilliance of her eyes. "I don't know how to satisfy a man like you," she confided, wringing her hands.

He cupped her hands and stilled them.

"A man like me?" He couldn't help a smirk. "What kind of a man do you think I am?"

"One with lots of experience and partners."

"I did once, but it was a lifetime ago. Haven't touched a woman in years, much less fucked one."

"Really? You weren't lying when you told me you hadn't had sex in three years?"

He frowned. "Why would I lie?"

She shrugged. "It's just hard to imagine, that's all. Not that I'm complaining, mind you."

A grin spread over her features, her eyes alight once again. He enjoyed her display of possessiveness. Taking hold of his hand, she prompted him to his feet. Her fingers went to her belt and she untied it from around her trim waist. Her shoulders shrugged off the robe. It puddled at her feet, like he was about to do.

In warning, he croaked out, "Better brace yourself 'cause I'm gonna bury my face between your thighs. Take me to your bedroom."

Her hand swam in his as she led him down a short hallway with a bounce in her step. He watched her tight, thick ass cheeks bounce up and down, holding back a long groan pushing against his lips to escape.

Pushing her bedroom door open, he stalled midstride. It was all pink. Every shade seemed to be present, from the delicate, pale pink curtains to the dark pink of her bedspread. The numerous shades didn't necessarily cohabitate well together. Thank fuck there weren't stuffed animals or lacy shit covering everything.

"I know, it's a lot of pink to take in all at once. If you didn't live in the clubhouse, and I wasn't embarrassed about doing the walk of shame afterward, I would've insisted on doing this at your place. Obviously, I didn't think about a man entering my bedroom when I originally decorated it."

As she explained, she tossed pillows off the bed. Ripping the coverlet off, she bundled it into a ball and flung it into a corner. The sheets were white, which was only marginally better.

Wringing her hands, she stood beside the stripped bed with a sheepish look.

Shifting his attention away from the bed, he focused on her, appreciating her lush tits and flared hips. Backing her up a step, her thighs hit the side of the mattress. He placed a palm on her sternum and gave a brisk shove.

Plopping down, her rear bounced on the mattress. Hands reached out for balance. He stepped back to enjoy the view. Traveling down her body, his gaze snagged on a lacy white thong.

"Didn't I explicitly state I wanted you naked?"

"Oops," she let out in a hushed tone. It was obvious she'd bought the lingerie on her way home. Although an indication of her nervousness, it directly countermanded his order. Normally, that required a show of dominance, but he pulled himself back. She wasn't his. That wasn't what this was about. He took in a deep breath to rein himself in and distracted himself by returning his gaze to her panties, the lace sheer enough to reveal the strip of curls underneath. He suppressed a groan at the wet spot seeping through the gusset of her thong. Damn *fuck*! The unique combination of pristine and sex-kitten left him momentarily breathless.

Hooking his index fingers into the sides of her panties, he tore them off.

And, there she was. Completely naked, sprawled on the bed like a little pixie goddess. It'd been so damn long since he'd had an aroused woman beneath him, but he was grateful it was Abby. The innocent, trusting way her knees dropped open beneath his intense gaze, her pink slit glistening with desire, almost brought him to his knees. He stared and watched and *sucked* in the vision of her, exposed to him as she was.

His cock ached so damn bad it was about to explode, but he was going to savor the moment if it killed him. Time to play. Trailing a finger down between her tits, he flicked a nipple and she gasped. "Tsk, tsk, not a very good listener, are you?"

Her chin dipped down, and her downcast eyes lingered on the torn panties in his clenched fist.

"Abby," he called. Her gaze inched up slowly to his. "Bad girls don't get their pussy licked. You want to get licked or you want to get a lickin'? Your choice." His eyes turned sober. "Remember, I'll always give you a choice."

She squirmed, closed her eyes, and let out a shuddering breath. "Licked. Definitely licked."

Her entire body flushed pink, matching her bedroom. He drew a knuckle down her patch of curls and twisted one against her clit. Her breath began to saw in and out. He wasn't above a little torture.

"Thought so. That was your first and only warning, sweetheart."

Scooting two hands underneath her ass cheeks, he

dragged her to the edge of the mattress, parted her thighs and dipped a hand between her folds.

Hot and drenched. Just the way he liked it.

Pulling away, he smeared her wetness over his lips with his thumb. Back and forth, back and forth. Her eyes followed the movement of his fingers. His eyelids shuddered briefly as he licked off the orange blossom vanilla flavor he was already addicted to.

A whimper escaped her.

"What do you want first, Abby?"

"Whatever you want," she replied, at once.

"No," he said, resolutely. "Tell me. I want to hear the words come out of that innocent mouth of yours. And be specific. Real specific."

She chewed her bottom lip for a moment, embarrassment and desire battling it out in front of him. Finally, she rasped, "I want...I want you to...lick me."

"What will I use to lick you?"

A shiver caught her shoulders like a fever. "Your tongue."

This young, little girl talking dirty lit a fire under his ass. His body shook with the need to beat his chest and crow that he was making her his.

Instead, he settled for a calm breath and asked, "Anything else you want me to use?"

"Your teeth?"

His torso jolted. Hadn't expected that one. "Yeah, I can use my teeth. Bite down gently on your swollen little clit. That is, after I tongue fuck it until you're writhing under my mouth."

She squeezed her eyes tightly, and the high flush of her cheeks deepened to a shade dark enough to match the bedspread she'd tossed aside.

"What about my fingers? What do I do with them?" he asked.

A crease notched between her light brows. "What about your fingers?"

This woman—he shook his head in dismay—*is going to be the death of me.* One moment, she talked like she was an experienced flirt, and the next moment she acted like an untried virgin. She obviously didn't remember he'd used his fingers on her last time. Christ, she may have given blow jobs, but she must not have gotten much action down there herself. Which was a downright shame with a pussy that tasted like hers.

Desire crawled up his throat. His fingers pressed so hard into her downy thighs they were outlined in white. There was a good chance he'd leave bruises and he didn't give two fucks. She'd have something to remember him by, besides the sore pussy he'd leave her with. Swiping his thumb back and forth on the very tip of her clit, he flicked it sharply with his nails, and watched intently as she wheezed.

"A little pain with your fucking. You like that, don't you, baby girl?"

She nodded vigorously in response. Bracing his arms on the bed, he took a deep whiff of the sweet scent of her pussy. Beginning with light touches, his tongue swirled around her swollen clit. He gave it a flick and then prodded between her folds. Her thighs began to tremble, and he lifted one leg over his shoulder for better access. Spread beneath him, he licked her from end to end slowly, parting her lower lips, delving in and inhaling her flesh. Her fingers yanked at his hair. Mewling sounds emanated from her.

He stiffened his tongue, pointed it, and stabbed inside.
Another harsh yank.
He let out a desperate groan, taking unbelievable pleasure in her taste, her wet heat.
Pausing against her pussy, he ordered, "Cup those beau-

tiful tits. I want you to fondle yourself while I suck the hell out of you."

Her hands instantly relinquished his hair, and he plunged back in, shrugging his shoulders for her thighs to splay open farther. Fingering the entrance of her sex, he slurped up her cream and laying down wet, dirty kisses. Fucking hell and damnation, but her juices were flowing. He lapped, sucked, and nipped until Abby's hips were off the mattress and gyrating against him. Ever so slowly, he entered her with his finger. Considering how primed she was, it slipped easily into the basin of her juicy cunt.

Lifting his face, he explained, "Lips, fingers. Now for the teeth."

Gently, he grazed her clit between his teeth. Her hips bucked against his mouth. He wanted her hot, wet, and mindless. Despite how careful he was, she was going to feel pain. His cock was too massive for it not to hurt her. The worst part was he was going to enjoy her pain. Enjoy causing it. He *hated* himself for it, but there it was. He was powerless to eliminate the pain, but he could control it by degrees, introduce her to it in stages. He slid another finger in, sucking on her clit at the same time. Her ass wiggled as her inner walls stretched to accommodate the two digits.

Pumping them in and out slowly, he complimented her, "Good girl, you're doing so good for me. Taking two fingers like a filthy little slut. Almost as inexperienced as a virgin, but dirty nonetheless."

"Don't stop," she begged. Hearing the strain in her voice puffed up his chest.

Smearing his face in her wetness, he continued to suckle and lick, while quickening the pace of his fingers until he was long past being gentle. Out of nowhere, she seized up on him. Her sheath clamped down on his fingers and she bucked against his face, smearing her release over his stubbled jaw and cheeks.

His hand snaked down to his pants, released his belt, and unbuttoned his jeans. He tugged on his cock a few times, but had to stop before he lost control and palm-fucked it raw. It was almost too much for him as she rode her climax on his fingers and mouth.

Once her breathing slowed somewhat, he rose to his feet. Belt free and in his hand, he clipped out, "Your snug pussy's going to hug my cock like a tight glove. Lay back, babe. Gotta tie you up."

Her pupils flared momentarily on her blissful features, but she obeyed immediately. God, it was beautiful, the way she responded to him. He divested himself of his jeans, leaving his boxer briefs on until the last possible moment, hoping it would slow him down.

Crawling over her prone figure, he lashed her wrists together and attached the belt to the highest, horizontal metal bar of her headboard. The slithering sound of the tightening leather prickled the skin of his nape, and he was seconds away from turning green and bursting through his skin like the Incredible Hulk.

Gripping her chin, he informed her, "I want to take you bare. Haven't fucked in years. Literally years. I was clean on my last exam. *Years ago*. Get my drift?"

She whooshed out a rushed, "God, yes, I'm clean too and can't get pregnant. Do it, do it, do it, Loki, please."

Fuck, the begging was unraveling his control.

Narrowing his eyes on her, he promised, "I'm gonna make this good for you, Abby. It might hurt in the beginning, but follow my instructions, and you'll end up coming on my cock."

Christ, he hoped he was right.

13

ABBY

Determination lined Loki's face: his lips flat, eyebrows furrowed, and scar taut with tension.

He said she'd come on his cock, and she implicitly believed. Not being a complete innocent, she was prepared for the pain. Although she was coming down from her climax, she was still keyed up. Stretched out beneath him, she kept her thighs spread open, painted with her release and the light scuffs from the bristles on his jaw. There was the delicious hurt on her outer thighs, where his fingers had grabbed her roughly. She liked that hurt. She liked it very much.

Imprisoned between his bulging biceps, Loki's huge shoulders blocked out the overhead light she'd forgotten to turn off when she'd rushed into the bedroom.

Her gaze raked down his sublime body. He looked ruthless, like a warrior brute. Add a loincloth and spear, and he could have stepped out from a time capsule. *Don't even get me started on his tattoos.* At some point tonight, she was going to trace every line of ink with her tongue.

Rising above her, he pushed his briefs down halfway, and his cock sprang out, long, thick, and proud. It *should* be proud of itself. She would be if she were his cock. Okay, the mind-blowing orgasm must have altered her brain chemistry, because she was rambling to herself.

Features austere, Loki stroked his shaft a few times. Eyes, reflecting a bone-deep need mixed with concern for her, fastened on her, burning her to the very depths of her soul.

Off came his briefs. He was instantly back on her and she luxuriated over every inch of his hot flesh that touched hers. Gripping the base of his cock, he pressed the flared tip against her slit. She couldn't look away as he teased her, spreading her juices over its crown. Dipping in briefly and then pulling away. Each time he pushed, he went a little deeper and stayed a little longer. Her hearing was muffled by the sound of blood pounding in her ears. She tried to reach for him, but her wrists were thwarted by the grip of his leather belt.

"I want to touch it," she whimpered.

"Later. I want you to focus on receiving. You'll be giving a helluva lot back, don't you worry."

A few inches inside her and she was more than feeling the stretch of his cock. The fullness, wow, was unexpected. It was nothing like the first time.

A little retreat, and then another press forward. Soon he was deep enough inside her that the next time he pulled out, he didn't come out all the way. An aching pulse began in her core, as if her pussy hadn't just come. As if it had a mind of its own, she began producing copious juices for lubrication. Aware that this cock, this instrument of pleasure, would reward her for her obedience, her inner walls began to melt under his careful assault.

Propping her knee into the crook of his elbow, he spread her wider. "That's good. Like that, baby. You were clenching hard, but I feel you stretching around me."

"Fill me up," she begged.

Her words caused his hips to punch forward and she gasped at the suddenness of the intrusion.

He froze. "Fuck, baby girl. Sorry."

"It's...okay," she paused, her breath coming in short pants.

Bracing himself up on one arm, his entire body was rigid as he waited. Tension radiated off him, but he made no move. She took her time, wiggled her hips in tiny circles as she tried to adjust around his shaft.

The sound of his teeth grinding were loud in the silence.

"If you were any larger, I'm not certain we'd fit," she admitted, relaxing into the intrusion of his hefty shaft.

In a husky tone, he rumbled in her ear, "Oh, I'd make damn sure we fit."

Blowing through her mouth, she consciously breathed through the pain until it subsided. The feeling of fullness was still there, but she eased back into the mattress and let out a *whew*. His fingers found her clit and twirled. Oh, God, that felt good. Along with the feel of the hard velvet of his cock, wet with her fluids, her eyes rolled to the back of her head.

Despite his girth, his cock felt like silk as he slid deeper, stretching and stretching until he bottomed out. Checking in on her, she nodded, so he began to pick up speed, his features tightening as his control crumbled. A tick at the corner of his eye, near his scar, beat a rapid pace.

The drag and pull of his shaft tantalized the walls of her vagina.

She released a low moan. "More. Please."

Pulsing her pussy around his cock elicited a flaming-ice shiver up her spine.

"That's right, beg for more. Fuck, this feels good. Your pussy's gripping me so hard, I'm not going to last long."

"Don't make me wait," she begged. "Faster, Loki."

Those last two words were all the permission he needed.

Exploding in a flurry of movement, Loki rammed into her with the intent to conquer. Mindlessly consumed with lust, he pummeled into her with strength and power, topping off the pleasure building inside her.

His crown repeatedly hit a particularly sensitive spot. *Tap, tap, tap.* Each time he knocked against it, she lifted her hips to meet his. Her nails scrawled at the leather belt as she hitched her legs up higher. With every downstroke, he rooted himself balls deep. His rhythmic grunts spurred her on, and the orgasm sideswiped her in a blinding rush.

A scream split the air. Perhaps it was her. She couldn't be sure because she was riding inside a huge wave, the atoms of her body splitting, detonating, and re-fusing all at once.

Minutes later—hell, might've been days later, who knew? —she came down from the stratosphere where she'd hung out like a blazing star. Her eyes popped open, and she found herself flat on her mattress with her legs high in the air and a huge, heaving body shuddering above her. Her pussy was still milking him. His widened eyes reflected the same shell-shocked expression she was feeling.

A lopsided grin cracked his pressed lips. It was the first true smile she'd seen on him.

Smug, he bragged, "Told you, you'd come on my cock."

She served him with a sharp kick in the kidney.

Dropping his head in the crook of her neck, he murmured, "You don't know how rare that is. To come when your body's so new to fucking." He lifted on braced arms and dropped a kiss on her forehead. "Your pussy did well. Second time in your life and you came, singing like an angel."

Rubbing his bristled jaw against her upper breast, she swore he said something like, "pussy knows who its owner is." Normally, she'd have a pert response, but she was too satiated to take him to task.

Tugging his cock free, he reached over and untied the belt. Blood rushed into her hands and she whimpered. He propped her up on pillows and rubbed her shoulders and arms until the pins and needles subsided. Delicious tenderness ached between her legs.

"Where's the bathroom?" Loki asked.

Bolstering herself up on her elbows, she replied, "I can do it."

Ignoring her, he walked out and found the bathroom himself.

Boneless, she collapsed on her back. Not only had she *finally* had sex again, and in the most incredible fashion possible, but she'd been completely consumed. Devoured. Used. It was a delicious feeling.

By the time he'd returned with a warm washcloth in his hand, her heavy eyelids blinked to stay awake. His hands spread her thighs open and dabbed gently. At first contact, she hissed and tried to snap her legs shut, but he held them open and gingerly ministered to her. The mattress pitched as he shifted his weight around and then, eyes shut, she heard his bare feet padding on the parquet floor. That was the last thing she registered before she went under.

14

LOKI

Waking up not long after six a.m., Loki found himself spooned around a pixie with a curvy ass abutting his hard cock.

His arm bore down on her waist and he nuzzled the feathery blond hair tucked below his chin. He hadn't consciously decided to stay the night, but there was no way she was waking up alone after the plowing he'd done to that tight pussy of hers.

She was awake. He knew because her butt wiggled against his erection, but he wasn't going to take her right away. Last night, she'd woken him up, and they ended up fucking two more times. She must be sore as hell.

"Go back to sleep," he mumbled.

Of course she disregarded his order, turned her head, and piped up, "You leaving?"

"Hell, no, but you need to rest. It's early yet," he growled.

Sticking out her tongue at him, she said, "I don't need more sleep. I'm not an old man like you."

"I'm not fucking you, Abby," he grumped.

She grimaced. "Because it was for one night and it's morning now?"

He'd forgotten about the dumbass rule. He'd known it wasn't going to stick, but at least he couldn't blame himself for not trying. "Because your pussy needs to recuperate. It got the pounding of its short little life last night."

"You promised all night and I distinctly remember you falling asleep. You owe me at least five hours."

"You want five *more* hours of fucking?"

Batting her eyelashes, she said cheekily, "Yes, please."

An unexpected laugh rose from his chest. Her mouth split into a smile. Yeah, he could see she was pleased with his laugh; he never laughed anymore.

"Since you asked so politely, I'll accommodate your request." He gave her a stern frown. "Once your body has a chance to recover."

"So, like a rain check?"

"Yeah, Pixie, a rain check," he replied indulgently. "Come on, go back to sleep for a while. This old man needs his rest."

She snorted but nestled back into him and dozed back off.

A few hours later, he rubbed his gritty eyelids and blinked. Rolling his head over toward the clock on her nightstand, he saw that it was past ten o'clock. He couldn't remember the last time he'd fallen asleep after waking up, much less re-awakened in the middle of the morning.

He rolled out of bed and followed the clattering sounds in the kitchen. Abby was by the stove, flipping pancakes. At the sight of him, her mouth fell open and her spatula dropped in the pan. He scratched his belly, bringing her eyes down his naked torso. She scrambled to grab the utensil while he palmed his erect cock a few times to watch the change of color in her eyes when she got aroused.

"I-I hope you l-like pancakes," she stammered.

"Love 'em."

"You're not going to get dressed?" she squeaked.

"Nah. You mind?"

"No. Nope. Nuh-uh. Stay as naked as you want," she replied, breezily. Her eyes zipped up and down his body, hunger licking at his skin. She was dressed in the same short, puffy robe that fell midthigh, buck naked underneath he prayed.

Before he realized what he was doing, he'd walked over to her and dropped a kiss on her forehead. He was surprised by his own actions. In the past, he was out the door as soon as he was done fucking.

She leaned into him, and his rock-hard cock prodded her hip like it wanted back in her sweet, snug clutch, but he held strong and didn't take it further. Knowing he was about to lose the battle to not strip off the fluffy robe, bend her over the counter, and take her from behind, he returned to the bedroom and donned his jeans.

Back in the kitchen, he sauntered over to her small table and she slid a plate of steaming, hot pancakes in front of him. Ginger twined back and forth around his legs. He reached down and gave her back a long caress.

"How do you like your coffee?"

"Black."

Depositing a steaming mug of black coffee near his hand, she rolled her eyes. "Why am I not surprised?"

He bit into a forkful of pancakes and melted chocolate burst on his tongue. Taking a closer look at the pancakes, he asked, "Are there chocolate chips in here?"

"Yup."

They were the best pancakes he'd ever eaten. "I'm gonna make you my espresso."

"I didn't take you as a specialty drink kind of guy."

He shrugged. "My mother was Italian. From Messina, originally. In the South. I learned from her." He peered over into her coffee mug, filled with creamy coffee. Winking, he said, "I'll give you a cube of sugar with your espresso. You put it under your tongue and suck on it as you sip."

"Sounds like I might get cavities," she teased.

"Not as many as me for licking that sugar puss of yours."

Sucking in a breath, her fork froze midair.

Chuckling, he inquired, "Cat got your tongue? Come on, eat up before it gets cold."

This felt good. Too damn good. Laughing, teasing, eating chocolate-chip pancakes and talking about his moms. These were not things he did, not things he deserved to do. Even if something rearranged in his chest, seeing his semen streaking her inner thighs last night. He was not one to take pride in making a woman come. With past females, he worked to make it happen out of a sense of duty and reciprocity, not out of a precise aim to have one specific woman come apart under his tongue or on his cock.

But, he reminded himself, he wasn't dealing with just anyone. This was Abby. She was something else. The way she responded to him, arching her back to rub her full tits against his chest hair. Nails scoring the back of his neck when he fed her his cock. Plundering her, inch by inch, until he was rooted deep, her cunt cinching his shaft. Christ, it'd been hot. Hotter than any fuck he'd ever had, and he'd had his fair share.

Too many new feelings bombarded him, and he shifted in his seat. He didn't indulge in carnal pleasure; he didn't dwell in a place of enjoyment and gratification. The fragile tendrils of control keeping his life together after Chopper were melting like a spoonful of sugar on hot blacktop during a summer rain. He wasn't certain he was ready to part with his oath. With his pain.

Since he was a kid, he'd been a cautious motherfucker, and he wasn't about to condone the toppling of thirty-eight years of walls, no matter how sexy and adorable the little pixie girl sitting beside him was. Since when did he use the word adorable to describe a woman? *Fucking never, that's when.* This was a novel position for him, and, for real, he was terrified how good it felt to release his tight hold on the reins.

His thoughts were interrupted when Abby reached across the small table and stroked the length of the scar that slashed down Loki's face. Starting high on his hair line, her fingertip traced along the curve of his cheekbone and halfway down his cheek. The soft brush of her touch sounded like a mourning dove taking flight near his ear. Her caress left a trail of crackling awareness on his skin.

"Tell me how you got your scar."

He grasped her wrist, her bones so delicate underneath his fingers. Abby ducked her head. Her shyness gripped at his heartstrings like nothing else. He didn't have the strength to shut her down completely, but it was time to regain a baseline of control, while putting some distance between them.

"What do I get for it?" he taunted.

"For what?"

"A story. What do I get for telling you a story?"

"What do you want?"

"You. Naked. Tied up. Pussy dripping and spread wide open for me," he bit out between tight lips.

"You've already had that," she teased.

"A bit of discomfort. A sliver of pain."

Abby's eyes turned the color of whisky. *Christ, this woman. Instead of running, she's turned on.*

"That's a lot to ask for," she breathed out.

"It's a good story. One I've never told before. Chopper was the only one besides Crispin who knew, and they're both dead."

"Crispin?"

Funny. She didn't ask who Chopper was. Bet Sammi opened her big mouth and told her his business. The two of them had gotten close lately. He didn't take to having his personal shit broadcast to strangers, but he was cagey, so it was to be expected that Abby would seek out details about him in other ways. A curious little kitten, she was. Sammi couldn't have spouted anything too fucked-up about him. Otherwise, he wouldn't be here. But he already knew she was too good for him.

"My violent, good-for-nothing sperm donor," he rasped out. "Strip. I want an incentive to start."

Abby shrugged out of her robe, exposing her heavy tits to the bright sunlight streaming in from the bay window of the kitchen nook. Her nipples puckered in the late morning breeze coming in from the open windows. The heavy perfume of summer roses drifted in and mixed with the bouquet in the vase on the counter. Yeah, the chick had roses everywhere like an English lady on a BBC special. He bet the rose bushes in the garden on the ground floor was her doing. Not surprised at all that she had a green thumb. His fairy princess was a perfect fit for nature.

Rising, he strolled around the table and tugged at the belt around her waist. From behind, he inhaled her natural vanilla fragrance, with a hint of something sultry, like their hot, dirty sex from the night before. The idea that fucking her had changed the way she smelled brought out a turmoil of feelings, something eerily akin to ownership. Ownership? The thought had never crossed his mind about a woman before. The burgeoning urge of possession required an outlet, and lucky for him, she was sitting in a wooden chair with vertical slates in the back, primed for a taste of bondage.

"I was fifteen," he began, as he dragged her wrists behind her. "My mother was a soft woman. Too soft. And Crispin liked to use it against her. He figured out that if he beat on my brother, she'd intervene to protect him. Then Crispin would have an excuse to beat on her."

Looping the belt around her wrists, he tested the tension to make sure her hands were lashed together while allowing for sufficient blood circulation. Her position caused those glorious tits of hers to jut out, and he couldn't help but take a taste. Bending over her shoulder, he stroked circles around one nipple with his tongue before giving it a few short, tight pulls. Blood rushed to the spot and flushed it a bright pink. Abby's mouth expelled a series of rapid pants as he admired his handiwork, or rather tongue-work.

"It was a weekend morning much like this one. Sunny. Warm. My mother got into it with him and he responded with his fists."

Taking his seat again, he sprawled his legs open. His mind detached from his body, went blank, and all that was left of him was a talking mouth, an instrument to deliver the past to the present.

"At one point, he had her over the kitchen table." His hand smoothed over the tablecloth. "Much like this one," he mused. "Shit went flying everywhere. I blinked and, suddenly, there was a knife to her throat. He was hungover, not drunk, so I don't think he'd have gutted her, but the second I saw the metal cut her skin, I exploded. We ended up on the floor, and in the middle of brawling, he sliced me. I don't remember feeling much. The adrenaline was pumping in my system, but blood began gushing. Face and head wounds are bloody by nature. Not realizing it was mine, I took advantage of his shock and got some good punches in before mom and Chopper managed to get Crispin off me."

Twirling a butter knife in his hand, he shrugged.

"That began my fascination with knives."

15

ABBY

Shock and horror reverberated through Abby's body.

He'd been only fifteen. Protecting his mother. Good God, he got the scar from protecting his mother. No wonder he was captivated by knives and weapons, strength, and self-defense. They'd been stitched together in his soul with blood and puckered flesh. Chopper had committed suicide, that much Sammi had revealed, but where was his mother?

Despite her arousal at being naked in front of Loki, her heart was bleeding for the boy he'd been, attacked by a psychopath of a father. She was fairly good at keeping her emotions in check, but this story, told in a blasé tone, as if he were talking about pancakes instead of getting his face sliced open, tore her cool to shreds. Loki was playing with the butter knife and, suddenly, she was inspired.

"Do you want to put the knife on me?"

His eyes snapped to hers. "I'd never hurt you," he snapped.

So, that was a bright line for him. He enjoyed having her under his control, more like craved it, and he'd liked to inflict a bit of pain, but no breaking of skin. No authentic pain.

"I don't doubt it. I trust you." Lifting her bound hands from behind, she said, "Since you have me at your mercy, do what feels right."

He raised an eyebrow, and his lips formed into a slow smile. "Got any ideas? 'Cause you're too sore for me to fuck you again. "

Abby huffed. Damn, she had been hoping to get another taste of his cock.

Loki leaned over the table, took hold of her chin, and said, "Don't deny it. There's no way you're going to dissuade me."

"Then think of something else?"

The butter knife twisting between Loki's fingers stopped. Swirling the knife in a puddle of leftover maple syrup on her plate, he leaned over and spread it over her areolas, leaving her stiff nipples untouched. Her breath quickened. As his hand pulled away, the blunt, slightly serrated edge of the knife scraped along the edge of her nipple and she whimpered. Holy fuck, that felt good.

He stood up, and bent down, his arms flanked either side of her, his face dipped near hers. "Impressive demonstration of trust."

She nodded, unable to speak past the lump in her throat. His head tipped down farther, and with a groan, his tongue laved the sticky, syrupy perimeter of her aching nipple. As he sucked harder, she squirmed, wetness streaming from her core, painting the chair beneath her.

He transferred his attention and captured her other nipple in his mouth. "Fuck, I love your tits. I've been wanting to see them molded around my cock."

Through a haze of lust, she heard more than saw the drag of denim down his trim hips. She licked her lips when the wide tip of his cock bobbed in her line of sight, a fat drop of pre-come shimmering in the bright kitchen. Quivering in the air, another drop popped out from his slit, pushing the first one over the head and down his shaft.

In a flash, she caught it with the flat of her tongue, moaning as the salty, musky flavor of him hit her. Widening her tongue, she slid it up like she was licking an ice cream cone. His thick thighs flexed. A hand landed on the top of her head, fist tightening around her curls, and her head was yanked away just as her tongue had taken another lap of his shaft.

"No sucking me off," he croaked out. "Yet."

She let out a soft hiss of denial, but he tutted, "Now, now. You got your story. Give that greedy mouth of yours a rest until I decide otherwise."

Gathering her breasts in his massive hands, he weighed them. There weren't many men who had hands large enough to hold them in their entirety. Quite a feat. His thumbs swiped at her nipples like they were video game controllers. Left-right-left-right.

"Is your pussy wet for me?"

"What do you think?" she replied hoarsely. "You have my breasts hostage and you're torturing them."

Chuckling, he twisted one and she yelped, although the aftereffect left her nipple with a deeper, pulsing ache. Divested of his jeans, Loki turned her chair to face him, planted his feet outside her knees, and kneaded her tits before molding them around his wide girth, her nipples brushing against the flat plane of his abs.

"You want something to do? Get your tongue out and start licking. Only the crown and hold it there. I'll do the rest."

Abby popped her lips opened and wrapped them around his blunt cockhead, although her tongue took a detour down the thick vein on the underside of his shaft for a quick second. Eagerly, she sucked as he pushed his cock through her squashed tits to the roof of her mouth. Head held in place, she breathed through her nostrils, hungry to capture as many sensations as she could. The taste, the feel, the *scent* of Loki's cock. Boy, did he smell good.

His pace accelerated and she suctioned around his oh-so-smooth shaft, sucking in as much as she could against the grip of his fist around her hair. Growly, male sounds emanated from the back of his throat, spurring her on. The belt around her hands had loosened and she wiggled them out, groping until she found his swollen, heavy balls. Cradling them in the cups of her hands, she rolled and tugged on them, sometimes pressing into the indentation separating them.

Writhing in her seat, she pressed her clit against the smooth wooden seat, seeking purchase, although the right amount of pressure eluded her. She was on fire from the feel of his velvety shaft rolling between her tits, come and spit having made them slippery, and gliding between her lips. Her mouth, moaning and humming, begged for more. Loki's use of her tits and mouth for his pleasure made her bold. Either the humming was working or he'd reached the brink of his self-control, because his thrusts became impatient. Peeking up, her gaze first landed on his scar, stretched taut, and then traveled to his lips, curled up in a grimace over clenched teeth.

Breathing ragged, Loki withdrew from the suction of her mouth. He jerked once, twice, and blew out jets of his load across her breasts.

His eyes, ravenous and half-crazed, bored into her and then dropped to her chest, covered with his seed. He followed the trail as it dribbled and dripped over the curve of her breasts.

Stumbling back, his palm smacked the top of the table as he steadied himself. "Fuck, that's a beautiful sight."

Then his gaze cleared and noticed her hands, one finger swirling in the liquid, shining in the light.

His expression turned cloudy. "Your hands."

"Oops."

"Mmm-hmm...yeah, no way you're coming. Hear me? Don't think of touching yourself, either. I was gonna rub my come into your skin, but I'm nixing that treat. Your second punishment is to wait until I decide to fuck you again."

"*Lokiii*," she protested.

Lifting her chin, he said, "I tied them up for a reason. You countermand an order; you pay the price."

She threw him a pout, but he lifted off the table and went to the roll of paper towels on the counter by the sink. Twisting a few off, he switched on the water, moistened them, and came to her. With a firm hand on her shoulder, he proceeded to wipe her clean. It was so sexy to watch Loki's furrowed brow as he diligently tended to every slathered inch of her. He may have cleaned her off, but, lucky for her, his scent still clung to her.

Shrugging her robe back on, she wondered, "How about we go out and do something?"

Loki's lips twisted into a hint of a smile. "Like a date?"

He rose and dropped the semblance of a smile. Going over to the garbage can, he stepped on the pedal and dumped the paper towels. "I don't do dates. Abby, let me make this clear. This is about fucking. Nothing more."

Striding over to stand in front of her, he braced his hands on the back of her chair, his arms flanked her head.

He crouched down until their faces were aligned and declared, "I'm not lookin' for an old lady. An old lady is what we bikers call our wives or partners. You'll be my fuck toy. Not lookin' for that either, truth be told, but there's no denying this pull between us. Mark my words, it will not go further than fucking."

Her breath caught in her throat. He was being crude on purpose, giving her ammunition to walk away. She was made of sterner stuff than that. If he thought she'd run away shrieking with anger and hurt, he had another thing coming. His harsh words were in direct opposition to his actions—the way he cleaned her up earlier, the way he crouched down at her level. Enveloped in his closeness, her nose quivered from his intoxicating scent, swirling around her like a cloud of hookah smoke. What he hadn't counted on, in this little display of his, was that she had a backbone beneath her touchy-feely mask. A spine layered with steel.

Her lips curled into a smirk and she assured him cheerfully, "Fuck toy it is, then. Anytime. Anyplace. But you better make sure *I'm* the only fuck toy you touch. You get the urge, you come to me."

Heat flared in his eyes, but he quickly fastened a noncommittal expression on his face before pushing himself off.

"Good to know we're on the same page. No misunderstandings. Next Friday. Same time. Same place." He smoothed a hand over her panties, his middle finger tapping her clit. "Until then, this pussy is mine. You don't get to touch it."

She clenched her teeth. Her eyes darted to her bedroom, where her vibrator waited in her nightstand drawer.

His eyes followed her gaze and narrowed. "Where's the toy?"

She blinked innocently.

"A vibrator," he ground out knowingly.

Dammit. He caught her.

"Where is it?"

"In my nightstand," she huffed.

He grazed his fingertips across her nipples as he swept

past her and went into the bedroom. Coming out with his shirt and shoes on, he waved the vibrator in his hand, stopped in front of her, he lifted her chin with the tip of the vibrator, and praised, "Good girl."

"I'm not feeling very good, actually," she complained.

"They you should've done what was asked of you. Don't worry, you will one day." He dropped a kiss on her lips. "When I decide, that is."

He sauntered out of the kitchen, plucked his cut off her couch, and pulled it on. Swiping his cell phone off the table, he gave Ginger a long, strong pet over her back. Lucky girl.

"Friday. Same time? Same place?" she confirmed.

"Yep."

"Sounds like a date to me," she sing-songed.

The sharp angle of his jaw jutted out like a carved statue of a warrior. Hand on door, he called out, "Sass will get your ass smacked, you know that?"

"No," she snorted.

"You'll learn, sweetheart, and I'm gonna enjoy teaching you every damn lesson."

The growly, raspy tone to his boasting held dark promises, and another flood of juices drenched Abby's panties by the time the door clicked shut. She glared down. *Goddammit.*

16

ABBY

Abby was already seated at their usual booth when Sammi slammed the entrance door of their favorite café open, pushed the waitress aside, and rushed toward her. Clapping her hands in glee, she beamed down at Abby for a moment before bending over to hug her. Two fingers popped up as she turned to the waitress and ordered, "Two mimosas and keep them coming! We're here to celebrate!"

Shimmying her butt down into the opposite seat of their booth, Sammi slapped her palms on the table and let out a celebratory whoop.

"Of all my friends, you're the only one who shares my obsession with *Sex and the City* and" —Abby waved her hand up and down—"who has the ability to come to a French café dressed in leather from head to toe."

"Bitch, people walk around wearing *Friends* T-shirts, but we know better. It's the aughts that produced the best of the best."

"I'd like to note, it doesn't take away from the fact that our obsession is bizarre. Neither of us live in the City and we're not in our thirties. Are you sure you're not a yuppie under-neath all that leather and lace?"

"Girl, I wish. When I was growing up, it was one of the only TV shows that gave me the escape I needed. Mr. Big, a fancy billionaire who rode a limousine around the City. Carrie with her walk-in closet and shoe fetish, like me." A nick formed between Sammi's eyebrows. "Anything to get away from real life, let me tell you."

Flapping her hands in front of her, she grinned at Abby. "As of yesterday, we've turned legit. Thanks to Loki, we get to talk about sex. Sex, relationships, and friendships. Going out for brunches and dinners and drinks, oh my! We're living our best life."

Leaning back into the booth, she gave Abby a pout and accused, "You've been holding out on me. How did it go from teasing to outright bangin'?"

"It was unexpected, I can tell you. We were talking after class, and seeing the way he handled my clients, yet again, did something to my head. I was super horny, and I just blurted out and asked him if he'd like to have sex with me." Abby gave a shrug. "I basically begged him to help me out of my predica-ment, you know. After losing my virginity to a guy I'd friend-zoned for years, I wanted to experience an orgasm during sex. I mean, Loki's hot as hell, my attraction to him is off the charts, and I trust him not to hurt me."

"Then what?"

"He said yes."

"Duh, you dirty whore. He'd be insane not to."

She beamed a smile at Sammi. "You're so sweet. Such a good friend."

Sammi rolled her eyes. "I wonder if you see what the rest of us see, because you're hot, girlfriend. Your tits alone are Playboy bunny–worthy." She leaned forward and mock-whispered, "And they're even real. Anyway, what happened next?"

"He had to finish up at the gym, so I went home," she held up her forefinger, "but not before going to buy lingerie. He came over after he was done."

"Have you ladies had time to look over the menu?" the waitress cut in, depositing their mimosas in front of them.

Sammi replied, "Eggs sunny side up with a side of sausages and wheat toast."

"I'm going for something lunch-like. I had breakfast with Loki. How about a turkey club sandwich? Thank you."

"Sure thing," the waitress said as she scribbled down their orders and moved on to another table.

"He swore it would be a one-time thing, but I finagled a way to get more," Abby confided proudly. "We have a little game going on."

"Damn." Sammi leaned back. "This is like a big deal. I mean, I've known Loki for years and he's never looked at or touched anyone. Well, except for Sage."

Abby's back snapped straight up. "Sage?"

WTF? He had a past with Sage?

"Yeah, it was quite a mess, back then." Sammi waved dismissively, although she stole a worried glance at Abby. "I'm sorry I even mentioned it. It popped out of my mouth without thinking."

Abby took a sip of her mimosa and placed a hand on top of Sammi's hand. "Tell me, Sammi. I can handle whatever you have to say but spit it out because I need to know where I stand with him. He's a mystery, but from the little I've found out about him, he's suffered."

"At one time, Loki crushed on Sage. He didn't hurt her, nothing like that," she was quick to reassure her friend. "Sage was going out with Kingdom at the time and I can't get into the details because it's club business, but he left her exposed and an outsider took advantage of Sage's insecurities. It led to big drama. Personally, I thought his punishment was a bit harsh, but I trust Prez had his reasons."

Abby placed her mimosa carefully on the table, aghast.

"Everything was cleared up," Sammi hurried on. "There was no long-term damage done. Sage and Kingdom are together and better than ever. I mean, Loki was at his worst then. Really, he wasn't himself. He was so full of rage and grief. He lashed out at Kingdom every chance he got. Don't worry, Loki was actually *in* love with Sage. Prez punished him, and over time he and Kingdom patched up their problems. They're quite close now, although, being men, they'd never admit it out loud."

Abby's shoulders slumped. "I could never compete with Sage," she concluded. Her ego was collapsing on itself, getting smaller and smaller the more she thought about what she heard. "She's stunning and luxurious. And smart. She's an amazing lawyer. I mean, there's no comparison."

That was his reason for maintaining distance between them. He was in love with the woman of one of his brothers. It didn't matter that Sage was completely unavailable. Since when did that stop a man from loving another? Especially Loki. He was the most authentic person she'd ever met. Despite his tough exterior, his heart was pure. His emotions raw. He couldn't stop himself from loving who he loved and he'd take that to the grave, regardless of whether the woman reciprocated or not. His reaction to Chopper was a perfect example of the intensity of his passion. Whew, thank goodness she was on birth control.

Sammi sank into the bench next to Abby and wrapped an arm around her shoulders. "Stop it, there's no comparison between the two of you. You're different people. Do you think I'm not as good because I'm a biker bitch compared to Sage?"

Abby pulled back in horror. "Of course not."

"Either you're lying to me or you agree you can't compare. Not only are you totally different people, but Loki was in a different place in his life."

Abby couldn't look at Sammi. Her gaze dropped to her hands. They trembled slightly as she picked at the napkin on her lap. "A man attracted to Sage couldn't possibly be attracted to me."

Sammi clucked. "Just shows how little you know about men. That's not how it works for them, and you can't tell me Loki isn't attracted to you when he ripped you apart last night."

"That's because I'm inexperienced and he's a big guy, if you know what I mean."

Sammi covered her ears and screeched, "I don't want to hear that."

"Oh please, you live among bikers."

Two plates clattered down on the table as the waitress deposited them and then whizzed away.

Sammi returned to her seat and tucked a napkin on her lap. "That may be so, but Loki is like an uncle to me. Normally, I'd say an older brother, but I already have one of those and he's overbearing enough to cover that label and more. Let me tell you, Loki has been celibate for almost as long as I've known him. It's unheard of in our world, with women throwing themselves at him. All. The. Time."

"Don't give me that look," she snapped. "It was not a pity fuck. Loki doesn't do pity. I'd say it's the opposite. He wants you. That is the one and only reason he'd fuck a woman. And he wants more, or he wouldn't have set up a date for Friday."

"But Sage—"

"Is the past." Sammi finished the end of Abby's sentence resolutely, hands clenched on the tabletop. "The past. She's Kingdom's old lady, and Loki has long since moved on. End of story."

Twiddling her fork, Abby shrugged. "It's not like it matters. Loki isn't marriage material, and I'm pushing twenty-three. When mom was sick, she lectured about how she wished she'd had kids earlier so we could've had more time together. We would've been older when she left us, motherless. Loki's only a distraction and to get experience for when I meet my real partner."

Liar. Dammit, she was so confused. Her heart kept calling to her like a damn siren, whispering dangerously, *he's the one, he's the one.* But everything else about that man was frustrating and difficult. She couldn't give herself over to a guy who didn't fall for her too. That would be intolerable.

Sammi arched a brow and drawled, "Oh, really?"

"Don't give me that look, Ms. Dubious. He's *not* husband material. Not because he's a biker, but I definitely want to marry a man who wants children and has a 401K, okay."

"Loki was in the service for fifteen years. He's getting something from that time. I'm not saying I know how much, but it's nothing to sneeze at, and he's established in the Squad. The man's able to provide for that kind of life," Sammi chimed in.

"A life with marriage and children?"

"Hmm...not sure about that, but then again, I've never actually seen him with anyone before you so I've got nothing to go on."

That was nice to hear.

"Anyway," Abby batted Sammi's hand to stop her interruptions, "I'm taking advantage of the chance at a sex life. Figure out what I like and what I don't like. Come to my life partner with some experience under my belt."

"Are you for real? You're delusional if you don't acknowledge you have feelings for him!"

Abby's fork flew out of her hand and made a loud clattering on the porcelain plate. Fisting her hands, she jeered, "Absolutely not. There is no way I could fall for him. He's emotionally unavailable. Damaged. Anyway, we kind of have a deal."

"A deal? Involving sex?" Sammi gasped. "A *sex* deal?"

"As a matter of fact, yes," Abby replied primly. "Nothing to embarrassed about. It's rational, actually. No one will get unnecessarily attached or hurt. It's transactional."

"You are the most nontransactional person I know, Abby. Three times you went to the animal shelter," she held up three fingers, "each time you were determined to leave Ginger because you said you worked long hours away from home. Each time, you came back home with her. You're the last person capable of keeping their feelings out of something. What you have isn't transactional, it's a recipe for disaster."

"Not necessarily, because there's another barrier. He's into kinky sex, which I don't even know if I like," she sniffed-slash-lied.

Sammi's fork flew out of her hand and clattered to the floor. She scrambled to pick it up and, waving it at Abby, burst out, "Damn, we can't keep utensils in our hands now, can we? Okay, now we're talking. Always knew that guy was too controlling for words. It explains so much about him, you can't imagine."

A knowing smirk slowly stretched across Sammi's mouth. "I shouldn't be surprised, though. Loki is a private kind of guy. Always wanted to try kinky. Never got the chance but, who knows, maybe in the future. It's hot as fuck you're getting to test-drive down that lane. As for a husband, you have got to give yourself a break. You can't magically conjure up *the* perfect husband because," she flicked up her forefinger, "first of all, they don't exist."

"Of course, they do," she replied emphatically. "My father was the perfect husband for my mother."

Sammi gave her a look of pity. "You cannot seriously believe that romantic bullshit. There is no such thing as a soul mate or a perfect love."

"There is too," she insisted, with a stubborn tilt to her chin. "My mom and dad fell in love at first sight at a music concert. They had to work hard on their marriage through the years, but the instant connection was there."

Sammi looked at her askance but was smart enough to not try to argue with her. "Either way, you're super young. Too young to be worrying about marriage."

"I'm not *that* young." Her voice dropped a few octaves. "You don't know when life is going to end. It can get cut off far earlier than you expect. You know this as well as I do." She and Sammi shared the experience of having their mothers die while still children.

"I know what you're doing. I get it, really I do, but life doesn't work out according to a plan. Especially one based on something as superficial as how old you are. My mother's death showed me the joke's on me if I make a long-term plan. With my luck, it would explode in my face. The best philosophy is to live day by day. Plus, I never want to be locked down to someone. Husband, wife, or child. I have my brother, my club and my friends. That's enough for me."

"Sammi, you were born to be part of a large family. You're so loving and giving and...communal. You practically grew up in the Squad."

"We're all one big family, for sure. There's no need to bring a child into this world so they suffer. If nothing else, my childhood taught me that tidbit of reality."

Stunned, Abby's spine dropped back against the cushioned booth. "I can't believe you came to the opposite conclusion as me."

"Maybe it's because I didn't have a father to fall back on." Sammi puckered her lips, and a frown creased the smooth skin of her forehead. "Although, Puck more than made up for a father. He's always filled those shoes, even if his way of doing it is overbearing as fuck. He protected me my entire life. Life gives no guarantees, so I'm not going to take a huge risk on something as fickle as a romantic relationship. Fucking? All over it. Relationship? Hard pass."

"You take a risk because nothing is better than real love and family," Abby insisted.

"I have real love and family with Puck and the Squad. It's dangerous to want too much," she finished in a soft whisper, her eyes downcast.

Abby reached for her hand and squeezed it. "I take your point. I don't need to rush anything. I'll live this thing between Loki and me, one day at a time."

"Yeah, and if that day includes a few slaps on the ass along the way, then I say, grab it and hold on tight. Don't miss out on the chances thrown your way. They may not come around twice."

Sammi grabbed her drink and, winking over the rim, said, "So, tell me all about dirty, bondage-y sex."

17

ABBY

After what felt like the longest week in her life, Friday finally arrived.

Class was over and Abby rushed out to the bathroom to change into a more appropriate outfit. Coming back into the room, she almost passed the threshold when she spotted Kerri sidling up close to Loki and looping her arms around his neck. She slobbered a wet kiss on his lips with a smack loud enough to make the remaining women by the door turn their heads.

Kerri was a new client at the Agency and had only recently joined the class. She was not one of Abby's clients, thank God. She was a bit of a handful. But right now she was a biker bitch coming on to Loki, looking sexy as hell, even in a sports bra and leggings.

A breath rattled out of Abby as she shuffled two steps back, behind the door. Her clients nodded and waved goodbye to her as they exited and walked down the hallway. Once the women turned the corner and were out of sight, she hurriedly took a step closer to the door.

"How about we go to the clubhouse and you can fuck me, Loki?" she purred.

Abby stifled a gasp behind her hand. Kerri had come on to Loki after every class, but tonight she wasn't pulling any punches. The urge to wrap her fingers around Kerri's throat and throttle her was pushing Abby hard. This was her man, dammit. At least, "her man for now." Although they had not had an extensive discussion on exclusivity, she'd bluntly told him to come to *her* if he had an itch to scratch.

A memory niggled at the edge of her consciousness. Didn't she see Kerri at one of the clubhouse parties with Tank. Of course, Kerri saw Loki as a brother first, an instructor second. She might not necessarily see this as a line crossed. Her mind ticked with different ways to have Kerri's social worker approach the subject of boundaries with her at some point.

Abby peeked around the door in time to see Loki hold Kerri's waist lightly and drop a kiss on her forehead. Gross.

"Not gonna happen, but thanks for the offer," he replied smoothly.

Such a gentleman. Although she was glad he turned Kerri down, what the hell? Aren't bikers supposed to be rude?

"Why not?" she whined. "Don't tell me you're interested in that little girl? She has no clue on how to take care of a man like you."

Did she actually say that out loud? Shameless, but apparently Kerri wasn't nearly halfway done.

Trailing a finger up and down Loki's bicep, she went on, "I know what bikers want, and especially you. You like it *rough*." Her hand dropped to Loki's crotch. "You need a bitch who can take it, not a midget who won't know how to handle a big cock like yours."

Abby clenched her jaw. The nerve of her. Thankfully, there

were no witnesses besides herself to this humiliation. He gave a low chuckle and her thoughts turned to throttling Loki. She punched her jealousy down, taking deep slow breathes to settle herself down. She had no rights on him, and God knew, bikers and bitches were a handsy bunch, but they *would* be having a conversation about this as soon as she was alone with him.

"Babe."

Abby ground down on her back teeth at his use of the endearment on another woman. "I know you'd take good care of me. That ain't the issue." She heard shuffling and prayed it was Loki extricating himself from that eight-armed, extraterrestrial octopus monster. "I'm in the middle of something."

After a pause, she heard, "Abby come inside."

Aww...crap. She shuffled back, her eyes darted from side to side.

"Come on in," he demanded in a stern tone as if he could see her backing away. She squeezed her eyes shut, feeling the flush of heat splash over her cheeks. She was mortified, having been caught eavesdropping on them, but there was nothing to do but walk in on them.

Two could play at this game.

Thinking quickly, she yanked the zipper halfway down her back. Thank goodness, she'd changed into a sundress that showed off her thighs and had touched up her makeup. Fluffing her hair, she threw her shoulders back, and stepped into the room.

Kerri's eyes narrowed and her lips curled up into a snarl. Loki, on the other hand, locked in on her gaping neckline. His gaze raked down her front, lingered at her exposed thighs and moved back up.

"Damn," he muttered, with an unblinking stare.

Grabbing her neckline, causing it to dip forward even

farther, she said, "I couldn't get the zipper all the way up. Could you help me?"

She turned around and cast a glance over her shoulder, about to bat her eyelashes for good measure, but his heavy-lidded stare on her bare skin halted her. She wished she had tresses of heavy hair she could gather in her hand and sweep over her shoulder in a sexy gesture, but whatever. The bold lust imprinted on his face had kicked off a flow of liquid fire in her belly and her head buzzed like she'd thrown back a few tequila shots.

Planting her palms on the mirrored wall, she watched as Loki moved in behind her. His hands dropped to her waist. Damn straight. His hands belonged on *her*. They caressed her hips and swept down her flanks. A shudder rippled up her spine and let loose on her shoulders. His grip tightened momentarily. Taking another step closer, his thigh brushed between her own spread legs.

He leaned into her and nuzzled her hair. "You're a naughty girl, Pixie."

"Who me?" she crooned innocently.

His palm smoothed over her ass, and she bit down on her bottom lip to quell a moan. "Not sure whether I should zip you up or down. Give Kerri a little show, that what you want, sweetheart?" he murmured for her ears only.

"Loki," Kerri spoke, in a shrill tone, from behind.

Seriously? This woman was a glutton for punishment.

"Mmm," he answered absently. "Gimme a sec." She was thrilled at his dismissal of the other woman. God, she was behaving so, so badly. It was vindictive, but when it came to him, she couldn't help herself. A flash of pride ran through her. She'd never had the guts to go after a man before. It was surprising and tantalizing to be so ruthless. The hard ridge digging into her lower back and the stretch of tension along his scar was...well...*yummy.*

Loki tugged the zipper up her back carefully, ensuring it didn't get caught on her skin. He swiped his hand down her spine and smarted her ass with a sharp spank before stepping away. Her nails scraped at the mirror as she gave herself a moment to get her runaway lust under control. A palm landed on her neck and pulled her around until her front was cradled into his side.

"Kerri, you got a ride?"

Kerri's eyes darted from side to side and she huffed out, "No."

Not missing a beat, Loki replied, "I'll get one of the brothers to ride over here and pick you up."

Casting a soft look down on Abby, he asked, "You hungry, babe? Come on, I could eat a fucking horse, and I'm gonna need the energy to fuck you out of this sexy dress you're wearing."

With her at his side, he walked them out the door. Bending down, his lips brushed her temple, and he murmured, "You conducted yourself very well in there." *Damn straight I did.* "You're both greedy and possessive." *Damn straight I am.* "I like when your claws come out, little girl." *Damn straight you do.* Her core hummed from his approval and praise and she snuggled deeper into his side.

As they walked past the ring, Loki called out, "Yo, Puck."

Puck put his hand up to indicate a break and sauntered over to the end of the ring, pressing his weight against the ropes.

"Whattup?"

"Do me a favor. Kerri's done with the class. Take her home."

Puck's gaze lighted on Abby, a gleam of mischief flickering in them. A wide grin split his face. "Will do, brother."

Loki hooked his arm around her neck and was steering her away when Puck piped up, "Taking off?"

Pausing, Loki hit back with a frown. "What the fuck does it look like?"

Puck raised his hands in surrender. "Bro, chillax. Askin' a simple question."

"One you know the answer to already," Loki retorted. His hand slipped down to palm Abby's ass, but his eyes slanted toward Puck, whose own gaze had drifted down to Abby's chest and stalled out there.

Loki seared Puck with a forbidding look. "Puck?"

"Yeah?"

"If you want to live another day, you'll take your fuckin' eyes off her tits."

Puck's loud guffaw echoed around the large, open gym, indicating he'd done it on purpose to taunt Loki.

Loki had them moving toward the entrance when Puck's voice drifted over to them. "Since when do you care, brother?"

"Since right fucking now," he threw back as he wrenched the front door open.

18

LOKI

Watching Abby's little kitten claws come out when Kerri hit on him was fucking adorable and hot as fuck.

Kerri had made it her mission in life to get as many brothers as she could. It worked for her, and considering the asshole she'd recently left, she should do whatever made her happy. But there was no denying it pleased him to see Abby go postal for him. She had a sassy edge, which would help her fit in with the bitches. He'd wage a bet Kerri had run back to the clubhouse and told every last one of them what had happened. Bikers could be as gossipy as a bunch of girls.

Abby swung up behind him and wrapped her arms around his waist. He enjoyed the feel of her arms around him. He couldn't remember the last time he had a woman on the back of his bike, it'd been so long.

He started the engine and rolled out of the parking lot. Seeing his little pixie in a short, flirty dress got his cock hard enough to jackhammer a fuckin' pothole in the street. First things first, though. They had to have a serious talk. He'd never enjoyed a woman getting possessive on his behalf before, and while he liked it, he quickly realized he could have easily been on the other side of that exchange.

If another man, even one of his own brothers—scratch that, *especially* one of his brothers—stepped to Abby, someone would die. Puck had made that point clear enough with his joke leering.

Which was fucking with his head. He didn't want an old lady. Their situation was...well, what was it? His fingers gripped tighter on the handles of his bike. He couldn't deny he enjoyed Abby riding on his back, pussy cradled up behind him, arms twined around his waist. Nor could he deny how good it felt to have her tight cunt wrapped around his cock, nails clawing up and down his back and sides, whimpers and moans egging him on.

And the only thing she wanted was a story about his life for access to that tight cunt. He shook his head in disbelief. Christ, how had he finally won the jackpot. It was a win-win situation. She got to feel close to him, because she was that kind of woman, and he got to be in absolute control of her body without giving more than was required by the terms of their agreement.

Abby shifted behind him and settled in against his back. A big inhale, and she leaned her head to the side, between his shoulder blades, and hummed. He could feel the vibrations through his cut. Jesus *fuck*, it was vibrating into his fucking cock is what it was doing. His balls were yanked up tight enough to spill. Swerving the bike sharply, he felt her gasp against his back. Five more minutes and they'd be at the bar owned by the Demon Squad. As much as he liked her teasing, walking around with a boner.

Propping the door open for her, Loki placed a firm hand on the small of her back. He braced himself for Abby to tease him about this being a date, but for the life of him, he couldn't muster up the indignation to deny it. It sure as hell felt like a date because he didn't need to feed her to fuck her, but he *liked* spending time with her. He enjoyed talking to her about anything, he even willingly revealed shit about his family, which was a first. She displayed no judgment or pity, two emotions he couldn't abide. Didn't mean he'd let on how much pleasure he took from her presence. It was his dirty little secret and it'd stay that way because, he reminded himself sternly, this was a temporary arrangement. *Temporary.*

Guiding her to a back table, he gave a chin lift to brothers at the bar. It was late and neither of them had eaten before class, so they'd grab some drinks and grub, and go. He had no intention of lingering when his cock was hungry for something else.

He sat her down, leaned close in and asked, "What do you want to drink? Order a burger. They're solid."

"I'll have whatever you're having," she replied demurely. She was so fucking adorable, it revved him up like nothing else. He bit back a moan as he stood up and ordered at the bar.

He came back with two drafts, a pint for her because, let's face it, Abby was a lightweight and he wanted her to feel every thrust when he pounded into her later. Once in his seat, she scooted her chair closer, extinguishing the distance between them. He loved that about her, her guileless pursuit of whatever she wanted. No posing. No airs of toughness.

Picking carefully at lint on the front of her dress, she peeked beneath her eyelashes and said, "So... I'm anticipating we'll end up in bed together."

He didn't respond and her little tongue darted out to lick her bottom lip nervously, concern flashing through her eyes. "We are, aren't we?"

Barely suppressing his laugh, he replied, "Hell, yeah."

His response elicited a sigh of relief. "Your place or mine?"

"Yours," he snorted. "No way in hell I'm bringing you to the clubhouse."

She crinkled her nose. "Why not? I hope you don't think I'd mind."

"You should mind. First off, the place is none too clean, but the brothers would be all up in my business. We wouldn't get past the front door without people waving at us to sit and drink with them. A not-too-subtle way of them sussing out what they can about you, and about you and me."

"What's wrong with that? After all, you live there, don't you?"

He lifted a shoulder in a light shrug. "Nothing except that I'm a grown man and my business is my own. You saw Puck before we left the Box. Asking stupid-ass questions, stalling me to find out as much as he could so he could run back to the clubhouse with gossip. Didn't matter when I was alone and had no business to share, but the brothers can be worse than the bitches."

He leaned into her and captured a strand of her hair between his fingers. "I'm not sharing you. We both work crazy hours, as is. I don't need to waste unnecessary time satisfying their curiosity." He gave a little shrug of his broad shoulders. "What can I say, I'm a selfish asshole."

A smile filled out her face. Time to get one condition of their arrangement out of the way. Folding his arms across his chest, he sat back and said, "Let's get story time over with so we can eat. Then I take you home and fuck you till dawn. What do you want to know?"

Abby's cheeks flushed, and she licked her pouty red lips as she studied the droplets of sweat on her beer glass. "How long have you and Kingdom known each other?"

"Since we were kids. I'm five or six years older than he is."

"What's the story between the two of you. Start with any story you like," she offered.

A bitter laugh bubbled up Loki's throat. "Since I'm telling you the gory details of my life, I'll relay the true story between Kingdom and me. One he doesn't know about," he began gruffly. His eyes slid away from Abby's fixed gaze as he sank back against his chair.

Focusing on the glowing fluorescent beer signs hanging on the wall behind her, he confessed, "I've never told anyone this before."

He fell silent, and Abby's mouth parted. He leaned over, placed his index finger beneath her chin and closed it. He was as surprised as she was that he was about to divulge this.

"My mom had been gone for two years, and shit at the house was unbearable. Crispin practically lived at the off-track betting place, a storefront about half a mile away from the shithole we rented out. I had one more year of high school. There was no way I was staying past my eighteenth birthday, but I had to do something with Chopper because he was only twelve."

He closed his eyes, remembering. "So fucking young. Not even in high school yet, but I had to take care of him. Chopper was starting to do what any son does, challenge his piece-of-shit father. I've already given you an intro to Crispin, so you can imagine what a day in the life of his sons was like. I had a part-time job at a garage, and I'd come home to Crispin knocking Chopper around so I *knew* I had to get him out of there. I just didn't have a good plan. Even if I turned eighteen, I was never gonna to get custody of Chopper. Although it was common knowledge up and down our street what was going on, Child Protective Services had never been called on Crispin. He sure as hell wasn't going to hand Chopper over to me. He lived for fights, and Chopper was biting at the bit.

Finally, I hatched up a plan. Chopper was a runner, and I figured he'd run off after Crispin gave him a solid beating. Hell, if you think I'm bad at being distant or shutting down, I had nothing on Chopper or my mother. A fucking fantastic family trait."

His vision hazed over as he snapped back to the conversation he had with his father and how easy it was to convince him to relinquish his son.

"As I predicted, Chopper ran to Kingdom's house, and his mother, a real good woman, took him in. Although Kingdom's dad was long gone, she had a close-knit family. You know Italians. Thick as thieves. Half of them lived on the same street, and they were in and out of each other's houses on the regular. They lived the kind of life where doors were never locked because houses were always full.

"The day after Chopper ran away, Crispin confronted Kingdom's mom and publicly rejected him, as per my plan. The following day, I went to visit Kingdom's mom. Explained the situation in greater detail, exposed my plans to leave for the military and asked for her advice. I should've stayed for him, but the moment she said she would take care of him... let's just say, I didn't need to hear it twice before I had one foot out the door."

Abby scooted her chair close to his and took his hand, lacing their fingers together. His body had gone rigid at the memories and ensuing grief surging up inside him.

"I stayed until the court dates for custody came through. Took a little longer than I'd anticipated, but I had to make sure Crispin showed up. The day after Kingdom's mom got the legal papers, I went to the recruiting center and signed up. My paychecks went to help Kingdom's mom, and whatever was left over after my meager expenses went to pay Crispin off."

By the time the last words left his mouth, Abby had a *holy shit* expression on her face. Mouth slightly parted, eyes blinking rapidly. He bet she'd heard some doozies of stories as a social worker, but this one had even taken her by surprise.

"Speechless?" he said with a twisted smile.

She surreptitiously wiped the corners of her eyes with the back of her hand, grabbed her pint class, and downed half of the contents. The waitress popped out of nowhere and deposited plates of food in front of them with an "Enjoy your meal," and a big smile for Loki. He gave her a chin lift, although his eyes remained fixed on Abby.

He knew she was a woman of understanding and sympathy but buying off his dad to beat up his younger brother to get him fostered into another family was downright dirty. He'd racked his brain to come up with that plan. A plan that would place Kingdom's mom in a situation where she'd never question taking Chopper in.

"You're an incredible person, Loki," Abby said softly.

He did a double take. "Say what now?"

"You figured out a solution for you and your brother." A small smile curved the edges of her lips, her whiskey eyes large and glimmering with unshed tears.

Roughly, he pushed the plate of food away from him. "Agreed, for me. Not for my brother."

"No? You think you would've done a better job than Kingdom's mom and her clan?"

"Of course not," he scoffed. "Don't look at me like that. With pride in your eyes for what I did. I did that for *me*, not for him." He pounded his chest with his fist. "I'm a selfish fucking asshole. What don't you get about that?"

Understanding washed over her face. "You like to think so. You like to think you're a selfish bastard who would pay off his father to renounce his younger brother so he could abandon his little brother."

"Those are the facts," he spat out. "No point in sugar-coating them."

"The facts are that you did the best thing for him. Seriously, you loved your brother. I've seen what happens when children bring up children, and it's difficult. Sometimes, it's disastrous. Even if you were technically close to being an adult at the age of eighteen, you weren't in a position to take care of him. Assuming your father would've let him go and assuming you were financially able to support your brother, living with Kingdom and his mother was the better choice. From what you've told me about Crispin, he was a prideful son of a bitch. The only way you could have freed Chopper from him was to pay him off. You were a clever kid and you succeeded brilliantly. I understand your feeling guilty about leaving your brother, but you did him a favor."

Although outwardly poised, Abby's eyes flashed with indignation on his behalf. "What's wrong with being clever enough to get out from under a sociopathic, abusive father? I'm proud of you, Loki." He dragged in a gasping breath. "Your tenacity saved him and gave him a chance in life. To be brutally honest, had he stayed with you and Crispin, chances are he wouldn't have lived long enough to be able to choose to die. You gave him the chance to make the final choice."

Loki's fingers white-knuckled the table edge. He didn't know what to make of her declaration, of her *pride* in one of the greatest shames. Her version had never once occurred to him. Granted, she had a point about it having been the best thing for Chopper. It was what he'd worked so hard for. Her blunt words about how he'd saved Chopper's life humbled him.

He didn't deserve her, but he was a greedy fucker, and he'd keep her for as long as she was delusional enough to stay with him.

"You know I don't believe you and the pair of rose-colored glasses you wear," he scoffed because he couldn't go there...he couldn't admit how much her good opinion of him meant to him. "Looking only on the positive side of the equation and never seeing the bad."

"Oh, I see plenty of bad, believe me. I may not have grown up in an abusive family, but I've seen even worse than yours in my profession. Maybe I have a better perspective than you. I know you don't believe it, but I'm telling you like I see it. I didn't say what I said to make you feel better. You can take it or leave it, but it's the truth as I see it."

His poor heart cracked at the conviction of her judgement, bleeding like it always did as he remembered what he'd done, the hard choices he had to make, and the way it had turned out for Chopper. But unlike any other time since his brother's death, there was a strain of inexplicable hope surreptitiously sliding into those gushing, bleeding cracks. It was a testament to Abby, to talking to her, to relaying this tragedy. She was a gifted listener, sympathetic, but without a trace of recrimination or pity. He'd never experienced anything like this before.

But he was nowhere ready to relinquish his pain, and only gave a bitter chuckle and replied sardonically, "Oh, I'm definitely leaving it. There's no redeeming what I did."

Locking up his story, his emotions, his pain, he picked up the ketchup bottle, he shook it, and squirted some on his plate. Holding it up, he changed the subject, "Want some with your fries? You got your story. Now eat up quick because you owe me a marathon fuck."

19

ABBY

"**H**arder," Abby moaned.

Loki paused midthrust, her pussy clutching his cock tightly.

"I said, harder. Fuck me rougher."

The usual placid blue ice of his eyes flared into a twin set of indigo blazes. Shaking his head, he muttered, "Fuckin' hell."

She'd ended up nude and tossed onto her bed minutes after stepping through the door of her apartment. Needless to say, he was in a hurry. Which she absolutely *loved*. Irate and impatient to fuck, Loki stripped off his cloths with a speed that left her a little dizzy and a lot aroused.

As soon as she told him to fuck her harder, he withdrew until his cockhead rimmed her entrance and slammed back in with a vicious, bone-shattering thrust, knocking the air out of her lungs.

Delicious.

He yanked her wrists to her sides, and holding them down, went into beast mode, pounding a hot, ferocious rhythm into her.

His wet mouth sizzled around her nipple, sucking with brutal tugs, matching the pace of his churning hips. The smooth glide of the hot, velvet rod of his erection had turned rough.

Demanding.

Her mouth sought purchase and found the crook where his neck met his shoulder. She bared her teeth and dug them in the side of his neck. A groan rumbled through his chest. He released her wrists and planted his hands on the mattress to lift her leg over his forearm and switch up his angle. An angle that had the root of his cock slamming against her clit, causing electric currents to shudder through her. She squirmed to adjust to the change and drove her hips upward to meet his thrusts.

"I was craving you before, but this is fucking..." he trailed off and she finished for him, "mind-blowing."

Concentration etched on his face, as if his sole purpose in life was to fuck her on him, when he grabbed her ass cheeks, and going back on his haunches, fucked her onto his cock. The raw strength of him, his ability to just pick her up and ruthlessly slam her into his body, unhinged her. A scream tore from her throat.

"God*damn*, your pussy's tight as fuck. You ever ride a man before, Abby?"

"Huh?" She couldn't concentrate on his words.

"You're cunt ever ride cock before?"

"No," she expelled in a puff of air, after a particularly harsh thrust.

"It will now." He withdrew his cock with a sucking sound that had her whining "nooo." The space, the absence, the ghostly feeling of his cock physically hurt. Loki propped himself against the headboard and patted his lap.

"Saddle up," he ordered with a challenge in his voice. She

looked at him, his hard, slick arousal vibrating as if in need of *her*. A heady thought, that one. This. Man. Defined ridges on his chest, abs and arms that could go for days. The thick slabs of his quads flexing, a nest of springy curls for his thick, bobbing cock. He wrapped his large, bruised fist around his shaft. Stroking it. Dear God, a huge man like Loki jacking himself off, watching intently for her next move, was unbelievably erotic.

"Come on, Pixie, you can do it," he urged. She wasn't worried, per se. More like stunned, but those words of faith, intertwined with the strain of desperation in his voice, quickly snapped her out of her haze. She scrambled onto his lap, took hold of his cock by the root, and notched the flared tip against her. Circling it around and around her clit, her pussy clenched and warm juices gushed down the sides of his shaft.

Abby raked her teeth over her bottom lip and dropped her weight down, her pussy spreading over his blunt head. The stretch was incredible, not easy, but incredible. She sank lower and lower until she was impaled. His hands dropped to her ass, lifted her a few inches, and spread her pussy wide over his cock. Another gush, and wetness slicked down his balls.

A sense of pride infused her chest. *She*, little, inexperienced Abby, was riding *him*, this older, experienced bad boy biker.

Puffing out a breath, she raised herself a bit and his shaft rasped her inner walls in the best way possible. A sigh of relief escaped. She slowly seated herself, slid back up, and repeated. Each time, she stroked down a little harder, a little rougher.

It wasn't just a sexual act, it was life-changing. Her on top of him. Taking him into her pussy, wrapped tight around his pulsing hot flesh. Their eyes locked. Vulnerability and love, tinged with fear, bled from his gaze. It felt like a claiming. Like he was letting her claim him, and Loki didn't let anyone do anything to him. Her heart split open. She was humbled by his willingness to release his body over to her.

If she could, she'd drop to her knees in thanks.

Writhing over him, she pulled back up. The emotions flooding her were on the edge of overwhelming.

To break the moment, she tore her gaze away from his and husked out, "Am I doing it right?"

"You have no idea, babe. You're a natural. Just look at you, fucking me like a porn star." His jaw tightened. "Now it's my turn to tell you, I want it harder. I can feel you holding back, so come on, take my cock, slam down on it, *take it*." His words did something to her, twisted something inside that made her goad him to come hard, under her hips, inside her clenching pussy. *He* was hers. The thought rattled her, and she faltered in her pace.

His hands came to her hips and brought her back in rhythm.

A wave of determination crashed into her Once she was back, she shoved off the aid of his hands and rode him hard. "Don't help. I'm the one fucking you."

"Fuck, babe, the words you use. You're killing me."

"Hopefully—*pant*—from—*pant*—pleasure—*pant*."

His hips punched up. "You have no fucking idea."

At his admission, she whipped her hips around, grinding down on his cock. Her tits bounced in the air and he filled his palms with them, kneading them with rough, demanding strokes. The feel of his calluses scrapping against her nipples and skin, the small jolts of pain from his too-rough handling began to spiral, and she bucked on him like a rodeo queen going for broke.

Tantalizing touches on her clit turned harder, too fast and firm for her oversensitized nub.

"Slower," she urged him, and he eased off until it was the perfect amount of pressure.

Abby moaned, a low, guttural sound from deep in her bell. Her inner walls fluttered around the hot steel she was riding like a jockey. Small tremors in her core reverberated outward, each one more intense than the last until her climax rang through her in earth-shattering shock waves.

"*Nuh, nuh, nuh,*" she babbled with each downstroke.

In return, raw, guttural groans escaped Loki. Gripping her hips, he took over as her rhythm became irregular. He jacked her up and down his cock, sparking aftershocks in her. His body hardened, fingers pinching her flesh so hard they penetrated her sex fog with the delectable thought of Loki leaving bruises in the shape of his fingers on her.

Streams of come shot into her by the short pumps of his hips.

Overcome, she reached forward and kissed him. Her fingers smoothed over the sweat clinging to his chest hairs.

Panting above him, she asked, "Was it good?"

He let out a puff of laughter. "Fuck, Pixie, you slayed more than my cock."

20

LOKI

Damn, had she ever.

Abby astonished Loki with her eagerness. She took it like a pro. He had to be the luckiest bastard alive because there was no way he deserved to keep this hot to trot fair-haired pixie girl with full tits to rival a porn star. Her eagerness to please, to ride him for gold, while seeking out her own pleasure, was an aphrodisiac like no other.

What she missed in experience she more than made up for in enthusiasm. A ravenous hunger like hers was unusual. Seeing her fall apart was humbling. Strands of hair slicked against her cheek with sweat, dripping from riding him so hard. And her pussy? Her pussy could squeeze him for days.

The moment that cut him at the knees, most likely hobbling him for life, was when she leaned over him, his softening cock still buried inside her, and planted a kiss on his lips. He wasn't big into kissing, but she'd ruined him for another woman's mouth. Not to mention another woman's pussy.

When her mouth moved over his, he instantly opened to

taste her delicate, honey-flavored tongue. What did he do then? He didn't pull back, no, he didn't. He didn't push her off him, put distance between them, and explain his dislike. No, instead he took it deeper, mating with her mouth, devouring her like he'd never get enough. She made him ache for more, for things beyond his reach. She stirred dangerous desires in him, desires of possession, of full ownership, and he couldn't have any of that.

He didn't know how long they made out like a couple of teens, but he would bet it lasted as long as their entire fuck session. Christ, he knew he was in over his head, but he didn't have the wherewithal to move her off him. His muscles failed him. He couldn't have left her bed if the building had caught on fire. That's how good it felt to be in the nestled with her. Her legs entwined around his and her chest resting on top of his, wisps of blonde pixie hair from her crown tickling his cheek.

And he realized, then and there that...

He. Was. Royally. Fucked.

He was, he knew it, and he knew he should extract himself from her, but he was too sated to do anything but draw her closer.

Gathering her in his arms, he said, "Our agreement's one-sided."

"I don't think so," she countered. "You get to boss me around however you want."

"Be that as it may, it's your turn to tell me a story."

She lifted her head, a spark of mischief in her eye. "Will I get to tie you up for a change?"

"Hell fuckin' no," he scoffed. "I don't want to give you the wrong idea. This ain't no democracy."

Her lips twisted wryly. "Sometimes, I ask myself why I put up with your pushy self."

"Because no one can fuck you like I can," he fired back teasingly.

"Come on, be my good girl and play the game," he cajoled. "Tell me something."

Abby pursed her lips. Her brows puckered together thoughtfully. "I guess there's one story anyone who knows me knows about. It's the basis of many of my decisions. When I was eight years old my mother was diagnosed with leukemia."

As if by instinct, Ginger landed on the edge of the bed, creeping delicately among their tangled legs. Circling a small space, she curled up on the pinnacle of the bundled sheet by Loki's side.

"I'm a little envious of my cat's ability to co-opt you, as if you were her property," she said wryly.

Her cat didn't much care for boundaries, he could say that much with confidence. She twirled around his legs as he walked through the door or sat on the couch. Jumped onto his lap, regardless of what he was doing. But he found he didn't care. Ginger was part of Abby's world and he'd do about anything to learn more about Abby, to be part of her life. Fuck, if Abby only knew how tightly wrapped around her little finger he was, he'd be screwed. He was sure as hell never gonna let her find out.

Reaching over him, Abby caressed the cat. "My parents were soul mates. They were super-liberal hippies who met at a Grateful Dead concert near the college they attended in Connecticut. They fell in love at first sight. But when she got sick, I took care of her. My father had to keep working, and my brothers were teenagers. They helped, but they were spooked by her illness, by the fac that she was dying, and the last stage of cancer is basically dying."

She shrugged it off. "So it fell to me. I turned thirteen when she died, and everything went hell after she was gone.

My father drowned in his work. He's an economics professor, a Marxist economist if you're wondering. I know, sounds like an oxymoron. He buried himself in his research and teaching while my two brothers ran. Couldn't get out of the house fast enough. I don't blame them. They were willing to do anything —*anything*—to forget the sickness and death clinging to the house. They're nosy and meddling busybodies in my life, out of guilt for having emotionally abandoned me as a kid. It's annoying, I can assure you."

A wave of shock blew over Loki. He had no idea. The image of his flaxen-haired pixie, dressed in black at the age of thirteen, watching a coffin being lowered into the ground. He knew what that felt like and it brought a shudder down his spine. He was a grown-ass man the day Chopper's coffin, draped in an American flag, was lowered into a pit in the cemetery, and he could barely get over it. Picked a fight with Kingdom afterward to blow off steam, and the bastard was more than happy to oblige. They'd rolled around on the floor of the clubhouse, throwing punches at each other before the brothers pulled them apart. His mother had left a long time ago, but he'd been grateful for it. Grateful she'd survive. Grateful she didn't have to know the grief of Chopper's death.

The exact opposite of Abby's experience.

"Christ," Loki blew out.

"Being a caretaker at such a young age formed me into who I am. I always knew I'd go into a helping profession, either a psychologist, therapist, or social worker. It was written in the stars. In the end, I chose social work because I wanted to provide holistic assistance to people in crisis. During my last year of graduate school, I took an internship at the Agency and I've never left. Assuming everything continues in the same direction, I'll retire there. I love my work."

Clapping her hands together, she finished cheerfully, "So, that's my story."

Loki blinked down at her. Ginger raised her head at the loud thwacking sound, but then settled her nose back into the fluffy fur of her back.

Loki's arms tightened around her. "Fuck, Abby."

He buried his face into her shoulder. "You're fucking killing me here."

"It's okay," she soothed him. "It was a long time ago. I've been through grief counseling and therapy to help me work through her death. One important life lesson I learned was not to take anything or anyone for granted. In a blink of an eye, one's entire life can change. The only thing that causes me a teensy, tiny bit of anxiety is..." she cast a bashful look in his direction, "children."

"My mother often said she'd wished she'd had children earlier so that she could've spent more time with my brothers and me. That we would be full-fledged adults by the time she passed. My brothers were older, but they were still immature and too young emotionally to deal with the early death of a mother. It would certainly explain some of their early choices in partners. Her words echo in my head constantly."

With an embarrassed shrug, she concluded, "My professional life is secure, but I feel like I'm behind in my love life, and in building a family life."

"Babe, you're what...twenty-two? Hell, I'm sixteen years older than you."

"We're different. I mean, I'm a woman, and I may be wrong but generally speaking, I think women are more often concerned about that sort of thing earlier on in their life. The pressure is doubled in my case." She sighed. "My brothers are already engaged or married, and my father internalized my mother's worry, so he brings it up constantly. As I've told him time and again, I'm holding out for someone special to have a relationship like he had with my mother."

✻✻✻

THERE, *I've said it.*

Covering his hand with hers, she assured him, "I'm not trying to put any kind pressure on you."

He snorted, "You couldn't if you tried. Abby, look at me." He waited until their eyes met. "I'm nowhere near where you need me to be, but I won't lie...I care for you. Don't ever doubt that. I mean," he grabbed her ass, "I'm fucking you, aren't I? Never thought that was gonna happen again in my lifetime."

Okaaay, wow. That was an unexpected confession. He could be obstinate as hell, but his simple honesty had brought her to her knees, hands waving in the air in a big *hallelujah.*

There was no denying the new developments in their relationship. Last night, their dinner out closely resembled a date. Their conversation, at the bar and in bed, was deep and personal. She would've never imagined confiding in Loki had she not felt close to him. And it was freeing that he knew her ultimate goals. If they included him, then he knew what she expected of him. If they didn't, then he'd understand if she walked away from him. Either way, acknowledging their deepening bond was a relief because she wasn't in stasis, going nowhere. Since the last two years of her mother's illness, which were the worst, the feeling of forging onward in her life was super important. She didn't need to be pregnant, but she *did* need the sense of moving forward, of progress.

Relaying the story of her mother and father made her

realize she'd fallen for Loki as hard as her parents had fallen for each other. She recalled her mother's description of not being able to look away from her father, of drifting toward him as if connected to him by an invisible steel cable that reeled her in like a fish hooked on a line.

Abby's fingers ghosted along the hard planes of Loki's chest, encircling his tightening nipples. The soft bristle of his dark hair stood out against his tanned, olive skin. Her palm glided down to ring his burgeoning shaft. The rise and fall of his chest accelerated as his features tightened. His face would never be splashed on a Calvin Klein ad with his jagged scar, heavy brow, and angular jawline, but at that moment, a smile broke over his face and the shifting of the muscles of his cheeks lit up his blue eyes. He was one of the most gorgeous men she'd laid her eyes on.

Abby ducked her face and buried it in his chest.

Oh, God. There was no denying it. He was the one for her.

He wasn't ready, but she'd throw caution to the wind and place a bet on this rugged, bristly, sexy man. His emotional depth and caring impressed her, surpassing her father and brothers. The tragedies and hardships he'd survived had forged a deep well in him. The deepest. For that reason alone, he was worth every effort on her part.

21

ABBY

The late August heat had long infiltrated the air-conditioned building and Abby plucked the blouse off the perspiration gathering between her breasts hours ago.

She felt the increase in humidity and temperature as she made her way down the long hallway to the open reception area of the Agency. God, how did Solange, the receptionist, handle it at her desk out front? Reaching the arched entrance of the larger room, her feet screeched to a halt and she backed up a step.

Leaning against a filing cabinet, Loki had his head bent down to catch whatever Solange was saying to him.

A breath caught in her throat. Good God, he was handsome. Dressed from head to toe in his uniform of black jeans and a black shirt underneath his cut, she inhaled the sight of him. Her gaze skated over his torso, his tricep flexing with tats running along the carved edges of each isolated muscle of his arm. His scar blinked at her as he grinned in response to a comment Solange made. The length of his body on display was a cocktail of hot, filthy sex blended with self-command and power. A devastating combination.

Solange grasped waves of her thick hair and shook it out. She couldn't blame the woman for preening under his regard. Abby stepped out of the shadows and into the bright lobby. The movement snared Loki's attention and his head snapped up, as if he'd caught her scent. A hungry stare clawed up her body, leaving a trail of heat in its wake.

He greeted her in a low, rumbling baritone. "Hey, Pixie."

Goose bumps traveled down her arms. Adding an extra sway to her hips, she sauntered over to him. The instant she reached him, he slid a hand beneath her hair, took hold of her nape and brushed his lips over hers. His fingers tightened and his lips pressed harder, as if considering whether to take it further.

At that moment, Solange let out a low whistle.

He gave an extra squeeze and pulled away.

"Do you have any single friends, Loki?" Solange quizzed him flirtatiously.

"Plenty, but they're not for good girls like you," he responded.

Fluttering her eyelashes, Solange crooned, "I'm not that good a girl."

"You're not bad enough, either."

She gave him a pout. "I can be for someone like you."

Tucking Abby into his side, Loki gave her reprimanding look. "You don't want to be that bad."

"Well, how bad is Abby?" she taunted.

"Sweetheart, I never kiss and tell, but I guarantee you that Abby," he gave her waist a squeeze, "is as good as they get."

Dismissing Solange, his attention switched to her and he asked, "Thought you might want to go for a ride. It's hot out there, but the breeze will feel good."

"Sure," she breathed out.

"Lucky girl," Solange sighed. Eyeing Loki up and down, she added, "You take good care of her, you hear? She's had back-to-back clients all day. Didn't even leave her desk for lunch."

Loki's expression clouded over, his voice taking on a dangerous edge as he said, "That so?"

Gliding a hand underneath his cut, she placed it over his heart. "It's not a big deal. A ride sounds perfect."

To her surprise, they rolled up to Abby's apartment complex first, where he told her to go in, change, and put on a bathing suit. She chose her most revealing bikini, shimmied a pair of short cut-off jeans over her hips and whipped on a tight, spaghetti-strapped tank top. Swinging over behind Loki on his bike, she tried to entice him to give her hints of where they were going with kisses along his neck, but he wouldn't budge.

Soon, they left the urban center behind, and drove through the country roads of the Adirondacks. One thing Abby never thought she'd enjoy as much as she did was riding. The sun beating down on her back, the wind whipping past, the hard abs bunching and flexing beneath her fingertips. All of it combined to create a magnificent sense of well-being.

After stopping at a roadside diner for a meal, they rode on.

Loki turned off on a private road, cut the motor, and they hiked up an overgrown dirt path. Private property signs popped up in increasing numbers as they ascended, but he assured her it was owned by a brother's family. They would be left undisturbed. Sounded promising to her.

The hike abruptly got steeper. Taking a breather after a particularly difficult ascent, she inclined her head to the side and heard the distinct sound of bubbling water.

She picked up her steps and minutes later found a break in the canopy of trees.

She gasped out loud, "A waterfall!"

Pointing over another ridge, she exclaimed, "Another! It has to be at least fifty feet tall."

Water cascaded over a series of ridges and roiled around flat rocks protruding into the wide stream.

Grabbing her hand, Loki helped her down a set of worn stone steps to a small swimming hole of swirling water.

Abby ripped off her tank top, thrust her pair of cutoff jeans down her legs, kicked off her sandals and waded into the pool. The sun was long past its apex, but the humidity of the day continued to cling to everything. The refreshing, cool water rushed around her waist and she splashed with delight, droplets flying everywhere.

Striped nude, Loki dove into the pool.

He swam past her and emerged in front of her.

"This is like an oasis from a fairy tale," she breathed out. Twisting around, she scanned the trees around them. "Can anyone see us from the trail, you think?"

"After the dozen private property signs we passed? Not likely, but possible. These waterfalls are known to the locals." Leaning in close, he mock-whispered, "Don't worry, I won't fuck you, no matter how much you beg."

"You arrogant prick," she cried out and gave him a hard shove. He sank in the clear pond, but quickly broke through the surface, jutting upward with a large splash. Flinging his head side to side like a puppy, he sprayed water in every direction. Screeching, she raised her hands to protect her face, peals of laughter escaping her.

Loki went farther in, and she followed him, her legs paddling rapidly to stay warm in the cold mountain water. She'd never seen Loki so carefree. Never expected to see him escape the strict control he demanded of himself. Normally, every move he made was economical, pared down to the essential. But here, he splashed and swam with ease. Tufts of hair stuck up in disarray, and the sexy crinkles she loved so much lined the corners of his eyes.

Swimming to the far end, she lifted herself up on the smoothly eroded edge of a granite boulder. Lying back on her elbows, her feet grazed the surface of the water, creating ripples that refracted the multicolored pebbles and rocks at the bottom of the pool. She watched as Loki swam a few laps, his strong arms slicing through the water.

Eventually, he came over by her. Water sluiced off his flanks like miniature waterfalls as he lifted himself out of the water. Her gaze skittered over the expanse of olive skin stretched over hard, yet refined muscles. His chest hair and the curls around the root of his cock were weighted down with droplets. Although not aroused, memories of what a powerful, pleasure-inducing instrument it was pinged in her mind.

Without realizing it, she smacked her lips loudly.

"None of that," he warned. "I don't care if anyone sees me naked, but if you keep lookin' at me like that, I might stop caring whether anyone sees you naked."

His own gaze migrated to her nipples, pebbled hard beneath her bikini top. Padding over to the bag he'd carried, he returned with a towel. Spreading it open, he prodded her to lie down and close her eyes.

Abby stretched her arms above her head and a low growl reverberated from Loki's chest.

Eyes closed, she said, "You better tell me a story quickly so that I can jump you when we get back."

"No more stories," he grunted.

Her eyelids popped open in surprise. Shielding her eyes from the still-strong light, she watched him curiously.

"No more games," he clarified.

Her heart rioted behind her breastbone. Flashing him a grin, she inquired primly, "Does that mean I get to have a story, free and clear?"

"Yep."

"Not that I'm complaining, mind you."

"We're past that," he replied soberly. "After Chopper died, I didn't want to feel again. Didn't deserve to. If I'm being honest, only thing that gave me comfort was my rage. Rage and fury made me powerful. Invulnerable. Always had two sides to me. Ultra-restrained and quiet punctuated with bouts of uncontrollable fury. That's why they named me Loki. Tricked the brothers into thinking I was cool and in control, until I wasn't. By the time I met you, I was mostly dead inside until you brought out a range of emotions in my. I fought it, but I'm done with that."

Although she had zero problems with the reciprocity of their deal, Loki's declaration was huge. It quieted the fears relentlessly whispering in the back of her mind. She swallowed over the wedge lodged in her throat. She learned early on that one's entire world could go topsy-turvy and to grab what happiness life offered you with both hands, quickly, quickly before it slipped away, in death or tragedy or just life.

Nerves and fear mixed with excitement made her jump to her feet and seamlessly plunge into the crisp, serene water. She hit the air and was startled to find Loki bursting out of the water right beside her. He must have followed her instantly. Grasping her by the waist, he effortlessly dragged her to the edge of a jutting boulder, placed his back against it, and brought her into the corral of his arms. She linked her fingers around his nape, lifted to her toes and kissed him. The words "I love you" pushed against her lips to escape, but she pushed them back at the last moment.

Abby splashed onto her back, arms wide, and allowed herself to drift down to the rocky bottom.

Kicking up, she resurfaced and taunted him, "Catch me if you can."

He lunged for her and caught her foot. It slipped free of his slick fingers and she laughed as she heard Loki's splash behind her.

22

LOKI

"Are you fuckin' serious?" Loki snarled. "I'll be stuck sharing my office with you?"

Cutter countered, "Yeah, yeah, keep up the act. As if. You fuckin' love sharing with me, you piss-poor fucker. Be serious, who else would share with you? You're a scary-lookin' motherfucker."

Loki gave him a dry, narrow-eyed glare. "Kingdom said I'd get my own office, you dirty son of a bitch."

Cutter let out a cackle. "And you were stupid enough to believe him? Christ, you've known him longer than I have. The asshole sells pipe dreams like a heroin dealer outside a druggy clinic. Easy pickings, bro. You were never gonna get a private office. We need as many available rooms as possible."

He'd only half believed Kingdom, since it didn't make financial sense, but he was sick of Cutter's messy clutter. Greta confided that he wasn't messy at home, so Cutter was doing it on purpose to piss him off. The bastard reveled in being a pain in the ass, through and through. It was payback for twisting Cutter's arm to become VP after Kingdom took over as president.

Loki said, "Swear to Christ, you enjoy fucking with me."

"That I do, brother," he quipped.

"If you weren't so damn big, I'd drag you into the cage and knock you out," Loki griped.

"That's why I'm big. So I can fuck with you and live to see another day," Cutter taunted as he pushed his chair back and propped one ankle over the other on the edge of his desk, allowing his feet to dangle off. "How are things with Abby, aka Pixie."`

Loki slowly lifted his eyes over his computer monitor and sent Cutter a warning scowl. "Don't call her that."

"Oh, is that right? How come?"

Loki pointedly ignored his question, although his typing had mutated into knifing motions on his keyboard.

"So. Was I right about her *nature*?"

Swear to fucking Christ and back, Cutter was the bane of his existence. Clenching his teeth, he continued to ignore him.

"Since you broke her in, she should be ready to move on to another brother, no?" Cutter pressed.

Loki vaulted to his feet and stabbed his index finger at Cutter. "Don't talk about her like that."

Wagging his finger back at Loki, he broke into a loud guffaw. "It's too fucking easy to get the drop on you. Like taking a lollipop from a baby."

Loki made a fist and casually punched the palm of his opposite hand. "Meet me in the cage. Be glad to drive you home afterward and see Greta's reaction when she sees you're busted-up face tonight."

Gasping for breath between belly-deep laughs, Cutter waved his hands in surrender. "Alright, I'll back off. Can't take a fuckin' joke no more."

Making a disgruntled sound in the back of his throat, Loki dropped back into his office chair and resumed staring at the spreadsheet on the screen. Taking a deep breath, he held it for four seconds and then expelled it. He was a stoic mother-fucker, but Cutter talking about Abby and other brothers was like ghosting a thumb over the hair trigger of a gun. Fuck it, who was he kidding? He was always sensitive. He was just ten times worse lately.

"You'll get a break from me this weekend. I'm riding down to Jersey. You can clean up the office," he swept his arm over the large space, "and bring it back to its anal cleanliness, once again."

Loki's gaze flicked up to his. "Why? Is it the Dark Horsemen?"

"Fucking Shadow. Kicking up a fuss about some bullshit with Kite. I'm going to see Kite at the Squad clubhouse and see what can be done to deal with him. I already knew he was an asshat, but this is not a good sign."

"Won't your ass rile him up more? After all, you got Greta and he lost her."

"Oh, I wanna go gangster on him, but instead, I'm meeting with Scudder at Kite's house. You remember him? He protected Greta when she was a kid. Like an uncle to her. Also the only sane motherfucker who has some power over crazy-ass Shadow."

"Of course, I remember Scudder" he scoffed. "Jesus, we were there last year. Not like my memory's blinking out."

Cutter shrugged. "Figured now that you've released the years of built-up sperm, all the endorphins gave you a brain fog. You know, endorphins are more powerful than morphine. Since I've never been abstinent for more than a week, I can't know what happens to a man who finally gets some after so many years. Permanent brain damage or some such shit."

"Ha-ha, funny man." He eyed Cutter. "You going alone?"

"Yep."

"Need backup?"

"From you? Bad enough if Shadow gets a scent of me, but the both of us? Hell, I don't know who he hates more. Anyways, who the hell is gonna clean up this shithole if you go? Nah, I'm counting on you to play maid with Abby in here and fix this place up." He broke out into a grin.

"This place is a pig sty because of you, asshole. Now, can you shut the fuck up so I can finish payroll?"

"Yeah, yeah." Cutter kicked his feet up on his desk and poked at his cell phone. Loki had refocused on the spreadsheet and templates on his screen when Cutter inquired, "So what's your plan for the anniversary?"

In the middle of punching numbers into a calculator, he replied distractedly, "What are you talking about?"

"The *an-ni-ver-sa-ry*," Cutter repeated, stressing each of the five syllables.

Loki glanced up.

Cutter's expression was stone cold sober. Not a trace of amusement lingered on his features. "You know, Autodestruct Week."

Loki's eyes flew to the top his screen. The Fifth was around the corner.

"Motherfucker," he breathed out.

Stroking the stubble along his jaw with his knuckles, Cutter observed, "It's a good sign you forgot. By this time of year, you'd be revving up to self-destruct for a whole week, either piss-ass drunk, shut up with that knife collection of yours, or picking a fight. I'd say it's a very good thing you forgot."

Thoughts struck him from all directions, fast and garbled. White noise drowned out everything and his body went numb. Fingers curled into themselves, the half-moons of his nails digging viciously into his flesh. His fist clenched tighter and tighter until the stabbing pain of his nails shook him out of his shock.

He checked the date on his computer again.

Un-fucking-believable.

The anniversary of Chopper's suicide was in two days. He'd forgotten. Completely fucking *forgotten*. A roar of guilt rushed through his chest. He heard Cutter call his name a few times, but it sounded like he was talking with cotton balls in his mouth. He couldn't move. He couldn't think. Everything converged around a widening chasm in his chest. A deep, gaping hole of roiling fury and fear.

"Loki, it isn't that bad." Suddenly, Cutter's face swam in front of his, and his palms were slapping him lightly on the cheeks. "Come on, snap out of it."

Loki swiped at Cutter's hands, and the brother retreated from his line of sight. "Don't tell me what to fucking do," he bellowed.

Cutter returned in front of him again. "*Brau*, don't do this to yourself. Don't let the monster take over and go on the warpath. Don't. Do. It. You'll regret whatever happens afterward."

From deep inside his chest came a bellow, "What the hell do you know about it?"

"Year after year, I've witnessed it. Don't let it take over and ruin your fucking life because you've got something good going on and you deserve it. You fuckin' deserve it."

"Get the fuck out of my face," he spat out.

Backing up a step, Cutter shook his head and released a weary sigh. "Here we go."

Then, he lunged over the desk and grabbed the front of Loki's shirt, twisting it in his fist. Getting right into his face, he snarled, "Listen motherfucker, deal with your shit because it's going to come and bite you in the ass. You don't want that to happen. You keep believin' you deserve the pain, but you don't. It's gonna wreak havoc and you've got too much of a good thing to lose."

Loki broke Cutter's hold and thrust him away.

Retreating behind his desk, Cutter kept a careful eye on him. "So, what's your plan?"

Loki's gaze drifted around the room. Everything looked blurry. His choices were limited. He had to dig deep, draw on his reserve of self-restraint and not instigate a fight these next few days. He didn't talk feelings and he wasn't about to start.

Focusing in on Cutter, he gave a one-shouldered shrug. "Simple. Ignore it."

"Ignore it?" Cutter repeated, his brows furrowed in disbelief. "I'm not saying I know fuck-all about how to deal with this shit, but shouldn't you talk to Abby about it. She's a sensible woman, and she's a social worker, after all."

"Hell fucking no. The last thing I want is for Abby to find out. I've got a distraction, so this year, I'm gonna let her distract me." Casting him a look of disgust, Loki went on, "What the hell is wrong with you, anyways? Your woman's got you turned into a pussy. We don't talk about shit like this. We break shit up. We brawl. Or don't you remember since the last time you were arrested for brawling in a bar?"

Cutter rolled his eyes. "Way to live up to a stereotype, why don't you?"

"Fucking sue me if I want to bury my cock in pussy the day my little brother took his fucking life. I have an option other than rage. You really wanna take that away from me? You want Trickster Loki to come out and play? 'Cause you know the kind of chaos he leaves in his wake."

Eyes bleeding pity, Cutter muttered, "Christ, okay Loki, you're killing me here."

Loki clenched his teeth. He hated seeing the pity in his brother's eyes.

Spearing his fingers in his hair, Loki grappled with the rage and fear warring in his chest, and let out a gust of air. "For fuck's sake, give me a break. It's the best way I know how to handle this."

"Yeah, all right. Pussy's definitely the right way to go, considering the situation."

"Glad we cleared this up for you. Now can you shut the hell up so I can get payroll ready, or what?"

"Yeah, go for it," Cutter affirmed, gruffly.

"Thank fuck," he snarled and plunged into the task like his life depended on it.

23

ABBY

Abby's gaze flicked to her cell phone. Sammi's name flashed. Huh, Sammi only ever texted, rarely picking up a phone and dialing.

Swiping at her phone and picking up, Abby greeted her, "Hey, what's up?"

"Hey," Sammi replied in a subdued voice. "Sooo...anything new going on?"

"Umm, nothing special," she replied, perplexed.

"And Loki?" Sammi prompted.

"Loki's good." Abby glided her fingers around the base of her throat. Sammi had never asked about Loki specifically before, especially right at the beginning of a call.

Running her fingers through her hair, she said, "What's going on?"

A deep sigh echoed through the speaker phone. "It's the anniversary of Chopper's suicide today."

"What?" Abby gasped, shaking her head. *Wow.* She had not expected that.

"Are you sure?" she asked, cringing the instant the question popped out of her mouth. "Never mind, of course you are."

"He hasn't told you, I see. Typical biker. I called to warn you because Loki doesn't usually make it through the day in one piece. In the past, he usually picks a fight with Kingdom. Last year, he got stopped for drunk driving."

Her belly fluttered and her chest tightened. Loki drunk driving? He was the most careful and responsible driver she knew.

Not good at all.

"He hasn't said a word to me. We were together last night, and he didn't seem any different." She went back through their night together. "Okay, maybe he seemed a little distracted, but we had another marathon night so it's hard to pinpoint anything specific. We didn't talk much, but I think I would've picked up if something was off."

"Oh, in the past, he'd definitely be off. Could be he's doing better, and it isn't wrecking him like it did the past three years. I wanted to make sure you were prepared. It's already a good omen he hasn't fucked someone up yet."

"Is it? The anger and grief is still simmering inside him. It hasn't gone anywhere if he hasn't dealt with it, and nothing tells me that he has. He's closed off," Abby mused aloud.

A little worrisome, to say the least. He'd opened up to her, but was it enough if he didn't broach the most important day of the year with her?

She expelled an impatient sigh. "Alright, I'm going to stop by the Box after I get off work."

"If he hasn't brought it up, maybe he doesn't want to bring it up. Everyone has their own way of dealing with grief."

"It's not healthy, Sammi," she warned

"Yeah, but it's his choice," Sammi reminded her in a gentle voice. "Don't forget that."

Abby's eyes squeezed closed. "Yes, you're right. You're right and I won't push or try to interven in anyway. Okay, I'm going to see how he's doing."

"Fine, but tread lightly, and step away if it gets heated. Don't get in over your head. If I've learned anything from living with bikers, it's best to back off if they don't want to deal with something," she counseled.

"Mmm-hmm," Abby responded absentmindedly as she plotted how she was going to get Loki to face his feelings about his brother, once and for all.

※※※

ABBY PUSHED OPEN the glass door and approached Whistle manning the front desk. "Hey, Whistle. What's going on?"

"Nothin' much," he replied with a lopsided grin. "The usual. Light day 'cause it's been raining all day. Slows down the traffic."

His gaze flittered to her chest and then jumped back to her eyes, a look of alarm on his face. *So busted.*

Smirking, she leaned an elbow on the counter and asked, "Is Loki in the back?"

"Yep," he replied with a knowing nod. "You know the way."

"Okay, thanks." As she passed by him, she said, "By the way, there are mirrors everywhere so I'll catch you if you check out my ass." She shrugged. "Just sayin'."

Whistle broke into a deep laugh. "I feel you, Abs. I'll keep my eyes to myself."

"Much appreciated."

With a laugh of her own, she walked across the floor,

passing the counter where members hung out, the weights and punching bags, and skirted around the large central ring before turning into the corridor where Loki's office was located.

Knocking gently, she waited until she heard Loki respond, then entered.

He was behind his desk. Elbows propped on the desk; his tatted forearms were in mid-air as he ran his fingers through his hair. Strands of hair stuck out of his head. He looked frustrated, but other than that, he had the sexy, lethal, bad boy look down to an art. She always got a little breathless the first moment she laid her eyes on him.

His brows sloped down over his piercing blue eyes. "Hey, what are you doing here?"

He half rose off his seat. "Everything okay?"

"Yeah, yeah, sit back down," she replied with a motion of her hands for him to sit back down. Walking toward him, she said, "I don't want to interrupt you if you're in the middle of something."

She reached his desk, and he scooted his rolling office chair backward and patted his lap. "Never. Come here."

He took her by the waist and scooped her into his lap. His hand grazed the opening of her button-down shirt a little south of her neck and smoothed over her breast, squeezing once. Her breath caught in her throat. She loved the way he just took what he wanted. He desired her so he grabbed her, settled her on his lap, and had his way with her.

He strummed her nipple over her clothing and there was a tightening in her belly. Languidly, he unfastened a button, paused, and then caressed the newly exposed skin. He unhooked the next button, repeated, and went for the next one. A warm throbbing unfurled between her thighs. She snuggled deeper into his chest, her chest rising and falling in greater excitement.

He spread the shirt, flicked open the front clasp of her bra, and her breasts sprang free. Biting her inner cheek to suppress a moan, her eyes fluttered closed. She fought hard to keep them open because she had to watch as Loki's big hand covered her breast, the contrast of his tanned skin against her pale one, adding to the crackling sexual energy between them.

She arched her spine to press it firmly against his palm.

His voice came out rough, harsh, tense. "You want my cock, baby girl?"

God, did she. Her response came out in a fast rush. "Yes, yes, please, Loki."

"I'm gonna be rough," he warned. His voice dropped further, a rough abrasion against her sensitive skin. "I need rough."

"Anything," she rasped out in reply.

Fingers trembling with anticipation, she struggled out of the rest of her shirt and stood to wiggle out of her pencil skirt. "The door?"

"No one walks in when it's closed. It'll be a cold day in hell before I let anyone see you like this because, this," he flicked his wrist, "is mine alone."

She hooked her fingers in the sides of her panties.

"Leave them," he commanded.

Her hands dropped off. Spinning her around, he grabbed hold of her nape and bent her over the desk. Skimming a finger along the edge of her panties, he gave her ass cheek a swift smack, just a little warning, and then drew them down over her hips and thighs.

Unbuckling his belt, he slowly slid it from the loops of his jeans, the slither of leather resonating in her ears. He slid a finger between the crack of her ass down to her pussy, which was already weeping for his touch.

"Goddamn, I love your peach-shaped ass," he croaked out, giving the other cheek a nice swat.

She let out a low groan.

Without warning, the belt cracked over one of her buttocks.

"Loki," she cried out. They had discussed this in depth a few days ago, so none of this came as a surprise but it was still the first time he'd smacked her with anything other than his hand, and for the record, it stung like hell. The strip of flesh where it had landed sizzled. The burn sped down her core and rushed over the back of her thighs like water dashing over rapids. His palm fell on her blistering flesh and kneaded it until the pain transformed into a low throb.

Pinning her down, Loki adjusted his grip on his belt. "Count for me."

The *whoosh* of the belt's arc through the air preceded the *whack* on the moment of impact. Abby puffed out the numbers as he lit into her, modulating the weight of each blow as they traveled over the surface of her ass. She twitched her butt from side to side, not exactly escaping and most definitely rubbing her pussy against the lip of his oak desk.

"Be still," he commanded. "Or you'll earn yourself more."

"What did I do to earn these," she panted out.

"Being a sexy little pixie angel, come down from heaven to torment me with your perfect cunt. Good enough answer for you, huh?"

Her top row of teeth instantly snagged her bottom lip and bit down hard. Once she nodded, he resumed, the belt reconnecting with her flesh. He stopped repeatedly to massage between his light smacks. But even a light smack with a belt packed a punch. The layers of pain melded together into a dark, luscious pulsing in her pussy, which was coated in liquid.

His husky voice broke through her haze. "Should see the way your fine ass bounces back after each smack. Fucking gorgeous."

The belt hit the floor with a clank. His fingers sought out her drenched core and worked them in and out of her slit. "Fuck this, I can't wait."

Yes, yes, please hurry up. She heard each metal tooth of his zipper separate, and, suddenly, his cock was nestled between her buttocks. Hot velvet steel alongside her quivering flesh. Turning her over, he set her blistered ass on the desk.

She whimpered, but his tongue lashed into her mouth, distracting her. She drowned in the sweet tanginess of his evening espresso on his tongue as his hips rocked into her. He hoisted up her legs and she clamped her thighs around his trim waist as the thick head of his cock pushed into her.

"Take it, baby," he demanded.

Her arms swept behind her and her palms smacked down on the desk, giving her the stability to oscillate her pelvis into his demanding thrusts.

"That's it, Pixie, take my big cock like the good slut you want to be for me. Take it and don't scream when I fuck into you and bounce you on my cock like the little fuck toy you are."

The glide of his cock caressed the inner walls of her pussy. Each withdrawal made her beg for the return of his cock. The perfect tilt of his shaft ground the base against her engorged clit on his upward thrusts, but it wasn't nearly enough. She snaked one hand between their heaving torsos and worked her clit. The rumbling, guttural and animalistic, rising from his chest drove her insane. Soon, her whole world shrank to the pain of her raw ass and the pleasure of Loki's cock in her cunt.

Suddenly, her body seized up and Abby lurched forward, screaming around his plunging tongue. Tremors radiated from her clenching muscles. Loki's pummeling turned short and harsh. Grabbing her ass, he plowed into her, his thrusts choppy.

Breaking his suction on her tongue, he roared as he came. "Fuck, fuck, FUCK," he thundered. Curved over her, he touched his forehead to hers, their harsh breaths dancing a tango between them.

She loved everything he'd finished doing to her, but she didn't like the desperate energy behind it.

She ran a hand down his chest and blurted out, "Your brother."

His body jolted off her as if something had slammed into his body and whipped him away. She gasped at the sudden absence, and reached to touch him, but he took another quick step back from her.

"W-what did you say?"

"I said, your brother. Why didn't you tell me that today is the day that he—"

His face twisted. "Because it's none of your damn business, that's why. Who the fuck do you think you are coming in here and bringing him up? You think 'cause we fucked, I'm ripe for you to pick me apart?"

Abby's mouth dropped open. The words sliced into her, leaving her gasping in pain. *Okay*, he was hurting. She got that. And her declaration was sudden, and maybe it wasn't the best moment to bring it up, but still...he was thrusting her away from him with as much force as he could. She was trying to help him, dammitt.

24

LOKI

Loki was aware of the snarling brutality in his tone, but he was beyond caring.

A fireball of rage barreled through him. He was lodged in her dripping pussy; she was milking him, and *that* was the moment she chose to bring up his brother? The audacity.

He actively worked to avoid bringing up Chopper every day of his life—agonizing guilt pounded through him—he sure as hell wouldn't have brought it up today, of all days.

Abby wasn't manipulative by nature, but it didn't mean she couldn't have done it instinctually. Either way, she'd taken advantage of his weakness by bringing up the one thing he desperately wanted to *forget*.

She was delusional if she thought talking about Chopper on the day he killed himself would bring about a fucking epiphany. Not fucking happening. He'd had three long-ass, hellish years, twenty-four seven for three-hundred and sixty-five days a year, not including a fuckin' leap year, of hellish guilt and grief. From the pit of his soul, he knew there was no chance of reconciling himself to Chopper's death.

What he did know was that she wasn't going to get half a chance to patronize him with her bullshit grief counseling. The pressure was building and building in his head, hunting for a way out—

"Fucking fuck," he exploded.

Grabbing a vase on Cutter's desk, he hurtled it through the air, and felt a twinge of satisfaction when it crashed against the opposite wall.

Ceramic shards, water, and flowers flew everywhere.

"I just mentioned his name," Abby spoke, in a subdued tone. Her arms came around her waist in a protective gesture that only fed his rage.

"Like hell you did," he spat out, spinning on his heel and storming toward her. "Since your mom died, you've had a rescue complex. Save the victims, save me, save every pathetic fucker that had the bad luck of stumbling in your savior path. You," he stabbed a finger in the air, "are not going to pull that psychobabble fuckery on me. Take your idealistic hippy dippy flower child bullshit and get the fuck out of my life."

Her mouth dropped open, her breath rattling out in pain. A slice of shame pierced his haze of fury, but he wasn't about to let it go, he wasn't about to step back, even though he knew it was the right thing to do. But his notorious self-control was in tatters and he couldn't backpedal. Hell, he could barely put a brake on it.

His chest heaving with heart ache, grief, and remorse, he stared her down as she arranged her cloths in jerky motions with trembling hands. Once she was decent, she stood up tall and threw her shoulders back. *Is she seriously challenging me, today of all days?*

"The time will come when you must face this, Loki," she pressed. "If not for yourself, then for us."

"There is no *us*," he lashed out. "Not once have I discussed a relationship with you. I told you from the get-go what I wanted, and it wasn't a girlfriend, a wife, or an old lady. Those exact words came out of my mouth so don't pretend like I led you on. I've been clear from day fucking one. You had no right to trespass on shit that has never and will never be any of your business."

He swore, "Never."

Abby threw her hands up in the air in exasperation. "Oh, really? Then, you're in as much denial about us as you are about your brother." She poked him with a finger. "You care about me. You've admitted as much to me before."

Yanking up his jeans, his quivering fingers wrenched at the zipper.

Abandoning the effort, he turned on her once again. "Come again? Newsflash, Abby, when a man doesn't tell you he fucking loves you, that means he doesn't. Let me spell it out for you to clear up any misunderstanding. I don't want you." His voice had risen until he blasted out the last of his rage and roared, "What I want is you out. Of. My. Life."

Ragged breaths panted out of her gaping mouth and her hand inched up and clutched her chest.

Loki jabbed his finger at the door and shouted, "Now!"

She strode up to him, planted her fists on her haunches and said, "The energy behind the way you smacked my ass today was different. Not that I didn't enjoy every part of it, but that's not the point. Your brother died today, Loki. You can't sweep the feelings under the carpet. I care about you enough to confront you about it, and *this* is how you repay me?"

It was a low blow, and true, which only gashed open the wound in his chest, where his heart should've been, if he still had one left. He absorbed her strike to make up for the harsh lies he'd spouted before, and let it stand without retaliating, but she wasn't done.

Eyeing him up and down, she assessed him, "You know what? Your bullshit is toxic and I'd done with it. You're willing to ruin your life for this grief. You're willing to hold on to the grief over everything else, even love. In the end, you're going to die an old, bitter man with only grief as cold company. I pity you, Loki. Truly."

He flinched as if she'd clapped him across the face.

Seeing his reaction, she wheeled back on her heels, but immediately rallied and stiffened her spine. Eyes flashing and chin tilted high, she spat out, "You don't deserve me."

"Tell me how you really feel," he drawled.

Jaw set, she waltzed toward the door and yanked it open. A sudden wave of panic seized him. "Where the fuck do you think you're going?"

Twisting around, she glared at him. "Go to hell, Loki. You've abdicated the right to know."

※※※

I'M DONE.

Finished.

Loki's damage was on a level even she couldn't reach, and yet her soft heart, her hopeless romantic optimism, and her sheer stupidity flouted the dangers of falling for a man who was unwilling to move on. Look where it got her? Hemor-rhaging pain. Grief was not something you could fix on a timetable, but nor did it mean she had to put up with being shut out.

It was the one thing she couldn't stand. She'd been sepa-rated from her mother by death. For years, grief had divided her father, brothers, and her. Her brothers' overzealous meddling in her life was their attempt at making amends for those terrible years. It would be a cold day in hell before she voluntarily re-enacted the same state of powerlessness and abandonment. Although he'd done it out of self-defense, Loki's actions were a form of desertion. He'd gone MIA on her, and she was not going to tolerate it.

Stomping through the gym, she stalked past Whistle, too fearful her voice would crack to risk answering his goodbye. She'd idiotically thought if she tried hard enough, Loki would trust her, would open up to her. Pausing outside the door, her chest trembled with emotion and she had to pound it a few times to reset it so she could keep going. Because she had to leave. He was stunted. He'd never give himself to her fully.

She wanted to rush back into the Box and run back to his arms, but no. *No.* She had to move on. There was no good future with a man who couldn't talk about his deepest pain. She'd survive. She'd survived her mother's death basically all on her own so she'd manage to survive this, too. Her hand drifted down to her belly. She'd direct her energy into building a good life, a life full of love and laughter and togetherness. It'd be without the love of her life, but it's not like Loki had given her any choice in the matter. She had to move on, dammit. *She had to.*

Striding between parked cars to get to her car, she squinted up at the broken streetlamp. Long shadows obscured the lot and her eyes hadn't adjusted from the bright lights of the gym's lobby.

Facing her car door, she clicked the fob on her key ring when she felt a wall of heat at her back.

An instant later, her small frame was engulfed by a heavy weight. The scent of unwashed male enclosed around her as arms wrapped around her collarbone.

Trapped.

Panicked, she twisted her torso, but the arms squeezed tighter, constricting her breathing. Abby shifted forward and she threw her elbow from side to side. It struck hard bone, perhaps a jaw, and a gnarled curse erupted near her ear.

The assailant's grip weakened.

She broke free.

In her rush, her feet got tangled around each other.

She tripped, the pavement flying up to greet her. Knuckles scraped the asphalt. Her cheek slammed against hard concrete. She hissed in pain.

Scrambling up, a heavy body slammed her chest into the car door, knocking the wind out of her. Fingers knotted in her hair, wrenching her head backward. A screech ripped out of her throat.

Flipping her around, her spine smacked the car, and his boot shot out and swiped at her knees.

She smashed to the ground.

He yanked her by her shirt, the sound of cotton ripping. *No, no, no rape.*

Abby fisted her keys in between her fingers and jabbed upward, at his face and chest. A rasped curse flew over her head. A boot swung up and caught her in the ribs. A burst of pain radiated out.

She doubled over. Another kick caught her in the chest. The boot shot up again and again.

In her belly. Her groin. Stabs of pain crippled her. Tears sprang from her eyes.

Wetness gushed from between her legs. Her hand darted beneath her skirt and came out drenched in a dark liquid.

Holding her hand, drops of liquid ran down her arm and she screeched, "Blood!"

"Fuck," came a harsh voice.

The beating stopped. The stale heat was gone. Suddenly, there was the sound of pounding feet on the blacktop. She keeled over herself as they receded.

Into silence.

Abby tried to call out for help, but a wooziness crashed over her. She gently fingered her temples as if to keep her bobble head balanced on her neck. The spinning sensation revolved in faster rotations until her head felt too heavy to hold.

Her vision joggled around, like she was looking through the lens of a shaky handheld camera.

Grasping the sides of her skull tightly, she staggered to her feet only to fall back down. Her hands slammed down on the ground to catch her fall, the sharp pain of loose asphalt scraping her skin. Nauseous, she struggled to her knees in time for her body's convulsions.

In the middle of an empty retch, she slumped over, and the world went black.

※※※

LOKI PUMPED his arms as he ran past Whistle, who had burst into his office, shouting words he could barely make sense of. *Abby. Unconscious. Parking lot.*

Slamming to his knees, he pressed his fingers to check her pulse. It was strong enough. She was lying on her side, knocked out. She'd have a mother of a bruise on her skull. Moving his lips, he prayed silently she wouldn't suffer a concussion. Her purse was gone. His hands raced across and down the length of her body, checking for anything that felt terribly wrong.

His fingers touched a viscous wetness on the hand lying beside her hip. His raised fingertips, gleaming beneath Whistle's cell phone light, were stained in blood. What in the fuck? Patting her bottom, he felt more. She was bleeding through her clothes.

"Motherfucker!" he thundered.

Fumbling with his cell, he held up his phone, but it was too dark for facial recognition. After several attempts, he swiped in his code while his other hand caressed strands of sticky hair off her forehead.

"Kingdom. Abby's been attacked in the parking lot of the Box." He barely comprehended Kingdom's reply until he heard 911.

"Ambulance? Yeah, okay. Kingdom, she's bleeding everywhere." He paused, took a massive breath, and resumed, "Between her legs. She's bleeding from between her legs."

Another volley of words came through the cell phone, most of them dissipating before they passed through his eardrums.

"Stay here? Of course, I'm staying. Swear to hell and back, if she dies, Kingdom, I'm going with her."

The cell clattered to the asphalt, abandoned. He laid down on the blacktop beside Abby's prone body.

Nuzzling her hair, he crooned into the curve of her ear, "My beautiful, pixie girl, you're gonna be okay. I'm here for you. Sorry, baby girl. Sorry, sorry, sorry. I'm a fuckin' bastard for fighting with you. I love you. Jesus, it's all my fucking fault. I'm never leaving you."

He swore the same word for a second time that night, "Never."

Sirens pealed in the distance, getting shriller by the second. Soon after, there were flashing red lights, slamming doors, and stomping feet. He was pushed off her, and he allowed it to happen for her sake. Abby's unconscious body was swarmed by medics, and he rolled himself out of the way. Hidden from his view by the medics, it was all he could do to keep from tearing them off her with his bare knuckles to stay near his pixie girl.

Numbness congealed around him, closing in on him like a shrinking box. Like a coffin.

25

LOKI

"I'm her *fiancé*, I'm telling you," Loki growled in the nurse's face.

Hands balled at his sides, he wanted to throw a punch in the male nurse's face. Kingdom had one hand clamped down hard on his shoulder and the other across his chest, holding him back from going ballistic.

Sage inserted herself between Loki and the nurse, and cajoled, "Sir, we understand the rules, but they're practically married and, as you can see yourself, he's beside himself. Is there anything you could tell us about her condition? Anything to relieve his mind."

Letting out a light snicker, although her eyes were stark, she attempted a joke, "There's no way you're going to get rid of him otherwise."

The nurse, who was young as fuck, was seemingly mesmerized by Sage's pleading, and finally said, "The wounds are superficial. The attacker was scared off before he got a chance to really hurt her. Sprained ribs is the worst of it. But...I'm sorry to have to tell you that...the fetus didn't survive. She might have been kicked or kneed in the belly. The trauma, a pulled muscle, who knows exactly. But, yes, she miscarried."

Loki stumbled back, clenching his pounding heart. Rage drowned his ear drums as loud as a fire alarm.

He inhaled.

Baby.

He exhaled.

Miscarried.

Dead.

His infamous rage shoved her away, then his infamous restraint almost got her killed. He hadn't trusted his instincts and gone after her when she'd rushed out the office. He should've followed Cutter's lead, a brother who lived almost exclusively on his gut instincts alone.

Instead, he hung back to give her time to calm down.

The blood drained from his face. His careful restraint killed their baby. He was reminded of something Abby once said when she recounted her mother's death, "In the blink of an eye, one's life can change." Her lesson: don't take shit for granted. *Too fuckin' late.*

Christ, the idea of Abby and him having melded together and brought another being into life cut him at his knees. Not only did she give him everything good in his life... Not only had she done that... She'd done more. More than he'd dared to imagine. After Chopper died, he whittled his life down to a smaller and smaller compact space. To control his grief-induced rages, but also because he simply believed it should be so.

Abby pounded away at the walls of that small space, banging them out to encompass a fuller life.

A baby had blasted them to smithereens.

The instant he comprehended she was pregnant, his life resembled the universe, where the scale of space itself expanded at a mind-blowing speed. But it was quickly followed by the images of her hurt, *his* Abby bleeding and unconscious on the asphalt, and the learning they'd lost their baby, that it has been *beaten* out of her—everything came crashing in on itself into a terrifying crescendo of destruction.

Guilt and shame tore at his gut like a wake of vultures, gnashing and ripping at his innards. Only one single unifying thought penetrated the chaotic tornado invading his mind. Do whatever you have to do to make it right. He'd been the reason they lost their baby. He'd almost lost her, but at least, she was alive. He'd drop to his knees and beg for her forgiveness. He'd accept any ultimatum. He'd do whatever necessary to keep her safe and make it up to her. He'd open up his heart. He'd bestow on her what he'd refused her before. He'd give her everything he had in his power to give her. He'd do what he was meant to do all along; he'd love her.

✳✳✳

LOKI WOKE up with a start in the cramped hospital chair of the waiting room. Sammi gave him a comforting squeeze. He had a dream of waking up in bed, with Abby in his arms. Her arms were wrapped around a newborn son, a shock of blond hair identical to Abby's waving at him like a flag.

"My life is fucking hell," he muttered as he jumped up and paced the length of the waiting room like a caged animal. As he passed Sammi, she grabbed his hand and tugged him down. Staring down at her with a frown, he sighed heavily and allowed her to draw him into the seat beside her.

His mask of impenetrability was crumbling. His stoicism

was in shambles. This was beyond anything he'd felt before, and he thought he'd already walked the path from hell and back.

"She's going to be okay," Sammi insisted. "She looks soft, but she's tough as nails."

"The baby." Loki sucked in a ragged breath. "She wanted one badly." He turned stark eyes on Sammi. "Did she know? If she did, then I bet she was gonna tell me our last time together, but I fucked it up. Didn't give her a chance. I never considered having a child before, but knowing my seed planted something in her and I destroyed it by my own stupidity...it's killing me."

Sammi shook his shoulders, staring at him with uncharacteristic anger flashing in her eyes. "Quit the drama, Loki. You did not kill your unborn child. It bears repeating. You. Did. Not. Kill. Anyone. It was a terrible and unfortunate attack, but it wasn't your fault. It could have happened to any woman. You know these things happen all the time. She was in the wrong place at the wrong time, that's it."

Loki pivoted in her direction and held her eyes. "Not you. It wouldn't have happened to you. Wanna know why? Because Puck would never stop watching out for you, never sit down on the job. He would *never* let anything happen to you, but I didn't do the same for Abby."

"First off, you can't compare yourself to Puck. Puck was my guardian, he raised me like I was his child. The situation between you and Abby was completely different. You told me you guys argued. Adults can argue, they can stalk off to cool down, and then come back together later."

"Puck would've never had you walk to your car at night, alone. Especially after an argument, no matter how heated, 'cause you know how loud you guys can get. Hell, you guys argue on the regular. If anything, he'd have stuck closer to you." He swallowed and confessed hoarsely, "And I told her to fuck off. I told her to get out of my life. Puck would never say that to you, no matter how much you pissed him off."

"Don't do this to yourself, Loki. It's Chopper's anniversary and you're always extra on the week of his death. As for Abby, shit happens to the best people. Sometimes for no apparent reason. Life can be wicked brutal. You know this as well as I do and this was an unfortunate, but random attack."

It seemed like a random attack, but whether it had been or not, he should've watched out for Abby, made sure she got home safe. He knew how dangerous parking lots were late at night. He'd fucking taught a class about it, for fuck's sake. Loki shook off her hands and curled into himself. "Babe, there's no excuse for what happened."

"Hush. You've blamed yourself once before and look where that got you. The moral of the story is *not* to fault yourself for shit that's out of your control. Yeah, okay, the best thing would've been to accompany her to her car, but it didn't happen. Millions of women walk to their cars at night. That's what they do, and they don't get attacked or beaten. It wasn't even very late. She was at the wrong place at the wrong time. Don't make more of it than it is. If there's someone out there who's attacking women, then I know you will find the threat and eliminate it."

Loki faced forward, his fingers gripping his knees tightly. "Oh, that's coming. Whoever did this is going to pay." His jaw clenched tight. "I'm bringing the knives back out to play."

26

LOKI

"Hello."

Loki's and Sammi's heads shot up in unison and frowned at a middle-aged man in a rumpled tweed jacket draped over a wrinkled button-down shirt.

Extending his hand out to Loki, he said, "The nurse told me Abby's fiancé is in the waiting room. I'm her father."

Fuuuck.

Standing up, Loki took his firm handshake and replied, "I can explain, sir."

Abby's father held his grip for an extra beat before releasing it. With a nod, he said, "Is there a cafeteria somewhere in this hospital? I'll buy you a coffee and you can update me on what's really going on."

"Yes, sir, although I'd suggest we go to the coffee shop around the corner. The coffee here is shit."

The man's lips curved upward slightly, reminding him of Abby. Now he knew where she got her smile from. "Sounds great. Lead the way."

Turning to Sammi, Loki asked, "Need anything, sweetheart?"

"Nah, I'm good. Just go with him, Loki. I'll stay here until you get back."

"Call me if anything changes," he warned her.

Sammi smiled softly at him. "Of course. Go on, now."

Giving her a squeeze on the shoulder, he gestured to Abby's father to follow him and they walked toward the elevator. "I go by Loki. And you're Mr. Sullivan, I assume."

The elevator doors opened, and they stepped inside.

"That's right, but please call me Tom. I don't stand on ceremony, and I'm guessing you don't either."

"Not since being discharged from the military, sir," he replied.

"I see some habits are hard to break with the way you call me sir."

Loki cracked a smile. The man was easy to like, but he was still a father talking to a biker who was more than a decade older than his daughter, and one who claimed to be her fiancé.

The elevator reached the lobby and Loki held the door open for Tom to step out first. They walked to the coffee shop.

Loki gestured to an empty table and said, "I'm getting this. What are you having?"

"Mint tea," replied Tom. "I don't drink caffeine in the afternoon or else I won't catch a wink at night."

After ordering with the barista, Loki paid and joined Tom at a table near the window.

The first question out of Tom's mouth was, "How is Abby really doing? She's acting brave and downplaying the incident, but she's in the hospital, so I can only assume she was badly hurt. She won't let me talk to the doctor alone but told me that her worst physical injuries are bruised ribs. Emotionally, I can only imagine how she's coping."

Loki scrubbed his hand over his face. Tom had his priorities right. His initial concern was over her well-being rather than going after more information over the shocking news that she had a fiancé.

"I'm not gonna lie," began Loki. "In my opinion, the attack was bad. It's up to Abby how much she wants to divulge to you, but it sure as hell dropped me flat on my ass, excuse the expression. Thank God for small mercies because she wasn't sexually assaulted." His voice cracked and he had to pause before continuing. "Still, any injury she's sustained is one too many in my book. You know your daughter, she's strong, but I'll make sure to help her get past this."

Loki regarded Tom, appraising his face. The clinking of ceramic cups and the low drone of conversation hovered in the background.

After a beat, he took a breath and explained, "I'm sure you've already guessed I'm not her fiancé. We *are* together, have no doubt on that score. She was unconscious when I found her. After she was taken away in the ambulance, I followed on my bike to the hospital, and told the ER attendant I was her fiancé to find out what was going on. Abby wasn't in a position to negate my claim, and when she was stabilized, she didn't correct the staff. We haven't spoken about it yet."

"Hmm," Tom said, in a contemplative tone.

The barista placed their drinks on the table and Loki murmured his thanks.

"Abby's my daughter and, in addition to my own concerns, I'll have to satisfy my sons. Let's just say, they aren't as respectful of Abby's privacy as I am. What exactly is the relationship between you and Abby?"

"It's complicated." Loki expelled a harsh laugh. "Not reassuring, I know, but don't doubt the fact that your daughter is mine."

"*Yours?*"

Fisting his hands on his lap, he clarified, "What I mean to say is that Abby is mine to take care of, and I will be taking care of *everything* that has to do with her. We're together."

Whatever happened last night between the two of them no longer mattered. The attack had shaken some sense into him and he had no intention of denying or turning his back on her ever again. He'd made that mistake once. Wasn't happening twice.

"We haven't been together long, but I'm one hundred percent committed to her. Fiancé is not far off the mark, in my mind."

Loki shifted uncomfortably in his seat. He wasn't one to confess, but nothing less than a confession was due to this man. He'd just walked away from seeing his only daughter in a hospital bed, and it was Loki's fault she was there. He owed Tom the entire truth.

Taking in a breath, he braced himself and said, "We had an argument just before her attack. She left the gym I manage and walked to her car alone. That's on me because I should've been there, making sure she got to her car safely. The attack would've never taken place if it hadn't been for me. I take full responsibility and will do everything in my power to make this right, I swear to you. Your daughter will never suffer again. Not while I have breath in my body."

Tom reeled back a little.

Yeah, he knew he came off as an intense motherfucker, but there was no way her father was leaving the table without knowing where Loki stood with respect to his daughter.

Loki waited, muscles tight, for Tom's judgment.

"It was a deeply unfortunate situation," Tom said, "but it doesn't seem like it was your fault."

Loki glared out the window at the passersby, jaw clenched.

"Like hell, it wasn't," he retorted, in a clipped tone. Batting his hand to end that line of discussion, Loki confessed, "The only problem is whether Abby will forgive me."

"Abby is not one to hold grudges. I can't imagine she would blame you for not walking her to her car after an argument. She may not have wanted you to accompany her. You know, she has a bit of a stubborn streak of her own," Tom suggested.

"Perhaps, but that's not the only issue between us. There was the argument itself. I spouted off some hurtful bullshit I deeply regret having said," Loki admitted.

"Listen, Abby didn't grow up in a quiet family. Her mother and I were young when we got married and," he chuckled fondly, "we had some loud shouting matches. I'd say a few a year. Yet, she knew how much we loved each other."

Loki wasn't going to go into any further details with her father. Shoving an unreadable expression on his face, he repeated, "Like I said, it's complicated."

"Did you cheat on her?"

Loki's eyes sliced to Tom's face. "Hell fucking no."

"I didn't think so. You seem like an honorable man, Loki, but I'm going through a list of the typical problems that crop up for a couple."

"It's definitely not typical," he grumbled. Because he wasn't typical. He was a fucking mess, is what he was, and he was an idiot for not realizing earlier what a lucky bastard he was for a gorgeous, sweet girl like Abby to even look his way, much less want to have a relationship with him.

"But you won't tell me," her father concluded.

Nope, he sure as fuck wasn't going to say a damn thing, but neither could he allow Tom to conjure up and mull over fucked-up scenarios. The man suffered enough. He deserved any amount of relief Loki could offer, but what was he going to say? *I was afraid to get close to her because of guilt I've harbored for years.* A choking sound came from the back of his throat and his hand covered his mouth and jaw to suppress it. Was he going to say *I was unable to protect my brother from self-harm*? No, he couldn't do it.

Loki cleared his clogged throat and rasped out, "Let's just say, we didn't have a smooth road up till now and it was my fault."

"You're going to make it up to her, I presume." Tom said.

Loki breathed out a huff of disbelief. "With every fiber of my being. I'll be there for her, show her how much I care for her, in any way I can. Work my ass off to deserve her. She's alive, thank fuck. I've been given a hell of a chance and I'm not gonna screw it up."

He'd spoken nothing but the truth. He was going to fight for her, tooth and fucking nail. For no justifiable reason, the universe had dropped her in his lap, like a gift from the gods. Unwarranted. Unjustified. Undeserved.

He'd almost tossed her away, but her survival gave him a second lease on life. He didn't get the chance to have a redo with his mom or Chopper, but he did with Abby. She was his for good and he was never letting her go. He'd do whatever he needed to do to earn her trust and regain her love. If he got it right, he might redeem himself from the wreckage of his past. The only thing keeping him from going insane was knowing he had the chance to turn it around and regain the gift he'd squandered.

"I'm not attempting to dissuade you but you're not going to have an easy time of it. Both of her brothers, they're twins, were overbearing during her final years of adolescence. She nicknamed them 'the terrible twins.' A year after their mother died, they went off to college, but as she got older, they'd routinely show up and attempt to make up for their absence by meddling in our lives."

He chuckled. "They saw themselves as adults, and they'd swoop in and strong-arm Abby into doing whatever they thought was best. Grief-stricken myself, I was quite unable to protect her. They were a deadly duo and regardless of how hard she fought them, she'd ultimately succumb to their demands. I believe her stubborn streak developed then, and it rears its ugly head, from time to time."

"Thanks for the warning, but I'm not too worried," Loki replied.

No one was a bigger stubborn son of a bitch than himself. He could handle a sweet little girl like Abby, and when it came to her safety, he had every intention of putting her under lock and key.

"Good luck," Tom offered.

"I don't need luck."

He'd use brute force if needed, but he had a full set of tricks up his sleeve. Like his tongue in her pussy. If push came to shove, he'd use whatever methods were at his disposal. He had no qualms whatsoever of playing dirty.

As he'd bluntly declared to her father, Abby was his to keep.

27

ABBY

The door popped open and Sammi peeked in, a soft smile on her face, and said, "Hey you."

A grin couldn't help but crack over Abby's face, causing her to flinch in pain from the abrasions on her cheek. It reminded her of Loki's scar slashing half his face. If road burn hurt, she could only imagine what his father's cut had felt like.

She waved Sammi in and said, "Hey you, back."

Holding up a brown paper bag with grease spots blooming on the bottom, Sammi offered, "I have a treat for you. Figured you deserved it after staying here overnight. How was breakfast?"

"Abysmal. Tasteless. Bland." She picked up a plastic container of fruit salad. "They tried telling me this is fruit, but I refused to believe them."

Plopping down on the edge of the bed, Sammi dropped the bag on Abby's lap and poked at it. "Take a look."

Abby tore the bag open and found two perfect chocolate croissants nestled at the bottom.

"Oh my God, you are the best friend a girl could ever have. Is it from—"

"La Boulangerie? Yep. They're both for you. I already had my fill."

Abby's lips turned down and she sniffed, "You're like my best friend ever." Tears embarrassingly popped out of the corners of her eyes, but she couldn't help herself. Her body was bruised, her heart was hurting, and she'd had loss on top of loss.

"I know I am," crooned Sammi. "Come on, eat them up while they're still warm."

Sammi dug inside and pulled out a croissant, tore off a piece of the brown paper bag, wrapped it, and handed it to Abby.

Moaning around the first bite, Abby closed her eyes and sighed. "Yummy deliciousness."

Demolishing the first delicacy, she reached into the bag for the second one. Her gaze flicked to the door.

Feeling better after the croissant, she dared ask the question weighing heavily on her. "Is he...is he still outside?"

"Nope," Sammi replied, "He went to get a coffee with your father."

Abby chocked on a piece of pastry, and Sammi gently tapped her back until Abby finished chewing and swallowed properly.

"That was not what I expected." She mock shuddered. "God only knows what they're talking about."

"I imagine they're talking about *you*. What are you worried about?" Sammi prompted gently.

Abby's jaw dropped open, practically swinging from its hinges. "I'm worried about my father talking to a guy that I sorta kinda dated for a bit, who proceeded to break up with me, and that I lost a baby to. I've never introduced my dad to anyone before. I don't want him to get the wrong idea. With his overblown romantic tendencies, he's going to come to the worst conclusion possible." She groaned heavily. "Then, he'll call up my brothers and spill my personal business to a pair of domineering men who are nosier than a couple of old women glued to a Brooklyn stoop during a heat wave in August."

Sammi reached out and clasped Abby's hand. "Is that really what you're worried about? Or are you upset about something else? Is there something you want to tell me, Abby?" she asked in a muted voice.

Abby's bottom lip trembled but she bit down on it, swatting away a few tears tumbling down her cheeks. "I was pregnant with Loki's baby and I lost it," she rushed out. "There, I said it."

Sammi wrapped her arms around Abby. "I'm so sorry, sweetie. Loki got it out of the nurse, but we weren't sure if you even knew."

Abby's flow of tears were unstoppable now.

"I knew," she mumbled into Sammi's shoulder. "I-I shouldn't have gotten pregnant. I mean, I was on birth control and I didn't miss any days. My doctor wasn't joking when she said it wasn't one hundred percent effective against pregnancy. I mean, what were the chances, huh?"

She pulled away and dropped her gaze to her hands fidgeting in her lap. "I'd missed my period, but it took a while for me to really believe I was late. I kept thinking, it'll come tomorrow. Tomorrow would come and nothing. After a week, I panicked and rushed to the drugstore for a test. Needless to say, I was pregnant." Abby looked up. "I'm sorry I didn't tell you,"

"You don't owe me an apology, Abby," Sammi cried out. "You were processing. You get to do that, you know."

"Yeah, I was. My emotions veered from ecstatic to terrified.

I always wanted children and I loved Loki, but I was afraid he'd think I did it on purpose. What if he rejected me or the baby?" She shook her head. "And then, we got into an argument about Chopper and he broke up with me anyway and now I've lost the baby," she hiccupped, and her face crumbled again.

Her chin trembled. Dropping her face into her hands, she burst into tears. "I wanted that baby," she wailed. Sammi wrapped around her, rocking her from side to side.

"Oh God, Abby," said Sammi. "I'm grateful he'll be able to comfort you in a way no one else can. He feels the loss so strongly, Abby, you can't imagine. But at least you'll have each other for support."

Abby reared back, her eyes with fear. She shrank back, shaking her head in denial. "No, no, I don't think so."

Sammi stared at her, fingers touching her parted lips. "You can't be serious?"

"Oh, I'm serious. He broke up with me just before the attack."

"He regrets whatever nonsense he spouted off. He regrets the argument. You know how hot-blooded he is beneath that mask of detachment," Sammi argued.

"Please, it wasn't nonsense. It was real. Yes, I pushed him about his brother, but when he lashed out at me... That hurt, but more importantly it proved he's incapable of authentically sharing his life with me." Her chin drooped onto her chest. "How did he react to the miscarriage? You said he feels it? I didn't think he'd want a child."

"I don't know if he intentionally wanted one, but he's crushed nonetheless," she insisted.

Abby lifted her head, arching a dubious brow. "I don't know..."

"Loki is the most soulful brother there is. He's got his

assholery image down pat, but he would never ever turn away from a child. And he blames himself for your attack," Sammi revealed.

A streak of shame flushed Abby's cheeks at Sammi's censure. Shaking her head, she replied, "Yes, of course, you're right. It must've re-traumatized him. Just more proof we can't be together. He'll stay with me out of guilt. After all, guilt and remorse drives most of his behavior."

"Guilt may ride him hard, but he's honest as fuck. He's not going to stay with you if he doesn't want to," Sammi reproved. "And he's deep in with you." Jabbing her thumb towards the hallway, she said, "I went home to catch some z's, but he's been out there all night."

"It doesn't matter," she said, her face settling in a stubborn expression. "He pushed me away, and losing the baby is only another sign it wasn't meant to be."

"Keep signs out this," Sammi snapped. "The argument and the attack were two separate incidents. Don't mix them up in your head. It will only cause unnecessary confusion." Her tone gentled. "I see what you're doing, Abby. You're choosing fear over strength and love. You're choosing to abandon what you have with Loki."

"He abandoned it first," Abby fired back.

"But he came back and now you're abandoning it," she replied softly.

With a flutter of her hands, Abby argued, "There are more important things happening."

"What could be more important than to comfort each other during this time?"

"No disrespect, Sammi, but I don't have the energy to argue right now." Abby's pressed her lips together to stifle the avalanche of sobs threatening to escape. She had been all in with Loki. Not only had he thrown her away, but she lost her baby. She wasn't going to get over either of those things any time soon. The bottom line was that she couldn't trust him. Sammi saw it as her giving up on love. It wasn't that...it was that Loki had hurt her. Then the baby...and now it was too much.

Scooting up to her knees, Sammi's arms soothingly wrapped around her shoulders. Swaying her from side to side, she murmured, "You don't have to make a decision about anything right now. Let's focus on getting you better and breaking you out of this white-walled dungeon."

Abby grasped her and let the tears flow over Sammi's shoulder.

"Let it out, sweetie, just let it all out."

28

ABBY

Abby heard the soft knock on the hospital room door. Lying on her side facing away from the door, she turned too swiftly and winced from the pain in her ribs.

"Come in," she called out through a wheeze as she clutched her side.

Loki was by her side in a flash, leaning over her, helping bring her to her back, and propping her up on the layers of pillows beneath her. Her eyes blinked up at the florescent light of the ceiling. Then they flicked over to his face, hovering beside her with worry lines etched on his forehead. Dark circles ringed his eyes, which had turned a shade of deep indigo. His hair was tousled, as if he'd raked through it over a hundred times. Sammi had told her that he'd slept outside last night, watching over her like an avenging guardian.

He caressed the hair off her cheek and greeted her, "Hey, babe."

She almost cried out from the pain of seeing him, showing such gentleness and care. Her eyes darted away. It was almost too much to look at him.

Swallowing around the lump in her throat, she replied, "Hey."

He took a seat on the edge of her bed and engulfed her hand in his much larger one. His distinctive spicy musk floated over her and swear to God, despite her cracking heart, she almost swooned with relief at the familiar scent. It was the scent of safety and danger, a heady mix that was Loki's alone.

"Why didn't you tell me?"

Loki's eyes didn't hold an ounce of accusation. Only deep sadness. His forlorn expression splintered her heart. She gulped, but it did nothing to alleviate the pressure practically choking her. How did she respond to him? Guilt plagued her for not telling him until it was too late. Fear that he would stay with her because of a sense of obligation.

Pulling her hand out of his, she twisted them together. "I was going to, but I could barely believe it myself. The chances of getting pregnant while on contraception are so small, they're practically nonexistent. You knew about my dreams of starting a family and I was afraid you'd accuse me of doing it on purpose, which was absolutely not the case."

Dropping her eyes, she focused on her fingers twining around the border of the bed sheet and continued nervously, "I was still processing. We've never had a conversation about a future, between the two of us, I mean. Heck, you explicitly stated your negative position on committed relationships."

"I regret that deeply, Abby," he intoned.

He reached for her, but she scooted back, and winced at the pain in her ribs. His hand dropped to his side. She was aching, aching for his touch, but she was going to be strong, if it killed her because if he stayed with her out of sense of obligation, that might truly kill her.

"I haven't touched another woman since being with you," he confessed.

"I know," she said in a small voice.

"I took you for granted and said some awful things, many of them coming from a place of pain, but I'm not excusing my behavior. But that's in the past and it's time I made my position crystal fucking clear. We're a couple. I lost my temper, lashed out at you, and I won't let that shit happen again."

Her head snapped up. Their gazes collided. Eyes narrowing into slits, she cautioned, "We were never officially together. As a biker, you could've made our relationship public with little effort, if you were so inclined. Tank declared to the club Kerri was his old lady and slapped a jacket on her back with "Property of Tank" on it. You wouldn't even bring me to the clubhouse."

"I didn't want the gossip and attention but I also didn't think you were ready," he said.

"*Hmph.* You or me?" Abandoning the bed sheet, Abby slashed her hand across the air. "Regardless of whether we were together or not, our argument effectively put an end to whatever was between us. I intended to tell you, but then it all fell apart. I was so angry with you that I *had* to leave. Once I had a chance to recoup from the fight, I would've spoken to you about my pregnancy."

"I believe you," Loki replied instantly, caressing her cheek with the back of his knuckles.

She bit down on her bottom lip. Damn, that felt good. Why, oh why was she so weak when it came to him?

"I also know that I'm gonna put another baby in your belly, Abby. I swear by it," he promised.

Abby gasped, and pushed his hand off her. *Okay, that's it. What the hell is he thinking?*

Loki said, "We will start a family, and it's gonna be a huge one."

"You can't just impregnate me again and think it's going to

fix anything. It won't," she snapped between harsh breaths. She felt like the air was being squeezed out of her lungs. "

"It's my fault. I allowed our baby to be killed," he murmured low, a voice dripping in remorse and agony.

Her anger crumbled, evaporated. Her lungs burned, but she forced herself to inhale deeply, hold it for a long moment and then expel it slowly. She couldn't stop herself from grabbing his fingers, crushing them in her grip.

"Oh, God. It wasn't you. I was the careless one," she said with a slight hiccup as she suppressed a whimper. "I didn't give you the chance to protect me, so don't you dare blame yourself for this loss like you blame yourself for Chopper."

"You know better than to blame the victim, which is what you're doing here. You fought back, baby, like a fucking champ. You can't imagine how proud of you I am. But, what happened with Chopper and you was exactly the same. Don't try spinning it any other way for my sake. I abandoned you like I did Chopper and look what happened." He twined his fingers with hers and held on to them tightly. "The miscarriage is on me. Your beating is on me. I fuck things up. That's what I do best."

"No, you don't," she replied, shaking her head vehemently.

Holding on to her hand, Loki took a seat on her bed and stroked her hair, playing with a dangling, loose strand of hair and said in a gentle, firm tone, "It was my duty to protect you, regardless of whether you were pregnant or not. I should've never let you go to your car in the dark, alone. I'd crawl over hot coals on my hands and knees to take back what happened to you. What I did was unforgivable. Unpardonable. Inexcusable."

The wretched pain twisting his beautiful features tore her heart to shreds. "We're human and we make mistakes. It was just as much my fault for leaving instead of asking you or

Whistle to walk me to my car. Regardless of how angry I was with you at that moment."

Tugging her hand out of his, she quelled the intense urge to take him into her arms and comfort him. Nothing good would come out of reconciling with him. She understood his reasons, but it didn't lessen the pain of his rejection, even if he currently regretted his words and actions. She hadn't been able to break through his shields, and he wasn't able to give himself completely.

After losing the baby, she needed all of him. Nothing less would do.

"The loss of our baby doesn't change anything between us, Loki. We broke up, and we're not going to get back together simply because I was assaulted a-and m-miscarried."

She drew in a deep breath, but then forged on. "I don't want you to stay with me out of some misguided sense of guilt and remorse. In fact, I think it's best if we don't see each other again."

Fingers clutching her bedsheet, he breathed out in a stricken voice, "You can't break up with me, Abby. I was wrong to lash out at you. I was shocked by the fact that I'd forgotten the anniversary of Chopper's death. I pushed you away when you were only trying to help me and when you called me on my bullshit, I snapped. But, baby, you're my fucking *life*. You can't mean what you just said."

"I mean every word," she choked out, clasping her hands together to prevent herself from reaching for him. "It's for the best. I want you to leave, Loki. Leave. And make certain you never come back."

✳✳✳

LOKI'S HEART was spurting blood as if a bullet had ricocheted against the cavern of his ribcage. He wanted to touch her, to caress her, to fuck her. He *needed* to fuck her, ravage her, pump her full of his come until his seed was lodged deep inside her womb and created another fetus to replace the one he made her lose.

At that moment, he wanted it more desperately than anything he'd ever wanted in his life. More than the return of Chopper.

Operation Abby was forming in his mind.

Nothing else mattered, and he planned to do whatever it took to get her back. And to keep her safe.

Tears rimmed the bottom edges of her eyes, and her body shook slightly as she white-knuckled the white bedsheet. Her skin was pale, her eyes strained, and her brows had been permanently knitted together since he entered the room. She looked even tinier than she was, drowning in a large powder-blue hospital gown.

But he feared he'd do more damage than good if he kept pressuring her. Stepping away was the right thing to do. For now. Unfortunately for her, he wouldn't leave without making one thing clear first.

"I want you living your best life, but make no mistake Abby, your best life is with me."

A strangled laugh was caught in her throat briefly before escaping. "You are so damn arrogant, you know that?"

He swiped his hand over his brow. Alright, that hadn't come out the way he'd intended, but the fact remained that they were meant for each other. Regardless of their argument, the attack, or her miscarriage. Those events only convinced him of how important she was in his life, of how close he'd been to throwing away the best thing in his life.

A nurse poked her head through the door. "There are only a few minutes left for visiting hours."

The soft click of the door sounded behind him. It was time to leave, but he couldn't walk away without a guarantee he'd see her again, and soon.

Heart in his throat, he said, "I'll leave you alone on one condition."

Abby puffed out a breath of surprised exasperation. "You have no power to negotiate with me here."

He leaned over her, caging her between his arms, and whispered, "Yes, there is. I see you home every night. I know you, the minute you leave here, you'll be back at work, even with your ribs hurting you. Until we find the bastard who did this to you, you've got yourself a tail. I'm gonna follow you wherever you go."

"What?" she cried out. Abby smacked at his chest in outrage, shaking her head vigorously. "No way, not happening."

"Regardless of how much you bitch, Kingdom will post a prospect or two on you. Even so, I don't trust them to do a better job than me, 'specially at night. Wherever you are, work, class, a bar—*I don't give a fuck*—I'll be the only one taking you home."

"Th-that's ridiculous!" she sputtered.

"Ridiculous or not, that's how it's going to be. I can barely live with myself as it is, but if anything happens to you…"

He shook his head at the memory of Abby crumpled on the ground in parking lot. "I found you lying on the pavement, unconscious and bleeding from between your thighs. I thought you'd been *raped*. I won't be able to go on. I'll go fucking crazy if you don't allow me to tend to you, to protect you. Do you understand what I'm sayin'?"

His mouth was a flat, grim line. Between Loki's arms braced on the bed near her head, she glared up at him and hissed, "This is emotional blackmail. You do realize that?"

"I don't give a fuck," he replied without skipping a beat. "We're talking about your safety and my sanity. If one goes, the other one goes. Been there, done that."

It was a flat-out lie. His sanity was long gone, but he wasn't above using any means at his disposal, and emotional blackmail was one of many in his arsenal. If she didn't agree, he intended to come back later and seduce her in this very hospital bed.

"Do you want to be the reason for me ending up in an inpatient clinic?" he threatened. "Because I promise you, that's where I'm headed if there's an inkling you being in danger."

"Blackmail," she spat out like an enraged kitten dunked in a bathtub.

"Like I said, I don't give a fuck what you call it. I need you to swear, Abby. Either you're on board with this or I get someone to cover me at the Box and I tail you twenty-four seven."

She threw her arms up in the air, "For the love of all that's holy, this is ludicrous."

"Promise me," he persisted.

She wiggled within his locked arms. He didn't miss the wince on her face from the pain the brisk movement caused her.

She folded her arms over her tits and glowered at him.

"Fine," she huffed. "I promise to let you follow me around like an idiot and take me home after dark. Satisfied?"

His nose grazed her cheek. She sucked in a sharp breath, and he was satisfied by the quickening pulse at the base of her throat. Touching her silken skin was a ecstasy and torture at the same time.

"I won't be satisfied until I have you under me again, screaming while coming on my cock." Her chest shuddered out her next breath. "Until then…" he forcibly ripped himself away before he whipped off the sheet and tongue-fucked her between the legs, "It'll do."

With that final parting shot, he stalked out of her hospital room.

29

LOKI

Forgoing the elevator, Loki stomped down three flights of stairs to the lobby and dropped into a round chair near the large floor-to-ceiling window by the entrance.

He'd had to get out of Abby's room and off her floor before he throttled her for her stubbornness or touched her because it was impossible to keep his hands off her. She'd let him take her hand but, beyond that, he didn't know how she felt about being touched, so it was best if he put some space between them. But he couldn't get himself to quit the building.

Elbows on knees, his hands clutched the sides of his skull as a pair of motorcycle boots stopped in his line of sight. Lifting his head, he found Kingdom standing before him, holding two cups of coffee. Holding one out to Loki, Kingdom took the seat beside him and stretched out his legs.

"Thanks," Loki grunted out and took a sip. "Espresso from the place on the corner. Nice."

Kingdom placed his coffee cup on the floor, propped his elbows on the arms of the upholstered armchair and steepled his fingers. "Only the best for you, asshole."

"Appreciate it," he replied, reflexively.

Debilitating guilt and self-recriminations cinched his throat. His emotions had blazed particularly high when he'd spotted the bruises around her arms. Her involuntary flinches of pain were straight-up excruciating to witness.

The man who did this was going to die a slow, agonizing death filled with pain and suffering. Loki already planned to take out and sharpen his most dangerous knives. Although he intuitively knew that nothing, *nothing* could save the mother-fucker who had dared hurt his woman, he felt as helpless as a captive panther, pacing the short length of a cage.

On top of the frustration and pain of knowing her attacker was still out there, alive and breathing, his harsh remarks during their last argument rattled incessantly in his brain. hte memory of those thoughtless words crushed his soul.

"Brother."

He glanced up at Kingdom, realizing his attention had wandered off and he'd forgotten that Kingdom was still there.

"You gotta stop driving yourself crazy over this," his president counseled. "We will find him."

"Have you found anything?"

Kingdom's eyes turned brittle. "Might be The Horsemen."

"What the fuck?" he thundered, crushing the ends of the sofa seat in his fists. "I thought Cutter was going there this weekend."

"One weekend too late. Last night, I had a gut feeling that wouldn't let me sleep. I reached out to The Dragoons MC in Newburg. There hadn't been sightings of Shadow or another Horseman, but following a hunch, I reached out to a few other people in the area. Turns out the Horsemen are doing business in New York. Not close by, but not too far either. New York's a big-ass state, so there's a lot of places they could go to drum up business. Shadow's been sighted and that's enough for me to suspect that he may be involved. I've got Cutter out right now, investigating more closely, but I think Shadow's exacting revenge."

"But why Abby? She's an innocent. It's not like she's an old lady."

"Not technically, but she's connected to you, and you're the one I sent down to Camden to negotiate the settlement with the Horsemen. It made him look bad. He's tolerated in his club, but not loved. Who knows what triggered him? For a fucker like him, it's enough his pride got bruised up. At the time, you were unattached and had no liabilities to exploit, but that's changed. Makes sense he would target you."

"Christ," Loki roared, as he shot to his feet.

Kingdom placed a hand on his balled fist and dragged him back to his seat.

"The assault is on me as much as it's on you, yeah? Shadow thinks he's a sly motherfucker, but he doesn't know what's coming to him. He saw an opportunity to take revenge and thought we wouldn't get wind of his involvement? Not fucking likely. Without further proof we can't rule out a random criminal, but my instincts tell me it's him."

Baring his teeth, Loki pounded his chest once. "The motherfucker is *mine*. Swear to me, Kingdom, he's mine to do with what I want."

Hands back in their steeple position, Kingdom turned his head and held Loki's stare for a long moment. Kingdom would want to get his hands dirty on this one, but this was Loki's kill. It had to be.

"Yeah, okay," he replied slowly, "but you gotta do something for me in return."

Loki grimaced. "What?"

"Give Abby time."

If Kingdom was insane enough to think Loki would allow

Abby to walk away from him, he had another thing coming. "What the fuck?"

"I overhead you with her, upstairs. You came down on her pretty hard." He held up his hand as Loki poised himself to launch out of his seat. "I've got more experience dealing with a woman who's miscarried than you do, so I suggest you listen up before you open your big, fucking trap."

"Stay in your fucking lane, Kingdom," he ground out between clamped teeth.

"Calm the fuck down and listen to me."

Loki blew out a long breath through his quivering nostrils, attempting to latch on to a shred of sanity before his head exploded. Any intrusion on his relationship with Abby was a dangerous proposition. Only a cocky bastard like Kingdom would attempt it.

"Her hormones are in free fall from the pregnancy and miscarriage. That's on top of the mental trauma of the attack and losing the baby. Even if her doctor gives her a rundown of possible symptoms, she won't always be aware of how her fluctuating hormones are fucking with her mind and her mood. Believe me, brother, I'm talkin' from experience. When Sage miscarried, I wanted to punch my fist through a wall more than once. Mind you, she wasn't suffering from the same physical or mental pain Abby is. I get it, you don't have it in you to stay away from her, but don't touch her. My advice to you is to let her initiate it."

"I can barely keep myself in check, as it is," groaned Loki, his hands tearing at the ends of his hair.

"You've got no choice if you want this to work. If anyone can do it, you can. She needs space to heal. I'm not saying you can't see her, but if you fuck her, it's gonna mess with her recovery, and put you both two steps back."

"Her ribs are busted up. I couldn't fuck her now if I wanted to," I retorted.

"Please," Kingdom snorted. "Like you wouldn't have your head between her thighs in a motherfucking heartbeat. I'm sure your tongue in her pussy wouldn't strain her ribs. Only reason you've held back this long is because she's in a hospital bed and people going in and out of her room all hours of the day and night. The second you get her alone, you'll be all up in her pussy."

Kingdom leaned forward, and locking in on Loki's gaze, his voice dropped to a deep baritone, "Don't do it. That's an order. It's for her own good, and her good is the priority right now. Besides her close friendship to Sage, Greta, and Sammi, the attack happened in the parking lot of the Box. There's a good chance it was because of her association with the Squad. That's *my* fucking lane, get me? She's under my protection, and you know what that means. It means she's like my own fucking sister."

The urge to grab Kingdom by the throat, fling him face-down and grind his mug into the carpet roared through him, but Loki clamped his jaws together with an audible clank. *Mother*fucker. No one intervened in his relationship with *his* woman. *No one.*

A vision of Abby, sitting alone in the large hospital bed upstairs, assaulted him. With skin so pale it competed with the whiteness of the sheets tucked around her, her eyes a dull brass color instead of their usual, golden amber.

Clenching his brows, he grimaced. He couldn't add to the heavy burden life had already hoisted on her shoulders. His only purpose in life was to help her. If he had to *not* touch her to achieve that goal, then he'd do it. This wasn't like when he was celibate before.

This was Abby. *His* Abby.

"Fucking fine, but don't ever give me an order that comes between me and my woman's pussy again, or so help me, I will end you."

A knowing smile spread over Kingdom's face. "Your woman, huh?"

"Goddamn, right. That bitch is mine. I'm gonna slap a property patch right on her ass and put another baby inside her. By the end of the year, I swear it."

Kingdom took hold of his cup and drained it. "You have my blessing, brother. The Squad's gonna make this right for the both of you."

30

LOKI

The door to Abby's apartment swung open and bounced off the wall.

Abby glared up at him, mouth set, arms crossed, and one foot thumping away like a deranged bunny.

Fuckin' adorable.

Loki suppressed a smile and moved past her, making sure not to touch her or he'd be mounting her from behind in one second flat.

Whirling around, she was at his heels as he sauntered into the living room.

"What are you doing here?" she asked in a tone doused with exasperation.

He didn't appreciate her accusatory tone. As if he didn't have the right to be there when she damn well knew he did. His initial burst of anger eased when he noticed the dark circles under her eyes and the lines bracketing the corners of her mouth. She hadn't slept a wink. He sure as hell hadn't, and he had no intention of a repeat of last night. No way was he leaving her alone again. If he had to sleep on her couch, so be it. But, considering the sharp edge in her tone of voice, he'd wait to announce his decree once she'd settled down a bit.

"You know I'm driving you to work," he replied blithely.

"Listen, Loki, I don't need this right now. I have a lot on my mind, and I don't need the drama of us," she waved her forefinger between the two of them, "the morning after getting discharged."

"You're lucky I'm fucking allowing you to go to work the day after you got out of the hospital," he growled in her face and then backed up a step and wiped his hand over his face. Antagonizing her would not help.

"*Allowing* me? Are you insane? You're not the boss of me," she retorted hotly.

He let that one slide because he was very much the boss of her, but it was a discussion for another time. If she derived comfort from denial, then he'd let her wallow in it for a while longer.

"I'm doing this, Abby," he said much more calmly. "We agreed."

"Our agreement was for you to drive me around *after* dark. It's eight o'clock in the morning. Nothing is going to happen to me on the way to my car, on my way to work, or from the parking lot to my office."

"Mentioning the word 'parking lot' is not bolstering your argument," he observed in a dry tone.

Instead, it bored into a mineshaft of fury and helplessness that made him want to take out the front door with his boot. He swore to God he would, if it were his door and he wasn't afraid it would scare her. He'd sparred for hours yesterday evening at the Box with one of the younger MMA fighters. *Many* hours and bruises later, it did next to nothing to lessen his rage—he eyed her pinned-up hair, strands of blond slinking down the sides of her face—or his desire to fuck her till she dropped.

"We agreed to the limited circumstance of you driving me around after dark, not anytime during the *day*," she maintained.

Tom had dropped Abby off after she was discharged and left to return to Ithaca yesterday afternoon. Last night, Loki swung by her apartment without her knowing, and realized there was no way in hell he could let her roam around the city on her own, night or day.

Planting his feet wide, he crossed his arms over his chest, fixed a pissed-off look on his face, and flat-out lied, "I don't recall that."

"I do," she rejoined without hesitation.

"Then we have a problem."

She folded her arms to mimic him. "We sure do."

He raised an eyebrow at her. "Positive you want to go toe-to-toe with me about this, Abby? 'Cause I guarantee there's no way you're winning this fight."

She threw her hands up in the air, stalked away, and then made a beeline back to face him. "I don't want to fight. I want peace and quiet, and to go back to my normal life. That's the only way I can put this behind me."

Pivoting around, she walked over to her briefcase laying on the counter dividing the living room and kitchen. Yanking it open, she began to stuff files into it. A soft sniffle mixed with the sounds of rustling paper and crunching file folders.

He was behind her in an instant and placed his hands on her shoulders. She stifled a sob and straightened. The crown of her blond head barely reached his shoulders, a few wisps of golden hair brushed the top of his cut. He massaged the tension from her muscles until her stiff shoulders dropped their resistance to him.

Sweeping his hands down her arms, he implored, "Please, do me this favor."

Her posture slackened further, and she cast a look over her shoulder.

"It's not a word I use lightly, and I never beg. You gotta let me do this. I won't make it through the day if I have any doubts about your safety."

Abby bowed her head. "For how long?"

"A week to start with. Then we'll reassess." Another lie, but he was beyond caring.

Her gorgeous golden eyes darkened to whisky. He knew what that meant, and he wanted her just as badly. Wanted to caress her smooth cheek. To trace that plush, bottom lip of hers, the one caught between her teeth, and prod it free. To wrap his fingers around her nape, pull her towards him and kiss her senseless. A blush climbed up her cheekbones under the heat of his stare. Her eyelashes fluttered down, casting long shadows over her cheeks.

"Okay," she agreed softly.

Her eyelashes trembled, lifted, and her eyes locked on his. Suddenly, he was drowning in the shards of yellow and green in her irises.

She turned to face him, her chin lifting a fraction in defiance.

"But I don't want you going after the man who did this," she declared, and the spell that bound them together broke.

He gave her a sharp look, half furious, half incredulous. "That's a fuckin' joke, right?"

She moved around him and walked away. He pivoted on his heels, following her while she continued to talk nonsense, "No, it's not. The police have opened an investigation. I don't want you involved in any way. I know how you operate, and we aren't together anymore, so this is no longer any of your business."

Shoving his face in hers, he took a firm hold of her rebellious chin and growled, "Are you out of your fucking mind? As if it's not bad enough you were hurt, it was my baby, too. Revenge is in order."

She ripped her chin out of his grip, and backstepped until her butt hit the back of the couch. Lips pressed flat, she argued, "More violence is definitely not in order, and that is what your kind of revenge will entail. I've dedicated my professional life to eliminating violence in this world, not adding to it. I need you to promise you won't do anything more or else you will not shuttle me *anywhere*. You will never *ever* see me again."

"You're trippin' if you think either of those things will happen in this lifetime. I am honor bound to protect you. Until my dying breath. That and finding the bastard who hurt you and neutralizing him are my paramount concerns."

"See!" she jabbed a finger in his face. "I knew it! I don't want this. I don't want you helping me out of a sense of duty and guilt."

"Reel in the attitude, Abby, before you find yourself face-down and ass up with my hand connecting with that ripe behind of yours. Fucking my hand is not nearly a worthy substitute for your pussy, so don't push me right now. You're out of your mind if you think that's what this is about," he thundered. "This is about your safety, and suggesting it's anything beyond that is an insult to everything I believe in."

"Will you stop making this about your ego? What about my peace of mind? I want this nightmare to be over with. I want my life back. I've spent my professional life dedicated to diffusing violence, not supporting it."

He stepped closer to her and reached out, but she bent over backward, cringing to avoid his touch.

Dropping his hands, he flexed them at his sides, willing himself to calm down. The urge to tear everything apart to release his rabid, pent-up fury would not help the situation. She was scared, and he had to fix that. *It's not about you. This is about Abby. Make her feel better, you asshole.*

"I understand you're scared, baby," he said in a softer tone, "but the only way to end this nightmare is to find the fucker who hurt you and take care of him. The police may be on it, but there's a possibility the attack was related to the club. If it wasn't a random criminal act, then it must be dealt with in club terms, and club terms mean retribution."

Abby's gaze slammed into his, searching his face. "Please, Loki, I don't want you to get hurt. We may not be together"—he growled under his breath, but she talked over his denial—"but, I don't want any more bloodshed. Promise me."

"Fuck, alright," he sighed. *Alright, I'm going to tear the bastard from limb to limb.* "I won't get involved." *Except, for the final knife to his throat.* He jabbed a finger in her direction, watching her keenly and taking advantage of his concession. "But I watch over you until he's caught." *And every day after.* "If I do this for you, then you don't fight me on protecting you." *Or fucking you, because I will plunge my cock into you as soon as you can take it.* "Understood?"

She nodded rapidly.

"The words, Abby."

"I won't fight you on shepherding me everywhere as if I were a child, even though I'm a grown woman."

His eyes lifted upward. "Attitude, Abby."

Her chin dipped to her chest. "I'm sorry but I don't think I can control my attitude. I'm too upset."

Bracing his hands on the back of the couch behind her, he

corralled her into his chest and whispered into the curve of her ear, "You'd better watch that sassy attitude of yours, for your sake."

He ground his arousal against the softness of her belly. "I'm hard every goddamn second I'm in in your presence. You don't want to test my self-restraint because I'm not far from flipping up that tight pencil skirt you're wearing and plowing into you."

Her breathing hitched and she rubbed her thighs together.

He let out a low moan. "For Christ's sake, I can smell your juices. Do you have any idea how difficult it is to not fuck you right now? *Do you?*"

Cinching her chin between his fingers, he raised her face up. "If you so much as mouth off to me, I'll tongue fuck, finger fuck, whatever fuck your wet pussy in a heartbeat."

Her gaze dipped to the floor and then fluttered back up to him. Hot breaths puffed along his jaw. "What if I want you to?"

Gritting his teeth, he clenched his fingers around the top of the couch to stop from gliding his fingers up her skirt and checking out exactly how much she was dripping. The very idea of leaving her clit pulsing and her pussy clenching on empty was driving him fucking insane, his oath to Kingdom aside, he was worried it was too soon for her.

Shoving off the couch, he said, "Get your shit together. I'll wait outside the door."

❋❋❋

IT WAS OFFICIAL. There was something seriously broken inside her. What other possible explanation was there for wanting to get mauled by Loki? Because mauled is exactly the word to describe what she wanted him to do to her.

Hello woman, do you not remember exactly how unavailable this man is?

Of course, her traitorous body had not one iota of common sense. Like a drug addict in withdrawal, it quaked from the deprivation of not having his hands on her, his cock inside her. Just his growly posturing had her clenching her pussy for dear life, feeling the ghost of the last time he thrust into her. Despite her fiercest self-reprimands, slickness drenched her panties. Her shameless body was on strike from her sensible brain.

Stepping out her front door, Abby sank a righteous glare on the back of Loki's skull. She was fumbling to fit the key in her lock when Loki wrapped his impossibly large hand around hers.

The roughness of his callused palms rubbed over the top of her hand in the most delicious way, and she had to tug her hand away before she did something regrettable. Like slam him against the wall, drop to her knees and have her way with him.

Her pulse kicked into high gear. One simple touch and she'd been reduced to a gooey puddle.

Ugh.

Crazy, mindless, lustful fucking was how she got into this predicament in the first place, she reminded herself sternly.

Body aflame, she relinquished the keys and took a few steps back to wait for him by the stairway. The more distance, the better, because the heat emanating from him made her want to slide her fingers over her already hot and bothered clit.

A hand connected with her lower back, and a husky breath washed over her cheekbone.

"Let's go," he murmured.

She blinked up at him. A shiver ran down her spine, and she hustled down the stairway into the bright early-morning summer sunshine. Glancing around the parking lot, she didn't see his bike.

With a Herculean effort, she managed to maintain an even tone as she asked, "Where's your bike?"

"I brought the truck." He prodded her in the direction of his black truck. "Didn't want you to be uncomfortable. How are the ribs?"

She almost stumbled when she caught the look of concern on his face, but they'd reached the truck and she managed to grab the door handle in time. Loki pushed her gently aside and opened the door for her.

"There's not much pain. Luckily, they were only bruised. I'm taking pain medication and iced the area before getting dressed this morning."

"Good to know, but I still won't be bringing the bike, if that's what your response was suggesting," he retorted.

Her eyes flew up over and connected with his. "But I want to ride." She missed riding.

It made her feel free. She swallowed before confessing, "Badly."

His expression softened.

"You must know why," he said softly.

"Not really but, whatever," she snapped irritably with a toss of her head.

He stepped into her space until her front was plastered against his. Her fingertips glided down his flanks and brushed against his taut abs. Oh *God*. They curled inward at the memory of raking her nails down his sculpted six-pack. Her gaze dropped to his lips and followed the path of his tongue as it lapped at his bottom lip. *No, no, no.* Her heart began to beat so hard it put pressure on her bruised ribs.

Abby dropped her hands, but her knuckles brushed against the hard ridge of his cock. *Sweet Jesus.* Despite her best intentions, her palm skimmed over the tent of his jean-covered shaft. *So, so wrong.* Yet, it felt so good. The heat from his thick shaft bled through the denim into the center of her palm.

Blazes of fire shot from his eyes, hot air snorted through his nostrils and the heat from his hands griping her waist turned her into a writhing mess of lust, wanting only one thing.

Him.

Better yet, his cock. In her mouth. She could practically feel his shaft spreading her lips wide. Thrusting inside as she swirled her tongue around the head. Releasing her, Loki slapped his hands on either side of her head on the car roof and leaned into her touch. The heat from his arms, so close to her face, sent pulses of electricity vibrating around her. She saw his biceps bulge from her side-eye.

"Abby," he warned in a low, gruff tone.

She wet her parched lips and rasped, "Yeah?"

"You can't ride on the back of my bike because I can't have your fine pussy grinding up on me. We aren't doing this. Not yet, anyways."

Shame slammed down on her, pricking her skin like she'd wrangled with a cactus and lost.

She yanked her hand off him. God*dammit*, she was doing it again. Falling for him. Arousal had clouded her judgment, *yet again*, making her forget everything bad between them. Mutual physical desire was never the problem. He was always attentive, especially in bed, and his sexual allure was as beguiling as ever.

She was even willing to admit her resentment of his protectiveness was a tad overblown. Last night, staying alone was hell. She felt like the attacker could jump out at her at any time in the dark and she couldn't deny her relief when she saw him this morning. Not once did she look over her shoulder since he'd arrived, and safety was a crucial element to healing from the assault.

Abby was taking that admission to the grave, but she still feared he'd pull away from her, put up walls, or use any number of tools to create emotional distance if he felt threatened. *For the love of all that's holy, would you just remember that?*

"Yes, of course. You're right," she muttered, involuntarily. Knocking his arms down, she scurried into the cab of the truck and slammed the door behind her.

31

LOKI

Motherfucker.

Loki was constantly torn between throttling Abby or throwing her down on the floor and fucking the ever-living shit out of her. He gripped the back of his neck and rubbed it.

Cutter plopped down on the seat beside him in Kingdom's office. Spreading his thighs wider, his knee knocked against Cutter's. "Fuck man. Can't you find somewhere else to sit, you big-ass motherfucker?"

Cutter pressed his lips together but didn't throw out a comeback. Aww shit, things were fucked if even Cutter was holding back out of respect for Loki's feelings.

"Don't pity me, asshole," he griped.

Cutter huffed. "Thought never crossed my mind."

"Liar," he grumbled.

Puck sauntered in and took his usual place against the wall. Behind him, Prez hobbled in on a cane. Vacating his chair behind his desk, he gestured to Prez to take his seat. Once Prez had settled in, Kingdom started their meeting. "It's Shadow. I've been in touch with Scudder, whose taken over leadership of the Horsemen for now. Shadow showed up back in Camden after the attack and bragged about beating Abby up. Then he loaded up on guns and money and hightailed it out of there."

Prez thumped the ground with his cane and snarled, "He's going down. I'm going to rip that motherfucker limb from fucking limb. There won't be enough pieces of him left to have an open casket."

Eyes snapping to Loki, he swore, "You get first shot, Loki."

Loki gave Kingdom a chin lift and said, "Tell them, Kingdom."

"Loki swore to Abby he wouldn't physically touch the cocksucking bastard."

Prez spat out, "Are you fucking kidding me?"

"Believe me, I'm not happy about this. She was fighting me on watching over her. Made me promise not to get involved, and I had every intention of ignoring it, but she's hurting bad right now over the loss of the baby. If she finds out I touched him, everything will be shot to hell." He shook his head. "My position with her is tenuous at best. We fought just before the attack and I fucked up. I've barely got my foot in the door, as is. My priority right now is Abby and our relationship. As bad as I want to kill this motherfucker, I can't afford one misstep. Not. One. Step."

Cutter clapped his shoulder. If anyone could understand, it was him because his woman was crazy stubborn, too. More than Abby on her worst day. "I feel you, brother."

"Anyway, Shadow's on the run. No one has a location on him yet. Scudder swears he wants Shadow gone, but some brothers are still loyal to him. It's a clusterfuck of maximum proportions. Once Shadow is taken care of, then Scudder can clean house. Right now, though, his hands are tied. He's got to play nice with the brothers who could lead him to Shadow. I don't envy the old man's position, living with vipers in your club."

"What's our next step?" Puck asked.

His jaw was clenched tight, a muscle in his cheek flicked away. He might not know Abby very well, but Abby had become close to Sammi, and anything that touched Sammi threw him in protection mode. "Abby hurt because of the Squad. She's just a girl. Nothing bad would've happened to her if it wasn't for her connection to the Squad. That makes her one of us. For life."

Turning to Loki, he said, "I respect you've got to do what you've got to do to get your woman's trust back, but she's club property."

His eyes locked onto Kingdom. "Right?"

"No doubt, brother," Kingdom replied, grimly. "What happened to her tears me up inside. Of all the brothers, bitches, or anyone aligned with the club, Abby's got to have been the most innocent girl connected to us. If we can't protect the weakest in our midst, then we aren't worthy to wear this patch."

He clutched his Demon Squad patch in his fist. "Cutter, I need you to go to Camden. Find out what you can. We need to hit up whatever contacts we have out there."

"I'm in touch with Abby's brothers," Loki explained. "One of them is a prosecutor in Manhattan. He's got serious clout. If Shadow interfaces with law enforcement anywhere in the Tri-State area, he'll find out about it."

"Good thinking, Loki," agreed Kingdom. "Operation Elimi-nate Shadow is in full force brothers, and we're out for his blood. I'm going to personally gut him like a hog on the killing floor."

※※※

THEY'D HAD a knock-down drag-out fight, and, needless to say, Loki wasn't pleased when Abby broke down and cried. In the end, he'd won. *That's what matters.*

Grateful to be in her apartment after a sleepless night followed by a long day, Loki lay down on her too-fucking-small couch, the pillow and folded sheet she'd thrown down before stalking away and slamming her bedroom door tucked underneath his head.

Might be uncomfortable as hell, but at least he had a fighting chance of getting some shut-eye. Thank fuck he'd stood his ground and insisted he sleep over because he was exhausted and he would've stationed himself outside her apartment if she hadn't allowed him to sleep over.

Abby had slunk out to use the bathroom, returned to her bedroom and, soon after, the light underneath her door went out. About an hour later, he silently crept up to her door and checked in on her. Dressed in matching bright yellow emoji pajamas, she was out like a baby.

His forehead creased into a frown. Her sheet and light blanket were twisted around her ankles, her pillows scattered on the floor. Normally, she was a peaceful sleeper.

Leaving the door wide open, he padded back to the couch and arranged himself as best he could. It felt like his knees were up by his chin, he was so cramped on the damn couch.

Letting out a sigh, he swung his hand over his head on the arm of the couch and shut his eyes when a nervous voice called out, "Loki?"

His head shot up, twisted over the back of the couch, and spotted Abby at the entrance of her room. Shoulder braced against the doorframe, she had the sheet wrapped around her body as if it was personal protective gear.

Eyes as large as an owl's, she peered over at him in the dark. The moonlight streaming through the uncovered bedroom windows lit her silhouette from behind, highlights framing her hair in an outline of silver.

"Whattup?"

She shifted from foot to foot, one hand clutching the sheet tighter against her breast.

In the silence that followed, he called out, "Need anything, baby girl?"

"No." She hesitated, shuffled some more, and then piped up, "Did I wake you?"

"Nope."

More silence.

"Trouble sleeping, Pixie?"

"I guess," she licked her lips nervously and bit down on her bottom lip.

Waving a limp hand, she noted blandly, "I closed the door."

And I opened it, to make sure you were okay.

"You made some noise," he lied. "So I went in to check on you."

Abby considered him for a long moment, and then broke their stare. Various expressions crossed the profile of her face.

He waited for a reprimand, but none came. His chest tightened.

"Wanna talk?" he asked, testing the waters.

Her eyes sliced back to his, a stricken look flashed over her face and she shook her head resolutely. Something had startled her out of her deep sleep. It hadn't been her open door or his return to the couch. She was too deep a sleeper for that. A nightmare? A flashback, maybe? His hands flexed open and closed. He'd do anything to erase the fucked-up memories branded in her mind.

His eyes cut to the clock. It was almost midnight.

"Wanna watch TV?" he prodded.

She hesitated for a moment, then, with the sound of the rustling sheet, Abby crossed the small apartment to him.

He sat upright to make space for her on the couch, but she plopped down on the rug in front of him, leaving a foot of distance between them. He balled his hands into fists to prevent himself from reaching for her.

"How'd you sleep last night?" he asked, conversationally.

"Not well," she admitted.

"Me neither. I selfishly insisted on staying here, hoping I'd finally get some sleep."

Her eyes snapped to his. "Why didn't you tell me earlier? I thought it was because you were being an overbearing prick. I might not have fought you so hard had I known."

"I wasn't in the sharing mood. And, for the record, I *am* an overbearing prick. It would help not to forget it."

He gave her a smirk, and one corner of her mouth curved up at his attempt at a joke.

"You can say that again," she snorted.

"What do you want to watch?"

Stretching forward, she patted the top of the TV and procured a remote control. "One of those late-night shows."

The TV clicked on and the sound of audience laughter blared loudly before she lowered the sound. Assuming a passive pose, he rested one hand on top of the other against his belly. She found what she was looking for and relaxed back against the couch.

He chuckled a time or two during the show, and each time, she angled her head to catch the tail end of his laugh before snapping it back in place.

The show ended, and another started. During a commercial, his gaze drifted down to her, and he found her slumped a little to the side, her head tilted back into the cushion of the couch, sound asleep.

Picking up the remote control that had slipped out of her hand, he turned the TV off, crawled off the couch and carefully lifted her curvy little body into his arms.

With a minimal amount of jostling, he laid her down on her bed. Mumbling to herself, she jerked once, and then curled onto her side. Concerned she might wake up again during the night, he rested beside her, leaving a few inches between them. He finished stretching his legs when she scooted over until her ass bumped and nestled into his waist. His cock rose to attention at her lush curves abutting him. Her honey citrus scent drifted over him.

Smoothing a hand over the curve of her ass, he muffled a groan in his clenched fist.

It's gonna be a long fucking night.

32

ABBY

There was bad news and there was good news.

Loki was staying for an undetermined amount of time. *Sigh*. A week later, he went through his so-called "reassessment" and decided to maintain the status quo. Problem was, she was secretly thrilled he'd moved in. The night she'd spent alone after returning from the hospital had been atrocious. Every little sound got her up and out of bed, irrationally flicking on the light switches in her apartment and placing her ear against her front door. She shuddered just remembering it.

The following night, he refused to leave after dropping her off from work. She was proud at how she'd fought him like a tiger, but he'd ultimately came out as the victor. Later, when he'd admitted he hadn't slept well alone either, the last of her resistance crumbled.

She hadn't made it through even one single night without him in bed with her. Thank God for small mercies he hadn't initiated anything sexual, otherwise, she would've found herself spread-eagled on her bed, blissfully getting the pounding of her life.

Abby was aware that, at this point, she was truly screwed. They were, for all intents and purposes, living together, and she was barely able to restrain herself from jumping him. Loki was intelligent enough to stay in the living room or kitchen, catching up on work or watching TV, and only joined her in bed after she'd fallen asleep. He was out of bed before she awakened, but she felt him, heard him, breathed him in when she routinely woke up during the night. Being a light sleeper, her wakings roused him, but he's always groggily lay a hand on her head, shushing and cooing until she settled down and fell back asleep.

As if spending nights sharing the same bed wasn't bad enough, their daily routine was genuinely, thoroughly killing her. She made sure to avoid the pronouns "we" or "us" at all costs, which was more difficult than it initially seemed. Instead of "We should stop and get groceries for dinner," it was "I need to stop at the grocery store because I'll be cooking up pasta tonight. Are you hungry, too?"

Speaking of dinners, he hadn't missed one. Not a one. *WTH?* The self-defense class had ended just before her attack, which she was grateful for. It would've brought up too many memories to return, but it would've at least kept him out later for at least one night a week. Shouldn't he be spending as much time away from her as possible, hanging out at the clubhouse with his brothers or working late at the Box. No such luck.

Not that she was doing any better on her end. She hadn't hung out with Sammi alone or gotten drinks with coworkers on Thursdays because she didn't want to skip prepping and eating dinner with him. It was beyond pathetic. *She* was beyond pathetic. Although they could never be together, there was no point denying his presence brought her a deep sense of relief and security.

Bleary-eyed, Abby stumbled out of the bedroom and walked to her briefcase on the counter just as her cell phone buzzed. She checked her phone and smirked at her brother's no-nonsense text.

LIAM: How are you? Why haven't you texted back yet?

ABBY: Because I'm fine, you stalker! [Smile emoji]

LIAM: Last time I checked, a brother checking in with his baby sister is not considered stalking. Just stating the law.

ABBY: Not like ten times a day. There's a law against that somewhere.

LIAM: Hardi-har-har. Stalking is if I followed you everywhere. Seriously, if I didn't have a kid on the way, I'd be there.

ABBY: Another reason to be grateful for my amazing sister-in-law. Why she picked you over all the other hot guys she works with, I'll never understand.

LIAM: Just because she works at GQ, doesn't mean she works with models. Anyway, from what I understand, they're assholes.

ABBY: And you're not? Ha! I've got to give her a call and tell her to snap out of it.

LIAM: You wouldn't dare with the baby coming.

LIAM: Homewrecker [Winking emoji]

ABBY: Good point. I'll wait until he's eighteen. Then, I'll get her to leave you, Mr. Bossy. She'll have a few decades to make up for, but what's a BFF sister-in-law good for otherwise?

LIAM: Ha!

LIAM: Is Loki there?

Abby scrunched her nose. *What the hell?*

ABBY: Why do you ask?

LIAM: Checking to make sure you're not alone.

ABBY: Why would you think he's here?

LIAM: We text.

ABBY: What?! You have his number?

Abby's head shot up and her gaze narrowed on Loki, standing shirtless by the stove, preparing scrambled eggs. His black jeans rode low on his hips, showcasing the Vs on either side of his abs. Goddamn him. What was he thinking walking around half naked. The man was either oblivious or purposely taunting her and her overheated libido.

LIAM: Thought you knew. Dad gave it to me.

LIAM: Why else do you think I'm not there with you?

She had to get off before she called him up and ripped him a new one. Pressing her lips together, she tapped out,

ABBY: I hate you.

LIAM: I know. Lucky for me, I'm immune.

ABBY: [angry devil emoji]

LIAM: [laughing emoji] Check in with you later.

Slamming her cell phone on the table, Abby glared at Loki's back and asked, "How long have you been in touch with my brother?"

Without turning around or missing a beat, Loki replied, "Which one?"

She ground her teeth together, inhaling sharply through her nostrils. After inhaling and exhaling four times, calming herself enough not to tear his head off immediately, she answered, "Liam."

"He contacted me the day you got out of the hospital. After he got some shit off his chest, I told him I'd give him updates. Been doing it ever since."

The back of her neck got hot. "What stuff did he get off his chest?"

"The usual. How he'd kill me if I hurt you. He's got one hell of an imagination. Gave me a rundown of the serial killer ways he'd dispose of my body. Pretty inventive."

"He's an assistant DA."

"Yeah, I got that. In detail," Loki responded dryly.

Shoving the heels of her hands into her eyes, she mumbled, "Oh God, they're like the worst."

Loki plated the eggs, along with toast and slices of tomatoes. "Nah. I respect his concern. It's good to know someone's been looking out for you these past years. Explains how someone like you survived, unharmed." A frown pinched between his eyebrows. "Until now."

Yanking open the silverware drawer, she dug for forks and knives. Ignoring his reference to the attack, she queried, "Someone like me? You don't think I can survive on my own?"

"Babe, you stepped out of a Thumbelina Disney movie."

"I'll have you know that I'm not as helpless and innocent as I look," she huffed.

"Hmm-hmm." Placing the dishes on the table, he gave her an arrogant smirk as he surveyed her with a heavy-lidded stare. "Oh, I know how dirty you can get."

Just like that, the air in the kitchen morphed into something heavy and hot. She had trouble inhaling full breaths of air through her constricted chest cavity and her body flamed with a head-to-toe flush.

Pretending he didn't realize he'd almost triggered a near-orgasm, Loki opened the refrigerator, pulled out the ketchup, and sat across from her at her tiny table nook. His pecs were peek-a-booing her, flexing every time he brought his fork to his mouth. The movement of his square jaw and the glide of his throat muscles with each swallow was distracting as hell.

"Aren't they good?" He asked with a tiny knowing quirk of his lips.

She blinked, realizing she was caught staring, fork frozen midair. Swallowing hard, she dropped her gaze and mumbled a disconcerted "yeah" before jamming a forkful of eggs into her mouth.

"Yummy."

"Don't moan and then say that word loud, Pixie. It's distracting," he teased.

Did she mention the sexual innuendos that volleyed back and forth between them?

Loki's gaze burned into her, and she stilled, midchew, as his eyes dipped to her mouth, held for a moment, and then traveled down her chest. The cerulean blue of his eyes darkened as he caught her nipples pebbling under her light cotton top. Under his slow perusal, she broke out into a hot sweat and plucked at her blouse. Barely able to stop from fanning herself, she quickly chewed the food in her mouth and gulped it down.

He scraped his teeth over his bottom lip, tugged on his chin, and cursed softly before picking up his fork.

The sound of his gruff tone sent shivers up her spine.

"Eat up," he commanded hoarsely.

Oh, I know exactly what I'm hungry for.

"Stop looking at me like that, Abby. I'm tryin' to do right by you, but I've got the kind of hard-on that could crush rocks to dust. Just sayin', you don't want me texting your brother to tell him how close I was to bending you over and fucking you over this table." He tapped the wooden surface for good measure.

Glued to Loki's face, she silently dared him to take what he wanted.

They stared each other down, locked in a battle of wills.

Her breathing turned ragged, the openmouthed rasps shuddering through the air between them. Growling low, he shoved off from the table and threw his dishes in the sink.

Taking long strides down the corridor, he muttered tightly, "I'm taking a shower," and slammed the bathroom door shut behind him.

The sound of running water permeated the door. Heat

curled up in her belly because she was certain he was taking his cock in hand. Pride filtered through her chest that she had the power to affect him like this. Hands clenched on the table-top, she moaned as the image of Loki's fingers wrapping around his thick shaft, stroking from root to crown, swam before her eyes. Her clit was titillated beyond reason, and she pressed the heel of her hand between her thighs.

Checking the time, she saw it was past eight o'clock and time to get ready for work. Appetite usurped by the kind of gnawing hunger that couldn't be easily satisfied, she gave up on breakfast and brought her half-eaten plate to the sink. The entire time she loaded the dishwasher, one ear pricked up in the vain hope of Loki calling her name from the bathroom.

33

ABBY

L oki held the clubhouse door open for Abby, and she stalked through mumbling about how she wasn't an invalid and could damn well open the door for herself.

Smart man that he was, he refrained from responding. After weeks of his persistent presence, her nerves were shot. He hadn't made a move on her, which was a source of endless torment to her. Meanwhile, he seemed to be in a more tolerant mood than ever.

She knew she was acting like a brat, but irritation scuffed her nape like a scratchy mohair scarf. It was her constant companion. This morning she caught herself tapping her foot impatiently during a session with one of her gentlest clients. Jenny looked up at her with an expression of hurt that had her blushing to the roots of her hair and apologizing profusely.

Seriously, her life was a hot mess.

Since he liked to torture her by touching her any chance he got, Loki guided her to the bar with his palm on the small of her back. She'd given up trying to avoid his touch. It only drove him to find novel ways to touch her.

Grateful to see Sage, Abby released a pent-up breath and quickened her steps toward her friend. Sage jumped down from a high stool and rushed over to her, arms spread open for a hug. Two other biker bitches at the bar had followed Sage and wrapped their arms around her as well.

Tears pricked behind her eyes as she allowed herself to be comforted by the women. Ever since her attack, even bitches who had previously given her the cold shoulder had warmed up to her. While she hated the idea they might pity her, they knew what had happened, and the possible reasons why. The fact she had suffered because of her association to the club, however tenuous, had transformed her status among them.

"I'll come for you after I'm done talking to Kingdom," Loki said, as he passed her on his way to joining Kingdom at the end of the bar. She nodded in response.

One woman noted to her friend, "Look how he watches over her. The change is like night and day."

Abby interceded with a flippant response, "It's more like duty."

"I don't think so, girl," the other woman replied. "He's actin' possessive as hell. That's not duty."

Shooing the other women away, Sage led Abby to one of the couches and got her settled before going to the bar. Returning with drinks, Sage dropped in beside her.

Looking her over critically, she asked in a tone lined with concern, "How are you doing?"

After another exhausting day at the office, Abby took a few sips of her drink. Lifting her shoulders a fraction of an inch, she said, "Okay, I guess."

Lips pursed, Sage made a noncommittal sound as she began sifting and sorting through bags stuffed with a haphazard array of Labor Day decorations on the low table in front of them.

"It's pretty much like the doctor had warned," Abby continued. "Mood swings, bouts of crying, fatigue. Work keeps me sane. Loki," her gaze slid over to the end of the bar where his head was huddled next to Kingdom's, "not so much."

"Tell me why," pressed Sage.

Her eyes dropped to the twiddling thumbs of her linked hands, laying on her lap. "It's hard being around him. He's living with me and, miracle of miracles, he's somehow convinced both of my brothers this was a good idea. He won't leave me alone and sometimes all I want is to be alone, but he refuses because he thinks I'll 'fall into a depression.'" The last words came out in an imitation of Loki's raspy growl.

"Sage, I don't feel comfortable being emotional around him. It makes me feel more vulnerable than normal. At times, it hurts to even look at him. Thinking about what our baby would have been like. He or she would've taken after him, for sure. His features are so strong."

An expression of commiseration filled Sage's face. "I can relate."

"I know you can, but there's a huge difference between us, and you and Kingdom. You were in a relationship when you miscarried. I am not."

"Are you not?" Her gaze coasted over to Loki. "I don't think Loki got the memo."

"Don't let his behavior fool you," she scoffed. "It's simply guilt over my attack."

Sage's eyes sparked with anger. "Don't say such ridiculous things."

Abby's eyes flared wide as Sage continued, "I know about guilt. Kingdom carried the same cross around for years after Chopper's death. He was a wreck when I first met him. Loki may feel guilt, but that is *not* the primary reason behind his behavior."

Abby's fingers fluttered around the decorations. She teased apart a tangled string of miniature flags.

Eyes downcast, she confessed, "I don't know what's going on. We're constantly together because he insists on driving me *everywhere*, but he hasn't initiated any intimacy, which can only mean he took me seriously when I told him that it was over between us. It's been three weeks, and I mean he touches me whenever he can, but he hasn't *touched touched* me, if you know what I mean. It's almost worse because I'm in a state of constant arousal. I had to get a change of batteries for my vibrator, and I can't remember the last time that happened. I shouldn't be upset since he's only following my wishes. It's for the best, really."

Sage abandoned her work and leaned back into her chair, watching Abby. "Is it?"

Sighing, Abby gave up on the flags and began unraveling a string of fairy lights. "I believe so," she replied with a resolute nod of her head.

"Well, I don't," remarked Sage. "I never thought of you as a quitter, but it looks to me like you're quitting on the two of you."

"Me? I told you about the argument before the attack. Loki isn't capable of opening up sufficiently and I can't dedicate my life to a man who can't share his feelings with his partner."

"I agree it's not easy for him, but you have to dig deeper into the reason *why*. It's not because he's in emotionally immature or frozen. Loki is one of the most emotional men I know. Still waters run deep and all that. His problem is that he feels too much, not that he doesn't feel enough. If he opens his heart, he won't be able to close it off again, even for self-preservation. I'm not going to pretend he's perfect, by any stretch of the imagination, but he opened himself to you and he can't shut you out. And, knowing him, he's tried hard. You should see the way he looks at you when you're not aware of him. He wears his love on his sleeve. The way he handles intense feelings is by controlling his environment. Deprivation is his fallback position. He wants you more than ever, but the safest way of handling those feelings is by suppressing them."

"Oh, no worries on that count," Abby offered. "He's definitely in control. To make up for our lack of intimacy, he texts and calls me constantly. God forbid I don't respond right away."

"The truth is you're both in love with each other, and you're letting the last argument, and everything that happened afterward, get in the way. I'm not trying to undermine the magnitude of those events, but you can surmount those challenges, Abby. You guys would've made up by now if it hadn't been for the assault and miscarriage. Are you really going to let this attacker change the course of your life? Don't you want Loki?"

Sage's question prompted Abby to gaze at him again. He was nodding in agreement to something Kingdom was saying, the rim of his glass tipped against his open lips. His throat slid up and down as he took a swallow of his beer. Even though he wasn't looking at her, the brilliance of his indigo eyes had a piercing effect on her. He was so raw. Intense. Powerful.

There was nothing he wouldn't do for someone he cared about. Despite the horrible times he and Kingdom had gone through over Chopper's death, he was fully committed to Kingdom and the Squad.

Abby rubbed her lips together thoughtfully. She hadn't realized how addicted she was to his taste and touch until it was gone. His scent alone drove her wild with barely repressed lust. In the truck, on their way over to the clubhouse, his scent wound around her, sultry and delicious. It was maddening. She'd been forced to crank the window all the way down. His eyes had darted over to her, and, without a word, he cranked up the air conditioning.

"I miss him, but I don't think I'm ready for anything like another pregnancy," she stated.

"Whoa, who's talking pregnancy? Take it a step at a time. Just think about the next right step. Put aside the heartache around these most recent events. Close your eyes," Sage ordered.

Abby looked at her askance.

"Humor me, please."

She let out a small huff and closed her eyes.

"Breathe in. Breathe out." Sage paused for Abby to follow her commands. "Don't think. Keep breathing and let yourself just feel for a moment. Free yourself from the pain. Let your mind focus on Loki's face. Are you there?"

"Yeah," she murmured.

"Good. Now, focus on his forehead, his eyes, his lips." Another minute passed. "His scar." A beat of silence passed. "Tell me, Abby, in the absence of pain, what is the first thing you want to say or do to Loki? Say the first thing that comes to your mind."

"I want to fuck him. Hard and fast."

Abby's eyes popped open and she slapped her hand over her mouth.

Sage's words had prompted a memory of his soft lips, brushing over hers, teasing her to open for him, but it rapidly devolved into an image of him, behind her, thrusting into her hard. Every day, she woke up ready to pounce on him. This morning she woke up with her mouth open, dreaming Loki was straddling her, feeding her his cock between her lips, ordering her to *taste it*. She almost came, there and then, and had to rush to the bathroom before she sought him out, slithered down his body, and went to town on him.

"I'm sorry, I never talk like that. I must be seriously sex deprived," Abby apologized, heat crawling up her cheeks.

Head inclined to the side; a soft smile lit up Sage's face. "Don't you dare apologize. You wouldn't be a healthy, young woman if you didn't want him. I don't know how you guys live together without having *any* sex. After Kingdom and I broke up, I tried everything in my power to get away from him, but every few days we'd end up having angry fight sex. Listen, you both need to get out of the house. After we finish decorating, go home, get dressed and come back to the party. Crazy shit happens at the Demon Squad clubhouse on any holiday. Some of the girls are going to get dressed up like Mardi Gras, just for fun. You can tease him for a while, get him nice and frustrated. Then, you can let him loose on you."

She eyed him dubiously and admitted, "I don't know if Loki will go for it."

Sage patted her hand with a knowing wink and stood up.

"I'll talk to him. Leave him to me," she promised.

Abby watched as Sage went over to Kingdom, who propped her on his lap and wrapped his arms around her waist.

Was Kingdom rubbing Sage's belly? She squinted her eyes but couldn't see a bump. Not pregnant. Yet. A pang of pain whipped through her. If they were pregnant, she'd be happy for them. She really would be.

Her gaze drifted over to Loki, who didn't seem pleased with whatever Sage was saying to him. Kingdom interjected with what looked like a command and Loki nodded tightly, once.

So, it seemed like she was going to a party and she knew just which outfit to wear to make him suffer.

34

LOKI

"What in the ever-loving fuck are you wearing?" Loki snapped, his eyes slitted in warning.

Abby had sauntered out of her bedroom dressed as—*get this*—a fucking fairy. His pixie girl was wearing a cocktease of a fairy outfit. Which was fitting, of course, it was. His cock was hard as a goddamn pike and Sage thought he would accompany her to the club, filled to the brim with drunken assholes so she could party? Think again, lady. He could hardly keep his hands off her plum-shaped ass as it was, these past twenty days. Twenty. Fucking. Days.

Fuck him, how did he know it was twenty days?

Because he was COUNTING.

But this? This was going too far. The flirty, short-as-hell skirt she was wearing scarcely covered her pussy. Top it off, he could see her lacy, white bra beneath her frilly, sheer fuck-me fairy top, paired with fuck-me kitten heels.

She had some nerve, thinking he'd let her mosey on out the door and strut around in public decked out like a luscious porn version of a nymph. Every hot-blooded male in the club would pounce on her. He had a succinct, two-word response for her when she asked him if he was ready to go: "Hell. No."

Her eyebrows puckered together as her head canted to the side, an expression of confusion gracing her pretty features.

He squeezed his eyes closed, it hurt to look at her, so fucking pretty and dainty. *Christ, could a woman be so fuckin' clueless?*

"You're not going anywhere dressed like that. I don't care what Sage says or does about it. It ain't happening. Turn that tight ass of yours around, strip that shit off, and put on your pj's. You're going to sleep," he commanded.

Her hand slammed down on her cocked hip and she sassed back at him, "Oh, I don't think so, Loki. Sage invited me to the party. I'm going and you can't stop me."

"You have no idea how batshit crazy it gets there. Wild doesn't begin to describe what happens. It's a fucking orgy, and I won't have you anywhere near there," he threatened.

"Considering I haven't gotten any in, like, forever, that's not a problem for me," she grumbled to herself, but loud enough that he could hear.

Heard it and about ready to whip out his gun to blow out the brains of any man who dared touch her.

Stalking up to her, he crowded her space, something he had proactively worked to avoid doing. Until now. Now, she'd stepped over the line and he couldn't take it anymore. He was going to teach her a lesson of who she belonged to.

"You got a complaint, Pixie? No one lickin' that sweet-tasting pussy of yours?" His voice dropped low. "Been making sure no man gets near you. No man but me, that is. Since I'm a helpful kinda guy, I'm gonna take care of it for you. Got an ache, babe? Tell me and I'll lick it better for you."

She must've been tongue-tied because her mouth opened and closed like a gaping fish, but no words came out. Her pupils dilated, leaving her eyes with more black pupil than gold iris. She wavered on her feet before stumbling back a step and landing on the edge of her couch.

"What. Do. You. Need? I want to hear the words," he demanded.

Considering she'd driven him right off the cliff he'd been skating on for the past fucking three weeks, he was *done*. She stood up, still dazed-looking, but he wasn't in a merciful mood. He'd been treating her like spun glass and hating every second he didn't have his hands on her like he wanted. The floodgates had been flung open, and the craving to dominate whipped him into a frenzy.

Loki dropped to his knees and glided his hands up her white thigh-highs. He snapped one of the lacy, elastic tops. A faint pink ring marked her milky skin where he'd snapped the band. See, this is what he meant by sexy virgin. Her outfit could double as lingerie, it was so damn revealing. His cock was tearing at his Levi's to escape, and that was saying something because he'd been living with a hard-on since the moment she walked out of the hospital.

His fingers dug into the outsides of her thighs and she pushed into them. *Fuck, yes.* The grip of his fingers deepened, and he face planted into her heaven-scented pussy. Drawing in a long breath, he was reminded of how fucking delicious she was. He ripped away the filmy layers of her skirt and panties until she was bare under his openmouthed kisses. Alternating between nipping and lapping at her clit, he lowered her onto the floor.

His head whirled with the elusive taste he'd been wet-dreaming about every damn night. Lifting his head off her, he straddled her as he wrenched off his cut and shirt. Abby clawed at his arms, frantic to touch him as much as he wanted her to. Holding onto her wrists, he looped them above her head.

"You've been a bad girl," he murmured against her lips. "Bad as can be, keeping this hot, tasty cunt away from me. Tell me, Abby, have you made yourself come without me?"

Watching him solemnly, she nodded in acquiescence.

"How often?" he barked.

Eyes aflame with lust and need and desperate desperate craving, she huffed out, "Every night, at least twice."

Surprised, he took his mouth off her. "When? I've been here every night."

"In the shower, in the bed, anywhere I could," she confessed. "I've been needing you so bad."

His lungs expanded with a sharp intake of air and he roared, beating his chest like a madman.

Raw fury pummeled him from all sides that his woman, *his* woman, was fucking herself with her fingers while he woke up drenched in sweat and come every morning from dreams of pounding into her.

"You're gonna pay for that," he promised darkly.

She lifted her chin defiantly. "You can't be mad at me. We weren't together."

"Like hell, I can't. Don't act like you don't know who I am. Who am I, Abby? Who the fuck am I to you?"

She twisted her head to the side, but he grasped her chin to face him. It wasn't about the damn orgasms, although that did stick in his craw. It was every moment he missed laying, sleeping, or nestling with her, inhaling her intoxicating scent, caressing her silky skin, squinting from the glare of her glossy white-blond tresses.

Between gritted teeth, he repeated, "Who do you belong to?"

"No one!" she spat out.

"Oh, yeah?" He glared down at her. "Keep your hands where they are. If you fuckin' make one move, I swear, you'll get stripes on your ass that won't let you sit down right for a week. Nah, make that one for every goddamn day I've been denied your sweet cunt. I'll make sure you feel what I've suffered without your tight pussy wrapped around my cock for the past three weeks."

❄❄❄

THE VIOLENCE PULSATING OFF HIM, coupled with his dirty, angry words, should've repulsed her, but they hit Abby's system like a blast of cocaine. His wide shoulder muscles bunched up, the thick slabs of his pecs flexed, and his abs rippled as his hand stroked up his hard shaft.

"Take off the rest of your fucking clothes and get into position," he demanded in a low, commanding tone.

She scrambled to her knees and tore off her top and bra. Reaching to roll down her thigh-highs, her fingers were interrupted by a rapid fire of rough-hewn commands.

"Leave those."

She dropped her hands.

"On your back, hands clasped above your head."

Flouncing down on the rug, she stretched her arms above her head and entwined her fingers together. Between her spread thighs, she watched with rapt attention as his hand raced faster and faster over his stunning cock. Stunning because it sure as hell stunned her.

Abby eagerly licked her lips in anticipation of sucking him off while his eyes gorged on her.

Abruptly he jerked, and ropes of come jetted over her breasts and ribs.

"No," she protested fiercely, but his hand kept going until he emptied himself out completely.

Tears pricked the back of her eyes. This was a punishment. An *insult*.

"That's your reward for your actions," he chastised, in a tone tinged with little regret. Breathing heavily through her flared nostrils, she was livid. "Next time, you'll know better than to keep what's mine from me. I fucking *own* you, you hear? You and every one of your orgasms."

His palms came down on her and proceeded to rub his come over her heaving chest. He was extra meticulous on her breasts, massaging around her nipples before giving them a quick twist. Loki didn't stop until not a drop remained.

"That was not a nice thing to do," she choked out.

Giving her a bemused smile, his hand snaked down her torso and thrust two fingers into her slick core. "Next time you'll think twice before coming without getting my explicit permission. This was one of our first lessons, wasn't it? Why? Because you don't take my prize out from under me like a fucking thief. Not to worry, though, you'll be paying me back for my losses."

The threat, in combination with his thrusting fingers, heightened her arousal.

He pinched one of her nipples and an electric shock lit a path down to her core, gushing wetness from her spread pussy. Stroking diligently, he examined her with a cool, detached expression. She recognized the dominant, controlling glint in his eyes. He'd made himself come because he was planning something diabolical, like keeping her on the edge for hours. Her belly roiled in response.

Reading her mind, he confirmed, "You don't come until I

give you permission. Ever. Clearly, you need a reminder of the importance of consent. Let me be clear, I'm talking about *my* consent, not yours."

Oh, G*od*. It was such a turn on when he bullied her. As wicked as they were, the words dripped with seductive intent. Her inner muscles clamped down on his fingers, silently begging for the cock she wanted so badly.

Moaning, she twisted her hips in circles, beseeching, taunting him to slam his massive cock inside her. She was dying for his special brand of power and ownership.

A hard smack came down on one of her ass cheeks.

"Quit humping the air with your cunt," he chastised.

The fierceness in his gaze lacerated her like the lashes of a crop. Withdrawing his fingers, he orbited her clit a few times, leaving the pulsing center of nerves aching with need.

Her eyes fluttered closed and she let out a low, plaintive mewl. He plunged inside again, withdrew, circled her clit, and dipped them back in, repeating the same pattern until Abby grabbed his wrist to keep his fingers embedded inside her.

Growling, he slapped her pussy lips and her eyes slammed open with a yelp.

"You don't control this pussy," he growled. "I do. You still on birth control?"

Eyes locked on his cock bobbing and weaving in the air, she nodded. He knew she'd been to her gynecologist since he drove her to the appointment. Not that contraception had protected them before, but she'd made certain to be on something.

"Turn around." Without waiting, he grabbed her hips and spun her around. She landed on her hands and knees, wheezing between outstretched arms.

His gruff voice trembled above her head. "Do you need a reminder?"

Rubbing her cheek against the inside of her arm, she replied in a small voice, "Maybe."

"I'll take that as a yes. Prepare for disciplinary action," he replied brusquely.

A hard smack landed on her upturned buttocks as he intoned, "You will not come without my clearance." The flat of his hand rained down on her. "That should have been self-evident. You've run rampant long enough and it hasn't done either one of us any damn good." His fingers ran over her inflamed cheeks. "Damn, pink is a good look on your ripe ass."

She felt the thick underside of his shaft nestled in between her ass cheeks, followed by a series of solid slaps, as if to punish her for his momentary weakness.

"From now on, you will sleep by my side. Every." *Whack.* "Fucking." *Whack.* "Night." *Whack.* "You'll wake up by my side. Every." *Smack.* "Fucking." *Smack.* "Morning." *Smack.* "How many was that so far?"

He was testing her.

"Seven," she breathed out.

"Good. Count off the rest."

There were three more blows, each falling brutally on her cheeks after she called them out. His harsh pants whispered over her raw flesh, sizzling like second-degree burns. The blunt crown of his cock slithered over her pulsing clit, coated in her juices.

"Two more," he said, although it seemed he was saying it aloud for his benefit more than for hers. Two fast ones came at her and then she was impaled, a growly baritone thundering in her ear.

Tangling his fingers in her hair, he plowed his cock inside her to the hilt. Back arched, Abby stared up at the ceiling and breathed out heavily. *Finally, finally, finally.* It dawned on her this wasn't a simple, cut-and-dried fuck.

This was a taking, a conquering.

His plunder was absolute.

Hips tilted up and ass pushed out, she met every one of his rough thrusts, as his cock flayed her from the inside out. Her butt stung like hell but her pussy squelched, sticky wetness running down his demanding shaft. His exacting finger slipped between her buttocks. She lurched forward, but he tightened his grip on her tresses to keep her in place as he continued his exploration. Her abdomen clenched and her smarting ass cheeks clamped shut.

"Relax, Pixie, I got you. C'mon, breathe."

She followed his command, relaxing with each exhalation as his digit rimmed her back hole, and then penetrated lightly. He must have lathered it with his tongue beforehand. The thought of his tongue licking the finger currently in her ass made her moan loudly.

"Fuck, I love this round ass of yours," he praised. His cock thickened inside her as his digit passed through the tight ring of muscles. In tandem with his finger, his cock took up a fast pace. This being the first time, she didn't know exactly what he was doing to her, but a delectable pressure generated tingles that exponentially sensitized her pussy. As her spine bowed lower, her hips opened farther, and she spread herself as wide as she could to get the most of his invading cock.

"Feel my balls slappin' you?" he grunted out, as his hips battered into her buttocks, pushing his finger deeper. Boy, could she ever. The head of his cock repeatedly stabbed at the magic spot inside her cunt, and she collapsed to her chest. A droning buzz invaded her ears. Her skin felt too tight. Her head detached from her body, floating up, up, up.

"Come for me," he ordered.

His command fit the last piece in the puzzle and *pop*. Like a helium balloon reaching too high up, she burst into a blinding climax. Her orgasm tore through her, stealing what remained of reality. Aftershocks rocked her system for minutes afterward, carrying her back to her body just in time to hear Loki roar above her and feel him spill inside her.

On trembling hands, she tried raising herself up, but crumbled onto her forearms and Loki tottered above her. His palms slammed down alongside hers as he caught himself before they both crashed to the floor. The hard ridges of his chest encased her back, the heaves of his harsh breathing shuddering through her. A set of teeth clenched around the soft flesh at the juncture of her shoulder and neck.

"Let there be no misunderstanding. You're mine." He licked the teeth marks.

"Speak," he commanded.

She simply stated what her bruised pussy, her sore ass, and her throbbing shoulder manifested as true.

"I'm yours."

35

LOKI

"That's right," Loki confirmed. "Thank Christ, we're clear on that point."

The intensity of their joining had left him dazed, but he managed to lift his weight off Abby before he crushed her. Helping her up from the floor, he placed a firm hand around her midriff and guided her to bed. Ordering her to stay, he went to the bathroom to get a washcloth for her.

Loki released a breath. It had gone better than expected.

Abby hadn't walked out of her apartment dressed like a fairy stripper.

She hadn't been accosted by hordes of drunken brothers at the clubhouse.

He'd fucked her hard and, most importantly, she'd accepted his ownership of her.

Life was starting to look up. He wasn't fool enough to assume everything would be smooth sailing. The beating, the miscarriage, and the weeks of spiritual and sexual separation had taken their toll, but at least they were back on the right track.

When he returned, Abby was sprawled facedown on her

bed. After taking care of her, he crawled over her, he trapped her inside his frame and pressed himself against her back. She let out a low moan, so he turned her pliable body over and arranged her against his chest.

Smoothing her glossy hair, he swept down to rub the handprint marks he'd left across her rear. She needed extra petting. Whereas adrenaline was surging through his blood, she required a stable presence to keep her tethered. The effort she'd made to cross the vast chasm and acknowledge his ownership would not go unrewarded.

"Abby," he murmured in her hair.

"Hmm..." she hummed.

"I'm dead serious about my promise to be by your side every day and night. Tomorrow, I'm moving my shit in here and we're gonna look for a new place."

She slanted her head to study his expression. He firmed his features into a stern look. Yeah, he was dead fucking serious.

She half rose in protest, but his hand urged her back down, and after a brief struggle, she collapsed against him.

"And I'm getting you an anal plug. To stretch you out."

Her nails dug into his forearm. "Umm, moving a little too fast, don't you think? You can't even talk about your brother to me but you wanna talk anal?"

"No," he practically bellowed, but tamped it down in time. "We lost almost a month of time together, time we need to make up for." He smirked. "Plus, your ass would've been stretched out enough to take me by now. As for my brother," his face turned serious, "I shouldn't have ripped your head off."

She harrumphed.

"I'm going to open up about it," he pledged. "Bring it up to me and I'll talk. I've let precious time waste away and realizing how easily you could be torn away from me scared me straight."

"I-I'm not sure I'm ready for"—she flicked her index finger between them—"whatever this is between us to move quickly."

Her eyes begged for understanding, but he wasn't going to allow her fears rule over them any longer. Been there, done that. It was a form of hell he had no plan of reliving.

"Too bad," he grumped out.

Her lips pressed together in a flat line.

Stroking the side of her face, he began, "I know I sound harsh—"

"That you do," she cut in.

"—but we've lost too much time. When I found out you lost the baby, it was a come to Jesus moment for me. Believe it or not, it was worse than when I found Chopper, and I never thought anything could compare. I was proven wrong. An image of you holding a baby boy with hair the same color as yours flashed before my eyes. For the first time, I understood the extent of what I had lost. I may not have known about the baby for as long as you did, but doesn't mean it wasn't real to me."

Soft whimpers crept out of Abby's throat and her eyes teared up.

"I'm not bringing this up to make you sad," he plowed on before he lost his nerve. "I want you to understand, I'm not giving up on you or the baby boy I saw in my vision. Baby boy, baby girl, I don't give a fuck. We could foster and adopt for all I care. What I do know, with every fiber of my being, is that I *will* have you and that baby in my arms. The sooner it happens, the sooner we'll be at peace. That's our future. Our destiny."

Abby had turned her face into his chest, clutched his

shoulder, and bawled into his bare skin. Her hot tears glistened, and his arms tightened around her. She reached over him, grabbed a tissue, and blew loudly. Scrambling to a sitting position, she scooted away from him.

Giving him big doll eyes, she confessed, "I don't know if I can do it again, Loki."

"You will," he replied resolutely, as he tucked her back to his side. "You need time. We need time together. I get it, it's too scary to get pregnant right away. We'll take some time, though not too much, I'm warning you, but enough for us to get our bearings."

"I appreciate you've thought this through, but what if I'm never ready?"

She extracted herself from his embrace, scooted her butt up until it hit the headboard and hugged her knees. "The GYN said there's nothing wrong with me physically, but I don't know if I can ever get pregnant again. The fear..." She swallowed and swiped at a falling tear. "The fear I won't be capable of bringing the baby to term haunts me. I have nightmares of miscarrying."

"You never told me," he murmured low, pain lancing him to the bone.

She sent him a wry smile. "We weren't exactly having heart-to-heart talks these past few weeks."

Loki took her hand and dropped a whisper of a kiss on the inside of her wrist. "I stand by what I said. If you don't want to get pregnant, then we'll foster or adopt. Whatever. There are children that need parents like us, and you being a social worker will outweigh the fact that I'm a biker. Not gonna coerce you to put your body through something you may never be ready for. You won't get any stress from my end. Chopper was adopted by Kingdom's mom and her extended family. My own family was worthless. I failed him, and I was his blood brother. It's not blood or genes that's going to determine what my family is made of."

Abby flung her arms around him and burst into another round of sobs.

"Pixie girl, don't be like this. You're breakin' my heart."

"The point is, I'm terrified by the prospect of my failure as a mother. I couldn't even keep a fetus safe in my womb," she sniffled.

"Oh, baby girl. That responsibility was mine, not yours. I'm the protector, whether you're pregnant or not. No one, and I mean no one, should've gotten close enough to my girl to touch a strand of her hair, much less brutalize her. Pregnancy is one small part of motherhood. If we ever have a kid, we'll probably become helicopter parents to make up for what happened."

Muffled against his pecs, she said, "I think I'm in love with you."

"Don't think it, sweetheart, know it. Honor it. 'Cause I'm pussy-whipped in love with you, and I wouldn't want it any other way."

36

LOKI

Loki was in his favorite position to date.

During non-fucking hours, that is.

Abby was wrapped in his arms as they watched the Giants whipping ass in one of their best games of the season. He'd moved in a few weeks ago, and all things considered, they were happier than ever. Once they'd stopped fighting, they fit together in ways he never would've expected.

"Have they been your favorite since you were little?" Abby asked, looking up at him expectantly.

"Fuck, yeah. Chopper and I were obsessed with the Giants when we were kids."

Chopper. His spirits sank, but this time he wasn't going to run from the conversation. He had his woman nestled against him, the fragrance of her shampoo teasing him, and it was no longer enticing to go down the same rabbit hole to the pits of hell. One conversation about Chopper wasn't going to fix him, but maybe it could staunch the bleeding and begin cleaning up the infection.

"I remember when I got the call about Chopper—I went fucking insane. I don't know what happened. I went into a rage so bad I blacked out. Next thing I knew, Cutter was throwing me into the cab of the truck, my arm in a sling. I'd broken my arm and he had to drive me to the hospital."

He paused and cleared his throat before continuing, "Chopper had been actin' cagey for weeks. Thinking back, I bet he had a prospect on duty to watch for me because each time I'd walk into the clubhouse, I'd get a text telling me he'd left minutes before. Knowing him, the bastard was slippin' out the back as I walked through the front door."

Loki's hand smoothed down the side of her throat before cupping the back. "Hard to say what was going on with him, but something was off. Figured Kingdom was on top of it. After all, Kingdom and he were tight as fuck since they were kids. I was always the older, distant brother."

He gave a derisive chuckle. "They both idiotically looked up to me, and I'd let them." His upper lip curled. "Thought Kingdom had it covered, like he and his moms had covered for my ass all those years ago. It was a fatal flaw, because Chopper was pulling the same shit on Kingdom as he was on me. My mistake was putting my faith in someone else to handle my job as his brother, as the father figure. Wiping my hands of my responsibility like the dumbass I was."

Abby turned to straddle him, grazing the sides of his face with her fingertips. Her finger ran down his scar. "It wasn't your fault. Of course you feel remorse, but he wasn't twelve anymore. He was an adult, and he'd made his own decisions. In the end, you would've never been able to stop him."

His fingers smoothed down the buttons of her shirt.

"I should've fostered a closer relationship with him. We were in the same club, for fuck's sake. I'd recently patched in, but he had seniority. Back together again after so many years and we were finally equals. You would've gotten along good with him. He was loyal, funny as hell, humble. Didn't have an arrogant bone in his body. Took after my mom that way. I took more after Crispin than anyone else," he concluded, with a bitter edge to his tone.

"Hush, that's not true," she rebuked gently.

"It *is* true," he insisted. "Especially with the rage issues. You once said I did right to leave him with Kingdom and his moms, but it was still a cold-blooded, heartless move. The average man would've fought tooth and nail to protect and raise their own brother. It was the Crispin in me, the cold-hearted callousness, that allowed me to do it."

"You're nothing like Crispin," she refuted, passionately. "As for comparing yourself to anyone else, you blame yourself for leaving, but your mother left, and you don't begrudge her for it."

"It's different. She would've been murdered by that bastard. She had no choice but leave."

"Assuming he didn't end up hurting you or Chopper physically, which is a big *if*, who says you wouldn't have died inside, every day you stayed trapped in that house with Crispin? Sometimes people do what they must to survive, Loki. Your life hadn't even begun yet, and you were skating by, surviving by the skin of your teeth. You had every right to seek out a better future for you and your brother. Was it pretty? No. It was dark. Really dark. But that doesn't mean Chopper's death is on you."

Abby laced her fingers behind his neck. "Yes, maybe you're right and you could've done more to get closer to him, but hindsight is twenty-twenty. You had no idea he had only a matter of months or weeks left in him. It's a myth to think a person with suicidal tendencies shows recognizable symptoms. You admitted, only after the fact, you recognized patterns of him actively avoiding you and Kingdom. Kingdom is a highly perceptive man, and if he suspected *anything*, he would've come to you immediately. Chopper hid very well. Do you know how I know this?"

Loki's heart stopped.

She canted her head to the side, looking at him knowingly, a tinge of sadness clinging to her.

"Don't—" His voice broke.

She pressed her lips to his, sweeping them back and forth gently, humming a little, as if to give him strength before she continued.

"I know because I went to a dark place after my mother died. I was thirteen years old and my brothers were getting drunk, acting out, desperate to escape the house. A year later, they were off to college and my father was lost in his own grief and depression. None of my friends understood. How could they? Sammi is the first person my age who lost a mother during middle school, like me. A few months after the funeral, everyone except my family had returned to normal and we were of no help to one another, existing in our separate bubbles. I wanted the never-ending pain to end and began researching different ways to die. I had no access to guns or pills, and I was too scared to cut myself, but I brooded over it for months..." she trailed off, creases forming on the edges of her downturned mouth.

"No one noticed?" he croaked out, his throat parched and painfully constricted. He swallowed hard.

Abby shook her head. "When I was seventeen, I got drunk with Liam during one of his weekend visits and confessed about that time in my life." She sighed. "Biggest mistake of my life. My brothers almost moved back in. Why do you think they're so protective?" She gave him a sly look. "Overcompensation."

He rasped out, "What happened? To get you out of it."

"Life happened. In my attempt to be the perfect daughter

and not be a burden to my father, I decided to fake being normal. I was on the varsity soccer team and got involved in theater. Showing up for practice and rehearsals, along with keeping up my grades, was a full-time job. Over time, the pain subsided. Eventually, not every moment felt like a mindless repetition of empty motions. I remember being in a movie theater with a friend and suddenly laughing at a joke an actor made on screen. A real belly laugh, you know the kind. It struck me if I had killed myself, I wouldn't be sitting there with my friend on a Saturday afternoon, laughing till I fell off my chair. At that moment, I was grateful I didn't kill myself. For whatever reason, Chopper hadn't reached the place where he could see past the all-consuming pain. Sometimes, it's the luck of the draw."

A shudder took hold of him. His hands framed the sides of her face. Frantic to taste her, he swept his tongue inside her mouth, and pressed her lush tits tight against his chest, feeling her steady heartbeat against his frenetic one.

Breaking off their kiss, she assured him, "It was a long time ago. I'm way over it now."

"Baby girl, you tear me up inside." He captured her lips again, kissed her soundly, and sucked at her bottom lip before releasing it with a pop.

"Promise me something, Loki?" she asked.

"Anything, Pixie."

"Promise me you'll stop whipping yourself over this and throw away the flogger. Allow yourself to live and love because I love you." She let out a half sob. "You deserve happiness. For me. For Chopper."

"For you and Chopper," he replied hoarsely, "I'll try."

His lips smashed down on hers.

37

ABBY

Abby knew something was wrong the instant she walked out of the Agency building and caught sight of Loki's stoic expression in the evening gloom. Waiting on his idling bike by the pavement, he twisted around to give her a deep kiss and place a helmet in her waiting hands.

Swinging her leg over his bike, she didn't hesitate to ask, "What's wrong?"

Quiet, Loki motioned for her to put her helmet on and settle into her seat. He zipped her jacket up to her neck and adjusted her collar. Facing forward, he gestured for her to wrap her arms around him.

Once her arms were linked securely around his waist, he shouted over the engine, "We'll talk at home."

The way he said *home* filtered through her soul and settled in her belly, wobbly-like. Good to know whatever was wrong had nothing to do with them as a couple. Anything else, she could handle. Loki revved up the motor and they flew down the avenue, the cooling wind whipping past her.

Inside the apartment, Loki tugged off his motorcycle

jacket, threw it over the couch, and stalked to the refrigerator. Wrenching the door open, he rummaged around and extracted two beers. Abby stood patiently in the small foyer, watching his every move, as she pulled off her gloves, one finger at a time.

He untwisted the bottle caps, threw them in the garbage, and came to her.

His lips grazed hers, and he whispered, "It's been a rough day."

"I can tell," she mused.

Abby dropped her gloves on the table by the entrance, and Loki placed the bottles on it to help her remove her jacket. Opening the closet door, she gestured for him to give her the jacket he'd left on the couch and she hung it up along with her own.

"Hungry?" he asked, handing her one of the beers.

She shook her head and, twining her fingers in his, led him to the couch. Sitting down beside her with a groan, he lifted the bottle to his lips and took a long sip. She followed the line of his profile as he swallowed. So sexy. Although it was finally cooler outside, Loki wore a fitted black T shirt under his cut. His and Chopper's military dog tags dangling over the defined ridges of his pecs. The cotton stretched tightly over his biceps, and her gaze lingered on his arm for a few moments before she forced herself to refocus.

Taking a sip from her bottle, she sucked on her lip to catch an errant drop.

Loki's eyes, at half-mast, paused on her lips, drinking her in.

Shaking her head to dispel her lust-filled thoughts, she said, "If I let this eye-fucking go on much longer, I know I'll end up in the bedroom. Come on, cough it up. What's going on?"

Loki expelled a long sigh and warned, "You're not going to like it."

Nervousness fluttered in her stomach. "You're scaring me. What is it?"

"We got intel on Shadow. He's in Brooklyn, in the City. I'm leaving tomorrow to go after him."

Abby sprang off the couch and began pacing between the low table and the TV. "Oh no, you're not. You're not going anywhere without me. I don't trust you."

He threw his hands up in a pleading gesture. "This is a biker's world, Abby. We may not be renegades, but we live by a code and that code says the fucker must pay for what he's done to you. It's nonnegotiable."

"It's toxic and I won't allow it," she retorted.

An eyebrow arched, and he mocked, "Won't allow it? You've used that word with me before. There's nothing for you to allow or disallow. You have no say in the matter."

Stopping in front of him, hands on hips, she shot back, "Oh, really?"

"Really," he ground out between clenched teeth.

Abby took in a deep breath and sat back down. "Okay, look, I understand something needs to be done to punish him and to prevent him from doing anything to us in the future—"

"He has no future," Loki interjected.

"—but I couldn't live with myself if anything happened to you. I can't have you implicated in a crime that will take you away from me."

"I won't be caught, but I *will* end him," he replied smugly.

"There's no way you can guarantee you won't get caught, or even worse, hurt!"

Abby grasped his hands and wrapped them around her icy fingers. "I can't live without you. I don't think I can handle another loss so soon after the attack. And you know my feelings about violence as a way of solving problems."

"I knew I shouldn't have told you," he griped, under his breath.

"As if you would've been able to keep me from finding out. I'd be furious if you vanished out of thin air."

Loki brought his hand to his brow. "I know, I know. Normally, I'd have taken care of it on my own, but I couldn't do that to you."

His eyes drifted away. "Even if I still think it's the best move," he grumbled under his breath.

She was touched by the effort he was making to include her, to accept her reaction to his plans.

"Thank you, Loki, for not shutting me out. I realize what a huge sacrifice you're making for me. I know you want to kill him, I mean, I hear it when you're mumbling in your sleep, but we can figure out another way to get to him."

"What other way? We have no proof that would stand up in court. I can't sleep at night knowing he's out there. You get that, right? After Chopper and the baby, I can't move forward until I know he's been finished off. I *need* you protected."

Abby slumped against him and he opened his arms to catch her. She crawled onto his lap and curled up in his arms, laying her head on his shoulder. Reaching out, she caressed his jaw, doing it as much to calm him as her racing heart. Perhaps if she hadn't grown up with the terrible twins, she wouldn't have such a high tolerance, but she understood where he was coming from. There was no denying his need to fulfill his role as protector. The problem was he was used to brute force. There had to be an alternative solution.

"We need to get footage of the attack as proof. And we need to contact Liam. It's been months and the Horsemen still haven't caught him. They need backup and he has connections with law enforcement in Brooklyn. With him in the fray, Shadow will get arrested. I know he'll do everything in his power to put him in Rikers for decades. No parole. No getting out."

"I don't think there's footage. That bastard was sneaky. He caught you in a part of the parking lot not covered by the outdoor security cameras."

"What about a neighboring building?" she suggested.

"The Box isn't located in a populated area, with nosy neighbors with Ring doorbells recording every damn thing that happens."

Abby sighed in frustration. "There are other businesses and every business has security cameras. Have you checked with them?"

"To be honest, no. I wasn't focused on getting Shadow through legal avenues. I was looking forward to a *very* personalized form of revenge," he pointed out wryly.

"Why don't we adjust our vision a little, from revenge to… oh…justice. Because I'm definitely down with justice. I love having you with me constantly, believe me, but I'd love to gain the freedom to do go where I want again."

Loki grunted. "Your days of freedom are over, Pixie. You're with a fucking biker, not a businessman. I'm possessive as fuck."

Abby giggled lightly. "Okay, some wiggle room then. Enough so I can go to a bar with the girls without having an escort. Is there nothing else? No other lead?"

Palming her breast, Loki seemed to consider that angle. "His club is pissed at Shadow for causing so much damn trouble. This could've turned into a bloodbath if the Horsemen hadn't been Greta's old club. Scudder took over as interim president and he's gung-ho on turning a new leaf. First, there was the reign of Scorpion, Greta's father, and he was a true cocksucker, that one. Then, Shadow took over and lost his damn mind when he went on a revenge rampage. He's confessed to a few of his brothers, but there's a strict code on snitching. I can't imagine the Horsemen working with law enforcement, but it's worth considering."

Abby thrust her breast deeper into his palm and he absently gave it a light pinch. A moan slipped out, catching his full attention. He slipped his hand beneath her shirt and twisted her aroused nipple. A thrill bolted down to her clit as if the two spots were joined by an electric current. Each end snapped like a live wire until he unclamped her peaked flesh.

Stradling him, she took advantage of her position to press her clit against his rock-hard cock beneath his jeans. Toying with the top button of her shirt, she teased it before slowly slipping it out of the buttonhole.

Abby popped each button open, and then spread her shirt open to reveal a new, pristine, see-through mesh bra, her hard nipples poking through. She grinned when Loki licked his lips. Her breasts felt heavy and quivery. She leaned forward and rubbed her peaked nipples against the rough cotton ribbing of his shirt. A little mew threatened to tumble out. God, the friction felt good.

His hand snaked in between their bodies, tugged at her skirt and tights, and found her wet center. He inserted a finger and she let out a muffled groan of complaint.

"Stand up," he ordered gruffly.

She struggled to her feet, almost face-planting to the floor, but he caught her by her elbow in time. Kicking off the rest of her garments, she stood completely bare in front of him. Fully dressed, he remained seated and simply splayed his legs open. It was arousing as hell, and she rubbed her thighs together as she waited for his next move. He leaned back and sat still for a moment, appreciating the sight of her naked and waiting for him.

Finally, he unbuckled his belt.

"Hurry up," she whined. He was going torturously slow on purpose. Her eyes bulged out as her gaze dropped to his hard cock wrapped in his stroking hand, his pace unhurried. She slipped her fingers down her torso and began fingering her clit. If he was going to tease her, then tit for tat it was, baby.

She heard a growl and then she was thrown down on the couch. Her cheek smashed against the thick weave of the bottom seat cushion.

With one hand on the back of her neck, he stroked two fingertips between her legs, a dark promise falling from his lips, "You're going to regret teasing me. I'm gonna smack that soaked pussy of yours." He slathered said juices on her clit, playing with it for a bit.

"LIFT your ass up and spread your legs open for me, beautiful," he commanded.

BEFORE SHE COULD SAY *BOO*, his hand smacked down on her pussy lips and clit. The shock reverberated through her. He knew what he was doing when he slicked up her clit, because the wetness added to the sensation. He swatted a few more times, the sound of wet flesh being smacked not one she'd forget anytime soon.

"SORRY FOR BEING A TEASE, LOKI—"

"You mean cocktease. Is that a nice thing to do, Pixie? Teasing your man?"

"No, no," she pleaded. "I'm sorry...j-just—" *Smack.* "Please, p-please— *Smack.* "Fuck meeee!" *Smack.* The last word came out more as a pathetic screech, but she didn't care. Gushing out, her juices painted the insides of her thighs

He let out a chuckle, low and ominous. "God, I love it when you beg. If you expect to come tonight, you better stay still," he said, in a stern tone.

She bit down on her cheek, adoring when he got bossy during sex. The more he let her in, the more he was coming into his own. His fingers disappeared, and she slapped her palm on the couch in frustration.

"Is that you staying still? I don't see you trying too hard," he chastised, a touch of humor in his tone.

Abby snapped her teeth at him. He was enjoying this a little too much. How was he showing such calmness while she felt like a writhing mess of nerve endings. Oh right, maybe because she just got her pussy slapped. The sound of Loki stripping off his cloths behind her increased her impatience and she shifted on her knees subtly with the pretense of positioning herself when she was wiggling her ass with the sole purpose of taunting him. His obsession with her butt was second only to her tits.

His hand curved around her bottom, letting it jiggle a little. She sighed at his touch. Then he brought his hand down in a hard spank that caught both cheeks.

Gasping, she jolted forward and arched her back. She could *feel* that intense gaze of his on her ass.

Soothing the burn away, he praised, "Look at that fine ass of yours."

He dipped his finger in her back hole and she had to consciously relax her backside for his probing finger. He'd been doing that more often lately. Another example of him coming into his own.

"So sexy, pushing those pink cheeks into my hand. I'm thinking this is your favorite position, Pixie. All in all, you end up on your belly more often than your back."

"Maybe it's because you like slapping my ass." she sassed back.

"Convenient 'cause you like getting this sweet ass slapped," he countered, emphasizing his point with a swat to her behind.

Her breasts had grown even more swollen with the anal play, and she rubbed them against the fabric to get friction on her tight, aching nipples.

Noticing, Loki ordered, "Play with your tits. My hands can't be everywhere."

She followed his order with a huffed, "Take me already!"

Loki chided her, "Now, now, patience. You wore that fuck-me bra all day, huh? Letting your heavy tits hang out. Hopefully, you weren't turned on during the day. Otherwise those dime-sized nipples of yours would've poked out for the goddamn world to see. You're lucky you work around women, otherwise I'd have to go down there and kick every man's ass who laid eyes on you. It'd be your fault some poor bastard's laid up in the hospital for staring at your fat tits."

She bit into the fabric of the couch. Her nails dug into the flesh around her nipples. Loki caught her ass in the clap of his hand three more times, giving her a slow rub between each smack. The heat billowed across her entire backside and drifted down to settle in her belly.

"Fuck this," Loki growled, yanking her hips up.

Her head snapped around in time to see his scarred hand slide up and down his thick shaft, leading it to stiffen further. His hand squeezed from base and tip, the tip oozing pre-come, which he used to lubricate his cock.

Her eyes rolled back. Grazing the crown of his cock at her

entrance, he punched his hips slightly forward between her clenching pussy, and she felt the stretch. She breathed out as the sweet scent of victory, of his come, was within her reach.

"Too damn sexy," he griped and then thrust in hard, bottoming out in one go. God, it was glorious having this man balls-deep inside her. He took on a rough pace from the start; his balls slapped her clit, his sculpted abs slammed against her scalded ass cheeks. Her thighs trembled, one knee slipped off the edge of the couch and hit the rug, but he didn't miss a beat, adjusting his posture to keep his pace.

The commanding manner he took, the silent way he demanded control of her body and pussy to do with what he wanted, ignited a bonfire in her. Her one purpose in life, at that moment, was to be bring him to the peak of pleasure.

"You're pussy's so wet, I can hear it sucking my cock. Hear that, Pixie?" he demanded, his voice strained with need.

She couldn't answer. She was too busy fighting to keep her orgasm at bay because she wanted to hang on just a little more.

"Eyes on me," he commanded. "I want to see you come."

He captured her jaw, and held it, his thrusts getting frantic. Their eyes interlocked. The harsh plane of his wide brow, his blunt cheekbones, stretched scar, and tight jaw pounded from iron showed he was about to crack. His breathing came out staggered, speeding up to keep pace with the pistoning of his steel shaft. She flew over the edge, thrashing from side to side, sweat gliding down her face as she twitched and jerked.

Triumphant, he ravaged her mouth with a blistering kiss. Her cunt milked him, and his pace became disjointed until he followed her with a low hiss and a violent jerk. Liquid heat spilled inside her, filled her up, and splashed down her inner thighs.

Abby collapsed, chest glued to the bottom cushion of the

couch, with Loki behind her. He enveloped her in his chest and arms as they caught their breaths.

"I can't sleep without you. I can't eat if I don't know you're safe." He rubbed his nose in her hair. "I'm fucking addicted to the scent of your hair."

She snorted. "How romantic. You can borrow my shampoo if you like."

"Fuck the shampoo. It's you. I'm hooked on *you*." Cupping her cheek, his expression grew serious and he swore, "I can't let anything happen to you."

"I know, babe," she conceded. "We'll be okay. I promise everything will work out."

She meant every word. Whatever happened, they'd work it out as long as they stayed strong. Together.

38

———

LOKI

Abby had been right about Shadow.

For the most part.

Loki should've never doubted her, and it was a lesson he'd taken to heart. Considering he didn't get the chance to choke the life out of Shadow, the story turned out better than he could've come up with on his own.

After decades of turmoil within their club and bad press among the MCs of the northeastern corridor, the Dark Horsemen were done with Shadow. Scudder finally convinced the few holdouts who were still loyal to flip and they got the deets on where Shadow was hiding out.

Unfortunately, the shifty bastard kept moving around the outer boroughs of New York City before a certain badass DA came to the rescue. No lie, it had been an ugly, stressful time for Loki. A desperate man was a dangerous man, and Loki was terrorized by nightmares of Abby getting attacked. In the end, Shadow had been too hounded to find his way back upstate to do any further harm to Abby or the Squad.

Cutter had finally convinced Scudder to collaborate with Liam, and eventually, it was Liam who caught Shadow. When word came down they were closing in on him, the brothers voted for Cutter to go down in Loki's stead.

At the last minute, thank fuck, Abby allowed Loki to go ahead with Cutter. The bastard was getting locked away, not killed. It was a huge sacrifice on his part because he'd gone to bat for her at Church, arguing it would damage Abby's mental state of mind. In the end, the brothers agreed. Shadow was to remain alive, but the Squad still had to make an example of him. Abby had tried talking to Kingdom, with Loki present of course, but there was no getting him to budge. As Loki had told her, she'd given it her best shot and had already achieved something unprecedented.

He and Cutter got to the Bronx in the nick of time. Guarding the abandoned warehouse where he'd caught Shadow, Liam allowed them access. The fact Liam was there to cover for them had been another big reason for Abby's acquiescence. They were guaranteed thirty uninterrupted minutes to mete out Shadow's punishment before the precinct cruise car came swinging by.

More than enough time for them to exact a healthy dose of vengeance.

Once inside, Loki's gaze landed on Shadow, lying on the floor, manacled to an old radiator. The man looked rough, to be sure, after months on the run.

His blood ran cold. Finally, fucking finally. The bastard who'd beaten up his woman. Killed his kid. In his hands, in his merciless hands.

Loki wasted no time waling into Shadow, who threw his feet up in hopes of protecting himself. Cutter joined in and held Shadow's legs down so Loki could get in as many punches as possible within their allotted time frame. He got to hear Shadow's screams, crying like the little bitch he was. Got to hear the crunch of bone when his face got smashed in.

Blood splattered across Loki's face and Loki grinned through it all, the smell and sight of blood driving him on.

Between punches and kicks, Loki gave him a detailed itinerary of what would happen to him if he ever got close to the Squad again and ended with a promise, "Motherfucker!" *Left hook.* "I will decimate you." *Right hook.* "If you come at me and mine again." *Front kick.*

The last kick knocked him out and Cutter's ugly mug drifted in front of him, grinning like the Joker.

"Satisfied?" he said with a smirk.

Shadow moaned and came back to consciousness in time for Cutter to taunt him. "Nice bruises, asswipe," as he poked and jabbed at the purple blooming across his face.

Sirens screamed in the background and Cutter smacked him in the chest. "Time to go, brother."

They ducked out a back exit, jumped a chain link fence and whistled their way to where their bikes were parked. Waving a good-bye to Liam from a distance, they hopped on.

"Been a while since we've done this, brother. It was dope, right?" Cutter gloated smugly as he started up his bike.

It was a Sunday afternoon so they were back in Poughkeepsie in under ninety minutes. He waved to Cutter as he took the turn towards the new place he and Abby moved into. He walked through the front door and on cue, Abby wandered from the bedroom and checked out his body for any injuries. Stripping off his cut, she dragged him back to the bedroom and pushed him down on the bed. He scooted up until his head hit the headboard. Crawling up and over him on all fours until he was framed by her arms and thighs.

Bending low, her chest rubbed against his and, tilting her head to the side, declared, "You have a guilty expression on your face. What did you do?"

"I'm satisfied with how it turned out," he replied evasively.

Abby snorted. "Satisfied? I know you, Loki. You may have followed the vow you gave me to the letter, but not half an inch more," she teased. "I'm assuming he's alive. Beyond that, I'm not holding my breath."

Loki put his hands out in surrender and then dropped them to her waist with a smirk on his lips. "Guilty as charged."

His cell phone rang. Checking caller ID, he saw it was Liam and put him on speakerphone. "Hey Liam, Abby's here with me so keep it rated PG."

"Hey, Abby," rang out Liam's deep voice.

"Liam," she replied with a warning tone in her voice. "What are you doing right now?"

"I'm making sure that son of a bitch gets what he deserves."

Abby released a long, belabored sigh. "Aren't you an officer of the law?"

"Fuck yeah, I am," he replied, "and I'm doing justice. That was the oath I took and it's the one I'm fulfilling."

"Within the bounds of the law?"

"Abby, get off my fucking case. If you thought for a hot second I wasn't going to be all over this from beginning to end, then you have no idea who your big brother is. I may not be as overbearing as my twin but, considering he currently lives outside of the States, it's on me to guarantee everything's taken care of. Plus, the bastard's riding my ass, and he's so much more violent than I am, so I don't need any added grief from you."

Straddled over Loki's prone body, she crossed her arms over her chest and huffed out, "Fine."

"Hey, why does he get a pass?" Loki groused. "I bet Liam got a punch in."

Abby leaned over the phone and asked, "Liam, did you get a punch in?"

Liam's voice came back smugly, "My boot may have connected with a certain part of his anatomy."

"Liam, how could you?" she cried out as Loki interjected, "See, told you."

"Is he in police custody right now?"

"Yes, the bastard's gone."

Loki grumbled, "Still don't see how he gets away with it and I don't."

She replied, "Because I can't manipulate him the way I can you. He's like Teflon when it comes to me and he's my big brother, that's why. But if he keeps it up I'm going to call his wife and plot out my own revenge with her. Bwahahaha!"

Abby steepled her fingertips and tapped them together like an evil villain. "She's always down for torturing him."

"Oh, for Pete's sake, leave Steph out of this already," cut in Liam's voice. "Anyway, got off a call with the Bronx DA and it'll be discreet, but I will be directly involved in Shadow's case. The fucker's going to spend a long-ass time at Rikers. Shunned by every club in the area, he won't have any brothers to back him up in prison either. It's going to be a bad, bad time for him."

"It'll be a miracle if he lives to see the end of his sentence," commented Loki.

"I'll make sure he doesn't have a shot in hell at parole," added Liam. "Thank you, Loki for bringing me into this and letting me take care of it. I promise. I won't make you regret following my sister's lead. She's too soft for her own good—"

"Hey, that's not nice!" interrupted Abby. Liam continued talking over her, "Anyway, I want you to know that I'm on it and that bastard will never harm her again. You can sleep in peace at night. That's my oath to you."

"Thank you, brother," Loki replied. "I'm lucky to be considered part of your family. I know you're part of mine."

"You've done well by her." After a beat, Liam added, "But, I'll still kick your ass if you hurt her in any way."

"Not gonna happen," Loki intoned.

His hands swept up Abby's flanks and cupped her heavy tits.

"Never," he swore again.

She bit into her bottom lip and undulated her hips as he flicked her nipples. He didn't allow Abby to wear a bra when they were at home so unbuttoning her shirt immediately got him hard.

"Time to go and celebrate this victory with my woman," he said distractingly. "She owes me for the sacrifice I made on her behalf."

Abby was nodding furiously as she batted his hands away to quickly strip off her shirt.

Liam groaned. "I do not want to hear that shit. Alright kids, I'm getting off the phone," and he hung up.

Chest rising and falling quickly, Abby declared, "Yes, baby, you definitely deserve a reward. What will it be? My mouth? Or I can get on my hands and knees."

Loki chuckled low. "You'll find out soon enough, pixie girl, but I can guarantee you'll be screaming my name very, very soon."

EPILOGUE
LOKI

A spontaneous party was brewing at the clubhouse, and Loki had Abby propped on his lap as he fed her munchies.

Her appetite was off the charts. His hand drifted over Abby's tits and skated over her ribs to settle on her round belly. She was five months pregnant, and not one day passed when he didn't send up a prayer of thanks for his old lady.

They decided the next one would be an adoption. Loki's luck had turned when he met her, and life had only gotten better from that moment on. After much pressure and implementing an organized line of seduction, he'd finally convinced her to buy a condo together.

Who would've thought he'd be insisting on marrying her, tolerating her eye rolls and hippie arguments about how "love was enough." She didn't want a big fanfare, although he suspected a tiny part of her feared the abundance, something he was doing his best to break her of. Since her pregnancy, she'd been understandably nervous. Worked for him, because she didn't fight any of his overprotectiveness, which even he was ready to admit was over-the-top.

It had been his mistake for waiting, assuming every woman was dying for a ring.

Apparently, not his woman. But he'd made it clear there was no way she was checking into the maternity ward with "single" on the admission papers. Not that there was a problem with that, but what could he say? He was a possessive motherfucker. She *would* be his wife before the baby came. It only made sense since she was already his partner in every way.

The front door cracked open, and Puck sauntered in. Plopping down beside Abby on the leather sofa, he matched Loki's bared teeth with a huge grin. The fucker was up to no good. He wouldn't have a big-ass grin on his face, otherwise.

Taking hold of a flyaway strand of Abby's hair, Puck said, "I don't know, but if I had a bitch like her, she'd already be wearin' my ring. A property jacket wouldn't cut it. Then again, we know what a cheap bastard you are."

Loki slapped Puck's hand off his woman's hair and bristled, "That's bullshit and you know it. I'm taking care of it."

A brow arched high. "Sure about that?"

Loki rubbed Abby's belly, which she promptly swatted away, but he simply placed it right back where it belonged.

She let out a tired sigh and let it go.

Smart girl.

Leaning forward to nuzzle Abby's hair, he murmured, "Pretty sure this baby's mine."

"Is it gonna have your name?" Puck piped up.

"Yes, you cocksucking asshole," he snarled at his brother. "Either say something useful or get the hell outta here."

Abby's belly trembled in laughter underneath his fingers. Man, Puck was more irritating than Cutter. At least Cutter had a motive for starting a conversation. Puck, on the other hand, popped out of nowhere just to fuck with a person.

"You're lucky you're making my woman laugh, or else..." he sniped.

"Hey, I'm saying out loud what everyone in this club is thinking. Sammi was goin' on about you at the breakfast table. Talk like that can cut a man's appetite, you know."

Puck gave him the stink eye, as if Loki were personally responsible for ruining his meal. As if Sammi wasn't a straight-up pain in the ass on her own.

The noise in the clubhouse had died and Loki lifted his head to find the brothers and bitches had paused their conversations to eavesdrop on Puck berating him.

Glaring at each of them, he asked, "Are you fucking serious?"

Jabbing a thumb toward Abby, he said, "You think it's me? Taking it slow and not committing to this woman? Anyways, you're bikers. Since when do you care about the institution of marriage?"

"We don't," crooned Kerri, sitting cross-legged over her bar stool. "But it's kind of a thing since Sage got married and Greta's marriage is coming up. With a baby on the way, we *assumed* you'd have locked it down by now."

Christ, shit was bad if Kerri was chiming in with her opinion.

"Our bad," Puck jeered from the couch.

Crunching his jaw together, Loki leaned back and whipped out a black box he'd been carrying around for weeks, waiting for the opportune time to ask her.

"No better time than the present," he muttered.

Setting Abby off his lap, he took a knee and popped open the box to reveal a pear-cut Mandarin garnet ring that matched her eyes. She'd already given him a lecture about the boringness and unnecessary expense of diamonds. More hippie shit. Thank fuck she'd never find out how much he'd spent on her vintage ring.

Abby's eyes turned round as saucers. A hand lifted to cover her half-open mouth.

"It's beautiful," she gasped. Then, her eyes ticked up to his. "You shouldn't have done this, Loki. Really."

"Shouldn't? I don't think so," he chuckled. "Been a long time coming, Abby, and it's time you woman up and become my wife."

Peals of laughter escaped as she cannonballed into him. His arm shot out behind him to steady himself on the ground and the other wrapped around her waist, balancing his bouncing pixie on his knee.

"Is that a yes, baby girl?"

Peppering him with kisses, she rushed out, "Yes, yes, yes."

The clubhouse exploded with applause, brothers and bitches alike descending upon them as Loki placed the ring on Abby's finger.

Whispering low for her ears only, he said, "You've made me a man, Abby, and I will do everything in my power to make you and our babies happy."

Her hands tangled into his hair and his lips found hers. After sharing a breathless kiss, he released her to be engulfed by the other women. Sammi exploded through the door moments later with a loud whooping screech before pouncing on Abby.

He smiled down at his woman, engulfed by his people.

Taking a celebration shot offered to him by Puck, Loki said to him, "You texted her didn't you?"

"Yep. Seeing the look of fury on your face after I messed with you, I told her to hurry up 'cause you were about to propose. She missed it, but don't worry," he held up his cell phone, "I recorded every second of your pathetic proposal. Woman up? Are you for real? I don't plan on fucking one woman my entire life, but if I ever propose, I'd do a hell of a lot better than the shit you spouted off."

"You don't have it in you to make a woman happy for her entire life so don't go hurting yourself trying. For the record, I feel bad for the man who proposes to Sammi."

Puck exploded in a laugh. "Sammi, married? You fuckin' kidding me, right?"

"What? Look at her," Loki said, waving his hand toward Sammi, who was cry-hugging Abby.

"She's happy for her friend, is all," Puck scoffed.

"Mmm-hmm." Loki left it at that. He wasn't about to argue with Puck on the happiest day of his life. Throwing the shot to the back of his throat, he handed Puck the empty shot glass and shouldered his way into the crowd of bitches that walled off his pregnant pixie from his view.

Wrapping an arm around her waist, he dragged her out of the clubhouse.

The sun was setting on a hot August day and he had plans to take her to the waterfalls. Watch her beautifully curved belly as she dipped into the pool of water. The orange glimmers of her engagement ring winking in the sunlight, rivaling the beauty of her sparkling golden eyes.

"Where are we going?" Abby queried as he hustled her into his truck. He'd enforced a "no more bike riding" rule until after the baby.

"The waterfalls."

Fist pumping the air, she let out a "Yes!"

Late-afternoon sunlight beamed into the truck and he rounded it in a hurry to turn on the motor and bring the windows down. Behind the wheel, with the gentle breeze airing out the August heat from the cab of the truck, he turned to her and she flashed him a smile.

"I feel like I'm living a dream. Pinch me and tell me it's real, Loki."

Cupping her nape, he plunged his tongue between her lips and took a good long taste. "It's as real as it gets, pixie girl."

"Chopper would be happy for us, don't you think?"

"Yes, baby, he sure would. He'd be bustin' my balls about how I didn't deserve you, and how good your tits look pregnant."

He gave her a huge grin. Only Abby would make certain to include Chopper on this day. If Loki had a hard day, he trusted her enough to tell her and let her catch him if he fell. But, he didn't need catching anymore. A monumental moment like this one, though plainly bittersweet, didn't lead him to a dark place any longer. Abby had a gift for gently weaving Chopper's memory into the fabric of their lives.

"The baby's going to be either a Gerard or a Geraldine," she said, matter-of-factly. "Gerry for short."

Chopper's birth name.

He nodded, unable to speak with the lump in his throat. He'd long concluded it was simple, inexplicable luck. What other explanation could there be for the life he'd received? He'd neglected his brother since he was a kid, lashed out for years, and turned away the woman he loved to be harmed by a vengeful asshole. Despite it all, Abby had delivered him from hell. She was a prize he'd spend the rest of his life striving to deserve.

Pulling out into the road, Loki swallowed the lump in his throat and rumbled, "Just when I think I can't love you more, you go and slay me again. I can't live without you and I don't wanna try."

Her hand glided over his and he clasped it tightly.

· · ·

THANK you for reading Loki's Luck! I hope you loved meeting Loki and Abby. The next book in the Demon Squad MC series is Sammi and Stanton's (Sage's ex-fiancé) story, Stanton's Sins.

A BIKER PRINCESS.

A broken billionaire.

Will his sins come back to haunt them?

THE DARLING little sister of the Demon Squad MC, Sammi loved everything about growing up in the club, including her infuriating older brother Puck. She'd do anything for Puck. After he gets arrested, she marches into the courtroom to give him a piece of her mind and marches out with the prosecutor's full attention.

CLICK HERE TO READ STANTON'S SINS >>

WANT A TASTE NOW?

STANTON STOOD inside the double doors of the entrance to the rehab center, tugging at the collar of his button-down shirt and adjusting his tie. Normally he'd have worn something more casual, but his mother was arriving any moment. Since he hadn't exactly been in a position to drive himself to Tully Drug Rehab a month ago, she insisted on driving up to retrieve him. Or, rather, being driven there. In the family limo, that is. One of the reasons he'd chosen this place was that it had a name among professionals and law enforcement, of which he was both. A close second was its reputation for privacy and seclusion. If he was going to do this thing, he needed to be as far from Poughkeepsie and his father as possible. Not that his father would have visited. The very thought of him and his accompanying barrage of recriminations would've been distracting, to say the least.

But there was no getting around the fact that he was an addict. Not some guy with a little cocaine problem. Not a guy who partied too much or had a bit of a control issue. Nah. He was a fucking addict, through and through. Stanton twisted the family signet ring on his finger as he peered through the frosted glass pane of the front door. He drew his cashmere coat collar up to cover his neck from a brisk draft coming from the entranceway. An addict who wouldn't snuff white powder up his nose again is who he was now. After four weeks in this place, and the hard work he'd put in, he had no intention of backpedaling and ending right back where he started. Not. Fucking. Happening. If for no other reason than that he didn't have it in him to take a month off work again. Being a high-powered, respected prosecutor did not allow for that kind of lapse of time. He shuddered to think of the state of his files when he got back to the office tomorrow.

Besides work, the thing he missed the most was the lack of fucking. Thank Christ he was back at court tomorrow. Hopefully, he wouldn't have too much trouble finding a soft woman he could sink his cock into real soon. His sponsor, who was about as much of an asshole as Stanton, did make one stipulation. Find a new woman. Cut off the old ones because they were potential triggers. Which meant no speed-dial party girls. Gregory made him delete every last female contact on his speed-dial list. Brutal. Unfortunately, that didn't include Melanie, the one he most wanted off his phone. He'd taken her off the cheat list during his miserable attempt at monogamy. He sighed inwardly. What a clusterfuck that had been. Old family friend turned other woman turned jilted fiancée. He'd have to make amends to her at some point in the future. It was a one-day-at-a-time program, so he didn't need to dwell on that hellhole right this moment. Or so Gregory told him when his thoughts tumbled down the rabbit hole. His sponsor was a man who'd been through exactly what he had been through and was willing to waste his time with Stanton to bolster his own recovery. Go figure. He never thought that was how shit would go down. For Stanton, sacrifice was sacrifice, without expectation of anything coming his way. Not approval. Certainly not an ounce of relief.

A limo rolled up to the curved driveway. He checked his Piaget watch. Just on time. Waving goodbye to the receptionist, he stepped out the door, towing his Rimowa rolling baggage.

Anthony hurried out of the limo, rubbing his gloved hands together as he walked around to open the back door of the limo for him. "Welcome home, Mr. Prescott," he greeted as he stood at attention in the frigid air of January in Upstate New York.

Nodding to the older man, he replied, "Thank you, Anthony. It's good to be out." *That's the truth, the whole truth, and nothing but the truth.*

Handing Anthony his baggage, Stanton slid into the seat beside his mother and placed a kiss on her right cheek. She squeezed his hand, giving him a quick but thorough once-over. "How are you doing, darling? You look well."

"Much improved from the last time you saw me, I'm sure," he said, squeezing her hand back.

"Now, now. Don't be so hard on yourself."

"Oh, Mother, only you would say that. You found me plastered in my own vomit, shielding Amy from getting a good look at me while calling nine-one-one. I think we're past suggesting that I was anything but a fucking mess."

"I see they didn't get you to stop cursing," she reproved mildly.

His mother. Always working to better others. She was tenacious that way. Never gave up. Certainly didn't give up on his father after Jax's death, and God knows he wouldn't have given the bastard a second chance. Then again, cast in his father's image, Stanton shouldn't be one to talk.

"You know your father can't handle anything *irregular*. It is the only reason he didn't come with me today," his mother said. *Yeah, right. Excuses, excuses.*

"For an alcoholic—"

"Former alcoholic," his mother interjected.

"There's no such thing, Mother. One of the many things I learned back there." He jutted a thumb in the direction of Tully.

His mother turned her face and gazed out the tinted window as the car started. "He stopped drinking quite a long time ago. That's past history."

If only past history stayed in the past. "He never stopped raging," Stanton threw back. "Or controlling everything." He expelled a weary breath. This was an old argument and he should know better than to go down this dog-eared, worn-out path. But dammit, he'd spent the past four weeks dredging up family ghosts. Outside of detoxing, which was *the* ultimate kick in the balls, he was done with burying shit or circumventing issues.

His mom turned back from the window, and her startling cornflower blue eyes locked on him. "In any case, I'm glad you're better and that you're home. I'll do whatever's necessary for you to remain clean. Anything," she vowed. He grasped her hand again and she weaved her fingers tightly between his. If nothing else, Marie Bethany Prescott, née Astor, was a good woman who'd go to any lengths to keep her family together.

Convincing his mother that he was better off going home and preparing himself for court tomorrow instead of swinging by his familial birthplace to see his father hadn't been as difficult as Stanton had expected. Marie had probably been too afraid to push, but he'd be damned if he wasted tonight on his father. He dropped the perfunctory kiss on his mother's cheek and exited the limousine. There was next Sunday brunch to serve as catch-up on his session of torture. Waiting for the elevator, he heard a *ping* and checked his cell phone.

AMY: What's up? Sorry I wasn't there to pick you up with Mom.

Yeah, right, like I'd put her through that for my ass.

STANTON: Stop apologizing. I specifically told you not to come. I wouldn't subject you to 4 hours in a car with Mom. 2 hours is one thing. 4 hours is to be avoided.

AMY: [Laughing crying emoji] You're my hero. [Winking kissing emoji]

STANTON: Always got your back, little sis.

AMY: How'd it go?

STANTON: Manageable. It wasn't bad.

AMY: I'll be there for Sunday brunch to act as buffer.

STANTON: I don't need you to do shit for me. I protect you, remember?

AMY: I like to help.

STANTON: Don't need you here. Take care of your life in the City.

AMY: You big brother. Grunt. Pound chest. Me little sister. [Winking emoji]

STANTON: Now you got it.

Stanton walked out of the elevator and down the hallway.

He'd put in the effort to develop a different relationship with his sister, but the *you scratch my back, I scratch yours* way of life was ingrained in them so young, he routinely had to remind her of the difference in their roles.

AMY: You're so protective! The best big brother a girl could have. You're going to make a great father one day. [Winking kissing emoji]

STANTON: Yeah, not going to happen. Ever. Hope you find someone soon to fill Mom's need for grandchildren.

AMY: Ugh. Whatever. I miss you, asshole.

STANTON: Can't wait to see you either.

IF YOU LOVED my biker series, you'll love my steamy mafia series, the Lupu Chronicles. Start this new series now with The Chosen Heir.

GET YOUR CHOSEN HEIR NOW>>

HERE'S A SNEAK PEEK...

"FUCKING HELL," I gritted out as I read the text over my grandmother's shoulder. Tasa was safe and she begged us not to look for her. *Really, Tasa?* As if I'd leave my baby sister to hang out to dry, regardless of whether she'd run away from home or not. Oh, and had she conveniently forgotten about her fiancé, Cristo? And what part of the term "dangerous enemies" had not penetrated her thick skull, despite my relentless repetition of that threat?

Bunică gave a nonchalant shrug of her skinny shoulders and a grin that showed off her gold tooth. That woman could get her teeth fixed a thousand times over, but she wasn't one to put on airs. As she always said, "I was born a peasant girl, and I'll die a peasant girl."

Peasant girl, my ass. She was as sharp as they came, and while she loved to ham it up with her country ways, she'd graduated from Romania's finest medical school. No lie, she could dig out a bullet and sew up the wound in under half an hour. It had come in handy on more than one occasion, when the doctor on our payroll didn't arrive quickly enough.

"What is she thinking?" I spat out. "She's roaming the country doing God knows what. No protection, no bodyguard, no—"

"Oh, hush, you act as if Tasa's an invalid instead of a smart young woman who can take on the world with one hand tied behind her back. She'll be fine. And you best leave her alone," she warned, poking at my chest with her bony finger.

I stared down at her, incredulous. Leave my sister to roam the country unprotected? *Is she insane?*

"Christ, *Bunică*, she's a female. Alone."

My eyes rolled up to the kitchen ceiling, seeking patience, as I took a seat on one of the stools scattered around the island in the kitchen of our family home. This was where *Bunică* practically lived so this was where family members came to talk to her. Was I the only rational one in this conversation? It wasn't like she didn't know who we were. It's not like she wasn't acutely aware that our enemies would start crawling out of the woodwork to kidnap Tasa.

"A *lone* female," I reiterated, emphasizing the word "lone" in hopes of getting through to my grandmother. "Of the *Lupu* clan." My gaze passed over the midnight-blue double oven range my father had imported directly from Italy when he busted out the back wall and extended the kitchen to please his mother and wife. The chrome from the state-of-the-art appliances gleamed under the bronze farmhouse lights.

We are the Lupus, the Romanian upstarts who quickly rose to the top of the New York City mafias. The speed of our rise was a point of embarrassment for the Bratva, the Russian mafia, and the main reason why they're so intent on destroying us. As for the Italians, they were a shadow of what they were before the takedowns and trials of the '90s. Which had left a vacuum for my father to fill when he arrived in New York, solidifying our foothold in Sunnyside, Queens. Better known now as "Little Bucharest."

Returning my attention to *Bunică*, I reminded her, "Enemies? Remember them? Why do I need to mention this? It's not like you don't know what I'm talking about. She's in real danger."

She let out a cackle as she whipped out a bottle of *palincă*, a traditional Romanian spirit from the region she came from. Plunking down two small glasses, she poured two shots and pushed one over the kitchen island to me. The other, she threw back like a pro.

"What's obvious to everyone but you and your mother is that Tasa is her own woman. She's smart, and she's not going to get caught by some two-bit *mafie* idiot. She'll be fine."

I narrowed my eyes at her. She was too relaxed by far, considering her youngest grandchild had just run off to god-knows-where.

"What do you know?" I demanded.

Fluttering her wrinkled hand weakly in front of her chest, she lied without a shred of remorse, "Who? Little old me? Why, nothing!"

"You're as deceitful as the day is long," I snapped, my patience finally fraying.

"Back off," she warned, her innocent features turning dark. *Ah, there's the real* Bunică. "I don't happen to know anything, but if I did, you bet your last dollar I wouldn't tell you. I won't help you drag her back here and keep her prisoner until she marries that worthless tâmpit, Cristo. *Uck.* He's barely a man. And he has a little two-bit hussy of a side piece. Each of you must marry in the *familie*, but why him? *Bah!*"

"You're unbelievable, you know that, right? Come on, out with it," I insisted, flicking the fingers of my open hand at her.

"Like I said, my lips are sealed." She made a gesture as if locking her lips together and flinging away an imaginary key.

My jaw clenched. Women. The bane of my existence. And those two stuck together like super glue. It was hopeless on my part to try to sever the unbreakable.

"Fine, then," I replied, releasing a long, exhausted breath. "You're not the only person I can press for information."

Her hand nabbed the sleeve of my jacket, crushing the fine wool between her bony fingers. "Leave that poor girl alone. You know she's in love with you. Don't you dare take advantage of her."

My grandmother was talking about Tasa's little best friend, the beautiful, supple Nina, of course.

Nina.

Damn, that girl. Smelled like jasmine and a hard fuck waiting to happen. Just the thought of her brought crackling heat to my skin and a stiffness to my cock. That woman was my Achilles' heel, if ever there was one. Sweet as could be, with large brown eyes and a chest I could face-plant in and suck on for days on end. Annnd...

And she's also like a sister to you, asshole.

Not.

There wasn't a shred of brotherly feelings toward that little minx. Unless one included the taboo kind.

Laying my forearms heavily on the smooth wood of the kitchen island, I warned, "*Bunică*, it's Tasa we're talking about here. My little *sister*. For some insane reason, you don't think she's in jeopardy, but I happen to know exactly what our enemies are capable of. I know exactly what they do during a torture session. Once it's out that she's gone, finding her and using her to get to us will be at the top of their list. This is like a nuclear arms race, during the Cold War." I tapped the watch around my wrist. "Time is ticking, and I can assure you that this won't finish well. Least of all for Tasa. Who's going to want to marry her if she's tarnished? Think about that and come talk to me when you've regained your common sense."

"*Băiețel*, don't speak to your *Bunică* like that. I wiped your bottom when you couldn't even feed yourself. Any man should be grateful for the chance to marry my little girl."

I snorted out an exasperated sigh. I hated it when she called me *little boy*. Deciding it was in my best interest to pretend I didn't hear her last comment, I bent down low and dropped a kiss on the crown of her head. "Do you think I enjoy this? Do you think I enjoy having to lay down the law and act like an enforcer with the people I love?"

"You *do* enjoy it," she shot back. "You always think you're right. In that way, you take after your father. Regardless of what everyone in this family thinks, he wasn't a saint, you know. He was human, and he made his fair share of mistakes."

Yeah, right. She always said that, but it was never quite believable. The man was a brilliant businessman and strategist. He loved his family and was the paradigm of how to behave in our twisted world. He was honorable to his core. If I could live up to half of the man he'd been, I'd die content. Which brought me back to the issue at hand: Tasa's marriage.

"I've been negotiating with Nelu on this marriage contract between Tasa and Cristo for *years*. It's more than a simple wedding, as you well know. What's going to happen when he finds out his future daughter-in-law ran away? It will be perceived as a stain on his honor. It could legitimately lead to war when we've only just begun our truce. Not only is business booming, but Tata would be disappointed in me. I gave him my oath that I would do everything in my power to make this happen. There's too much on the line," I finished with a frown.

The responsibility of taking care of my family fell heavily on my shoulders, but on days like today, the weight was crushing. Although *Bunică* was whip smart, the truth was she couldn't relate. She'd always been taken care of. First by my grandfather, then my father, and now me. She could afford to focus solely on the personal, not the big picture. No, that fell on me.

"Pfft. And so you had to sell Tasa to do this? Of all people, you chose to sacrifice your little sister?" Reproval shimmered in her eyes at me.

"*Tata* would've commended me for it. *He* would've thought it was a brilliant move. With the Popescus, Tasa will be taken care of. She'll be protected. And it would solidify a peace that's eluded our families for decades."

Bunică stared at me like she was about to spit on the ground. "Don't make it seem like you're doing this for Tasa, Alex. It's beneath you to lie."

"I *am* doing it for her," I ground out, fists balling at my sides. Christ, this old woman was never satisfied. She was spoiling the girl with notions of love. Our life was based on duty and, for women, that included the duty to marry a man chosen by her family. As the boss or *șef* of this family, I might be given a leeway regarding this rule. But for a princess of marriageable age like Tasa, it was unthinkable.

"She's the baby of the family. The Popescus, curse their name, are worthless mongrels. Animals. Unlike the Lupu clan, they didn't gain power until the fall of Communism. That's a blink of an eye in the span of history, and you sold your precious sister to those heathens?"

I snorted. "They're powerful enough now; I can tell you that much. We can look down on the Popescu clan all we want, but only a fool would underestimate their potential to do damage. They're *vicious*. Ruthless. You know this as well as anyone." It was also common knowledge that their tempers were like hair triggers. One wrong move and *kapow*. I made a dismissive wave. "In any case, it's done. My hands are tied. There's nothing I can do but retrieve her and make sure her marriage goes off without a hitch."

She stalked up to me. Barely five feet tall, she went toe to toe with me and spat out, "Then, you will get no help from me. I will do everything in my power to thwart you. The marriage be damned."

"You're impossible," I heaved out, throwing up my hands. "You know the situation."

When Tata was bleeding out in the ambulance roaring through the quiet streets, his dying wish had been for me to take care of the family. I'd already failed on that promise, with Tasa stranded somewhere out there, alone and vulnerable. Possibly hurt. My back teeth ground together at that last possibility.

The second oath had been to reconcile our family with the lowbred Popescus. I didn't disagree with *Bunică* that every one of them was a bottom-feeder. No education, no class, no nothing. Violence was their greatest attribute. The two families had been at each other's throats for generations, clawing their way to the top by throat-punching the other. We may be at the pinnacle, but they came in at a close second.

Nelu, their *şef*, and Tata were always vying to be the top dog. Tata often said that it was too late for their generation, that there was too much bad blood. But at his death bed, he declared, "There needs to be a marriage. It's the only way." Those last words were the proverbial nails in my coffin.

"Go back to your fancy apartment in Columbus Circle, Alex. I don't want you under my roof until you come to your senses."

Goddamn, this woman was impossible. She refused to acknowledge the possibility of a looming war. Instead, she was banishing me to the penthouse floors of the two towers of the Time Warner Center building in Manhattan, where my brothers and I lived.

Tasa had moved in with Nina a few avenues over, in a nice high-rise building overlooking the Hudson. Of course, Tasa, always with the rebellious streak, couldn't share an apartment with her twin, Nicu. Oh no, our building was too snooty and fancy for her. And Tasa was as opinionated as the day was long. Thank Christ, she had her little best friend living with her.

My back teeth ground down harder, my fists flexing by my sides, but there was nothing I could say when *Bunică* got into one of her fits. Turning on my heel, I marched out of the kitchen, grabbed my coat from the hallway closet, and stalked out of the house. What in the ever-loving fuck?

Tasa gone.

Contract in ruins.

Potential war on the horizon.

Everything I'd worked for gone.

Gone.

I was an abject failure. No, I refused to let that stand. I didn't care what it took to make this right. I'd fulfill Tata's oath. I'd drag Tasa back by her hair to marry the Popescu if need be. I'd make my father proud if it fucking killed me.

I APPRECIATE your help in spreading the word, including telling a friend. Reviews help readers find books! Please leave a review on your favorite book site.

Sign up to my newsletter to find out when I have new books!

MORE BY MONIQUE

Steamy Biker Romance Series

Kingdom's Reign (Book 1)
Cutter's Claim (Book 2)
Loki's Luck (Book 3)
Stanton's Sins (Book 4)
Puck's Property (Book 5)
Whistle's War (Book 6)
Her Hidden Valentine, A Squad Novella
(Book 7)

Lupu Family Mafia Romance Series

The lives of these powerful men revolves around three core elements: duty, sacrifice, and family. There's little time for women, and no time for love.
Each one of them will be cut off at the knees, humbled by a woman. Oh, how far these mighty men will fall before they learn the age-old lesson that the only way out is through…

The Chosen Heir (Alex's story)
The Recluse Heir (Luca's story)
The Savage Heir (Nicu's story)
The Perfect Heir (Tatum's story)
The Secret Heir (Prequel to Sebastian's story)
The Bastard Heir (Sebastian's story)
The Princess Heir (Emma's story)

Empire Academy Series
A High School Bully Mafia Romance Series

UNFORGIVABLE (Starlene's story)
UNREGRETTABLE (Crina's story)
UNFORGETTABLE (Gabriela's story)
UNDENIABLE (Zoe's story)

www.ingramcontent.com/pod-product-compliance
Lightning Source LLC
Chambersburg PA
CBHW072054190726
48294CB00005B/1503